KU-181-386
30 AUG 2019
SOUTHWARK LIBRARIES
SK 2484551 5

Praise for *Her*

'Deliciously nasty, *Her* belongs to an emerging "women beware women" sub-genre indebted to Zoë Heller's *Notes on a Scandal.* Yet it is distinctive in its domesticity and its missing formulaic elements: a violence-free psychological thriller in which the victim doesn't even know there is a threat' John Dugdale, *Sunday Times*

'Harriet Lane, author of *Alys, Always*, specialises in scheming women. Her new novel of psychological suspense asks how you can tell when your friend is really your enemy . . . She's a clever creation, this villainess, like a deadly spider waiting to pounce . . . One unanswered question keeps the reader gripping that seat-edge . . . The answer and the novel's outcome do not disappoint' *Independent on Sunday*

'As seductive as it is chilling, *Her* is quality literary fiction meets psychological thriller, the devil of which is in the detail' Lucy Scholes, *Observer*

'If you loved *Notes on a Scandal*'s brand of toxic camaraderie, you'll love this' *Grazia*, Summer Reads

'Lane's writing shines a spotlight on life's domestic flotsam. Lego under the fridge, damp laundry, crumbs in the toy box: these details of middle-class parenthood are picked out in Hitchcockian detail, gathering weight, promising imminent horror. Lane's first book, *Alys, Always*, was one of the most talked-about thrillers of 2012, a psychological drama exploring deceit and manipulation. *Her* is another study of spiteful female friendship, unwinding slowly and subtly over a year . . . Lane's writing is always careful and elegant, loaded with significance and often beautiful'

Charlotte Runcie, *Daily Telegraph*

'The author is good on atmosphere, observing lifestyles, ratcheting up the tension and keeping her readers guessing'

Choice

'Tautly written psychological thriller . . . there is forensic social observation here. Her London is recognisably real. Both Emma and Nina feel like women you might pass on a leafy Islington street. She has a sharp eye for telling detail . . . Then the endgame, when it comes, is shattering'

Independent

'This unfolding story of a toxic friendship . . . will have you racing through the chapters. A gripping and thought-provoking psychological thriller'

Nimmi Maghera-Rakhra, *The Sun*

'Dual narrators and their different perspectives on the same events create a distinctly sinister and uncomfortable atmosphere in this gripping novel. Sympathies and allegiances shift with each chapter, keeping the reader unsettled, yet hooked . . . A cautionary tale that could make you re-evaluate those friendships made by the swings'

Victoria Clarke, *The Lady*

'The exquisitely sinister psychological thriller that is going to take us all by storm this summer, Harriet Lane's *Her*, has a *Notes on a Scandal*-type relationship between an exhausted young mother and her rich sophisticated neighbour'

Amanda Craig, *Daily Telegraph*

'Another taut, tense psychological thriller from the author of the acclaimed 2012 debut novel *Alys, Always* . . . A compelling revenge drama that will make you think twice about getting too chummy with the neighbours'

Sebastian Shakespeare, *Tatler*

'Harriet Lane's *Alys, Always* was one of the most memorable fictional debuts of recent years, a seemingly simple story that discovered subtle ways to unsettle, and which found elegant, disturbing insights into familiar English obsessions with class and status. Lane's new book, *Her*... promises to be this year's unmissable summer novel. Among Lane's antecedents is the pin-sharp prose of Patricia Highsmith'

Tim Adams, *Observer*

'A fabulously creepy thriller from the author of *Alys, Always.* Nina recognises Emma on the street from 20 years ago, but doesn't reveal this, and Emma treats Nina as a new friend. But what happens when it comes out that Nina remembers?'

Viv Groskop, *Red* magazine

'Driving the plot are the reciprocal forces of revenge and provocation: we want to know what Nina will do next and what Emma has done to deserve it. Lane inspires a terrible dread as Nina's threat looms larger, combined with a slender hope that Emma might realize the danger in time. Lane also intrigues her readers with the puzzle of Emma's past... a fine mistress of suspense' Emily Rhodes, *TLS*

'A sharply observed relationship with a sinister plot line of hand-in-the-mouth proportions... psychologically nuanced... Lane excels at everyday detail. Emma's total absorption by motherhood is rendered with beautifully stinging observations' *Metro*

'Harriet Lane's debut, the subtly unsettling *Alys, Always*, was a chilling psychological drama of power privilege and manipulation. In this, her equally compulsive follow-up, similar sinister shenanigans are spun out in Lane's elegant, poetic prose... Unlike conventional thrillers, the perverse pleasure of this compelling novel is not a big reveal but the pin-sharp unpicking of personality' Eithne Farry, *Sunday Express*

'Harriet Lane is a deft conjurer of menacing middle class scenarios, and her second novel a taut revenge drama with a shattering endgame' *i* newspaper

'Nina's a control freak, Emma's a mess. What happens when their paths cross – and is it really the first time? Psychological page-turning follow-up to *Alys, Always*, Ms Lane's best-selling debut' *Grazia*

'Like a fly caught in a spider's web, struggling naive mother Emma is drawn further into sophisticated Nina's life. The ultimate frenemy thriller' *Now*

'When frazzled mum Emma encounters sophisticated Nina, she thinks their meeting is down to chance. But, as this cool, controlled thriller reveals, the truth is far more sinister. With wonderfully fleshed out characters, this is a chilling study in revenge' *Sunday Mirror*

'Struggling young mum Emma is grateful when her glamorous neighbour Nina befriends her. What Emma doesn't realise is that Nina recognises her from the past and has a score to settle. In *Her*, Harriet Lane keeps the reader on the edge until the last page' *Good Housekeeping*

'Struggling mother of two Emma doesn't recognise Nina, but Nina recognises her. She infiltrates her way into Emma's life gaining her trust. But what is it that she wants? The story is told by both women, with an underlying tension that builds and builds until the last horrifying scene. I loved this slow-burning tale of revenge' Fanny Blake, *Woman & Home*

'This spare, tense psychological thriller opens when a wealthy woman finds a struggling young mother's purse in the street of the London suburb they live in. Returning the purse marks the start of an unlikely friendship' *Harper's Bazaar*

Her

Before the publication of her debut novel, *Alys, Always*, Harriet Lane wrote for the *Guardian*, the *Observer*, *Vogue* and *Tatler*. She lives in north London with her husband and two children.

Also by Harriet Lane

Alys, Always

Her

HARRIET LANE

A W&N PAPERBACK

First published in Great Britain in 2014
by Weidenfeld & Nicolson
This paperback edition published in 2015
by Weidenfeld & Nicolson
an imprint of the Orion Books Ltd,
Orion House, 5 Upper St Martin's Lane,
London WC2H 9EA

An Hachette UK company

5 7 9 10 8 6

A CIP catalogue record for this book
is available from the British Library

ISBN 978-1-7802-2002-4

Typeset at The Spartan Press Ltd,
Lymington, Hants

For Poppy

Nina

It's her. I'm almost sure of it.

It's late afternoon, a Friday towards the end of July. I've just left the off-licence with a cold bottle wrapped up in paper, and I'm crossing the square, thinking about the afternoon's work, whether I'm getting anywhere or whether it's going to be yet another dead end. The sky, through the shifting canopy of plane leaves, is still saturated with heat, and the golden air is viscous with pollen; but it's tainted, too, with the disquieting scent of the urban summer: the reek of exhausts and drains and sewers, the faraway stench of the ancient forgotten streams that seep through the rocks and silt deep beneath my feet.

I'm thinking about that exact shade of violet – wondering if I've got it quite right against the greens and muddy browns – when I see her. She's on the other side of the square, stooping a little, reaching out to a toddler. The sensation of it, of finding her there in front of me after all this time, is almost overwhelmingly powerful: like panic, or passion. I feel my hands curl into fists. I'm very conscious now of my lungs filling with air, and then releasing it.

Quickly I change course, walking over to the community noticeboard and standing in front of it, as if I'm taking an interest in yoga workshops and French conversation classes, and all the time, while the scene unfolds right there in front of me, I'm watching her, noting the thin matelot top and the rolled-up jeans, the ugly German toe-post sandals they all wear around here, the hair hooked behind her ears.

I watch as she takes something out of her pocket, a tissue or a cloth, and spits on it and bends over the child, wiping its face. 'Oh, goodness, Christopher, look at the mess you're in,' she says. 'Ice-cream in your hair! How did you manage that?' and her voice is still the sort that carries, so I hear how tired she is, the way she finds the words without thinking about them. When she tucks the tissue in her pocket and straightens up, I can see she's pregnant, maybe four months.

The boy breaks free from her hand and staggers off unevenly; a rolling gait, a sailor's, or a drunk's. He's reeling across the square towards me, and now I feel a moment's terror: Emma's heading in my direction, she'll smile at me in a spirit of ersatz apology as she comes level, expecting me to be charmed by the boy, and maybe she'll recognise me. Or maybe she won't.

But then he saves me by falling over, stumbling on the gravel and pitching forward onto it, almost comically, like some creature in a cartoon, and in the dreadful moment of silence that follows this she moves swiftly and strongly towards him.

I walk away across the square, not looking back, as the high scream begins, and I'm thinking: *Emma. It's you. I've found you.* And when I pay for the bread and cheese at the deli, my hands are trembling, just a little.

I go home. Without Sophie and Charles in it, the house feels exotically empty and novel, as if it barely belongs to me; it always takes me a few days to get used to solitude, on the rare occasion when I'm alone. Lenka has been and gone, leaving the scent of detergent and ironing hanging agreeably in the air. I wander through the rooms, opening windows and correcting Lenka's corrections, switching the flowers back to the side table, removing the drinks coasters she has placed fussily under the candlesticks. In Sophie's room, I find Henry curled up on the bed. He pushes his head against my hand as I bend over him, then lies back, patiently exposing his throat, allowing me to give him more attention. I oblige, and then I go to the chest of drawers and find the packet of cigarettes Sophie has forgotten about, hidden under her school jerseys.

I take the Cook's Matches and a glass of the Sancerre out onto the terrace and sit there looking out over the garden, smoking. I haven't smoked for several years, and the cigarette is stale and dry and burns strongly, with a sort of crackle, making me feel a little giddy and sick. The smoke drifts through the honeysuckle and the white poppies, whose papery petals will soon litter the grass.

Charles rings when I'm on the second glass, and I'm glad to hear his voice, glad of the distraction, so glad that I wonder whether to tell him, to try to put it into words.

He is in an expansive mood, on the verge of excitement: the flight was delayed, but he made the meeting by the skin of his teeth, and the pitch went well, he and Theo were the last team to go before the panel, and the contractor just rang to say they've made it on to the shortlist. 'It's a great scheme,' he says, 'A fantastic site, not far from the opera house. We could really do with landing this job. I'm going to stay out for a few days, speak to a few people, do some drawings. I can't draw in the office, everyone's on my case the whole time. Would that be OK with you, if I extended my stay?'

Fine, I say. We've nothing planned.

'How are things with you, did Sophie get off OK?' he asks, and as I say what is expected I'm wondering how to mention Emma – although I don't know quite how to explain it; it's more of a feeling than an anecdote – when he says, 'Oh, just a minute, I'll be with you in a minute . . .' and then he says Theo's turned up and they're due somewhere for supper. So I say, *fine, let's speak tomorrow*, and hang up.

Later, I lie there in bed and go back over the scene under the plane trees, analysing it, looking for clues, trying to remember what else I saw. She had a worn brown satchel on a long strap, which banged against her hip as she hurried after the boy. Her hair was lighter than it used to be: dyed, probably. The matelot top. The rolled-up jeans. The bronze sandals. It doesn't seem enough.

After that, I'm a little on edge when I'm out in the high street or the park. I'm scared of seeing her, and I'm scared that I'll never see her again.

Charles comes home. The state schools break up for the holidays; the roads empty. The sound of the neighbours laughing in their gardens keeps us awake at night.

My father calls from the house in the south of France: 'Why don't you and Charles fly over for a few days, Clara's learned to swim.' 'Yes, yes,' calls Delphine, a little way away, 'Tell Nina we want to see her, don't we, darling?' There's a rustling and scratching on the line, and now I can hear Clara's breaths, her mouth against the receiver. 'Is that you?' I say. 'Clara, is that you?' And then my father takes the phone back and says, 'Well, bear it in mind, you'd be very welcome, either here, or in Paris when we get back.' I say how lovely, I'll think about it, but we know this is where we'll leave the matter. Nothing will come of it.

Sophie sends me duty emails, telling me about the work experience her father has arranged in a midtown art gallery, and throwing in the occasional joke about Trudy's horror of dairy. Once a week I ring my daughter at the apartment, and if Arnold picks up there's a little starchy conversation: she's grown so tall, she has been making cupcakes with the kids, the Crawfords have invited them all to the Hampton Classic so could she stay on for a few days? If I'm especially unlucky I'll get Trudy, with her up-talk, her noli mi tangere formality, her relentless chirpy competence. I'm afflicted with a hateful shame when I speak to Trudy, when I imagine her imagining me: the Englishwoman, the first wife, the rogue Mrs Setting. A woman who retains Arnold's surname, 'for professional purposes, apparently'. Of course, Trudy has kept her maiden name, both for her psychotherapy practice and for the social aspects of the life she shares with Arnold and their rigorously scheduled children, Astrid and Otto, whom Sophie calls the brats – though she finds them tolerable in smallish doses.

'She paints a little,' Trudy probably tells her friends. 'I'm told she's quite well known, in England.'

The weeks go by, rolling into deep summer. Emma, I imagine, has gone away, like everyone else: maybe to Dorset or Norfolk, maybe to Corsica or Crete. I picture her sitting by a stretch of glittering water in a sunhat and (her bump neat and firm) a practical navy one-piece, while her husband – with freckled shoulders and a few days' worth of beard – takes a mouthful of beer and gets busy at the barbecue, observing that the charred bits add flavour.

So I stop watching for Emma, and it's a relief to have the neighbourhood back, the freedom of my familiar haunts. I like London in the lazy grip of August: the empty streets spotted with shade, the grass in the parks turning sparse and yellow, the heat coming in hard shimmering waves off parked cars. I turn down invitations from Kate Farrar and the Sharpes, quite glad to be left alone with my work during the day and spending the evenings at home with Charles, eating supper outside as the dusk brings its cool down over the garden. Making the most of the peace.

During these slow hot weeks, as I walk to and from

the studio, my mind has started to fill up with colour and texture: greys and browns and sometimes a startling blue. There's a softness there, and a roughness too. A coldness. Something has started to happen.

As ever, when I feel this, I try not to think too hard about it, in case it vanishes into nothing. I've lost too many possibilities this way and those losses always hurt. I do my best to concentrate on the impulse, rather than its implications. For now, in the studio, the brush feels good in my hand and the canvases collect in the racks: the bands of earth and air and water. One sky after another, low indistinct horizons, the smudged bruised suggestion of the landscape.

Michael from the gallery drops in one morning and goes through the finished pieces, nodding and frowning with what I now recognise as approval. 'You're on a roll,' he says eventually, standing back to look at one of the largest paintings, propped against the wall. 'They're very atmospheric. I like the way you're dealing with the emptiness of the place.'

'It's a part of Kent I used to know,' I say, spooning instant coffee into the mugs, and as I say this I realise it's true: if it's anywhere, it's the marsh. Those broad expanses of scrub, the wind-whipped tussocks and trees shaped by the weather, the dark inlets and drainage ditches and channels pock-marked with birds. And somewhere behind all of this, under all of this, is the sea; and above it is the sky.

Because the work is satisfying, it's a happy summer. Charles lands the Vienna job, and this fills him with relief and good humour. I doubt he's conscious of it, but he's glad Sophie's out of the way. He does things he doesn't often do: stopping by the Turkish greengrocer on the way home to pick up wooden boxes of flat white peaches (I prefer the cheaper orange-fleshed ones, though I keep this to myself), ringing me up to say he's managed to get tickets for the Almeida or the Duchess.

Walking down Dean Street as evening falls, I'm as aware of his vague contentment in being here with me as I am of the sticky residual heat of the pavement beneath my thin-soled sandals. In the old days, he would have kissed me here, near a dark doorway that smells of piss. The realisation almost fills me with melancholy.

The relief of finding a new direction in the studio means my sleep is deep and luxurious. I'm spared the dreams. When I wake up, there's a point to the day.

I try to put Emma to the back of my mind. But she won't stay there.

It's nearly September now. The sun has bleached most of the colour out of the city. At night, I'm woken by the sound of police helicopters wheeling round to the estates at the bottom of the hill. It's a dangerous time of year: tempers are short. The open windows are an invitation to burglars.

Anything could happen.

I'm in the dry cleaners collecting a silk dress and some of Charles's suits when I glimpse her through the glass. For a moment, she's caught unseeingly in my reflection – tall to my slight, rosy to my sallow, bright where I am dark – and then she's moving past while I stand there in the doorway. We're so close that I can see the silver bangle on her golden wrist; so close that I can smell her, the freshness of the detergent on her clothes (a green cardigan over a pink linen shift, scuffed white plimsolls). Her hair's loose this time, rather unkempt-looking, as if she hasn't had time to brush it.

She's pushing one of those big triangular buggies, its handles hung with hessian bags, and there's the child, Christopher, ferociously constrained by the safety harness, his face set with resentment. 'No biscuits,' she's saying briskly. 'It's lunchtime.' When the lights change she crosses the road by the pizza restaurant, and I see the movement as someone seated in the window half-rises and waves at her. I feel in my bag for my sunglasses and put them on so when I walk past the restaurant a few moments later I can look in without anxiety. Emma is seated at a table with a few other women, and the kids are all in highchairs, throwing things on the floor, while the waiter stands back, smiling with pained tolerance, attempting to take the order.

I'd like to know where she lives.

Of course, it's not the first time I've done it, but when I google her, the same thing happens: nothing comes up. She may have someone else's surname now, but even in her historical incarnation she left no trace, lost among all the other Emma Halls. I shouldn't judge her for this. We both came of age before the internet, so I can find no evidence of how she spent her teens or twenties or even her thirties, though really I don't need the proof of what I've gleaned from these two brief sightings: the arts degree, the job in magazine editorial or publishing or possibly some sort of curatorial role, and then – just as she was beginning to despair – the chance to bolt, to try out a new life for a while. Transport systems, controlled crying, soft play and coffees in the park with the other older mothers.

Are you enjoying it, Emma? I find myself thinking as I unscrew the cap from the tube of purple madder and squeeze a shiny worm of pigment onto a saucer. *Is your life the one you were due?*

Sunlight slides relentlessly over the studio's concrete floor. The metal-framed windows are open and a few storeys below people are talking, popping car boots and lugging things in and out of the storage unit opposite. I don't have much of a view: the studio overlooks the black windows of empty workshops, a series of flat gritty roofs seamed with lines of asphalt, weeds colonising cracks in the brickwork.

I look up, into the white burning sky.

Emma

In the end, it comes down to luck. I must have dropped my wallet as I came out of the greengrocers', and she finds it on the pavement.

'Oh, it's no trouble,' she says on the phone. 'Your details were on the library card.'

'I can't tell you what a relief it is,' I say, although I hadn't even noticed I'd lost the bloody thing, in the usual confusion of shopping bags and getting the wilting lettuce into the fridge, and Christopher's disgust with his green beans. 'Are you local? I could come round to collect it once my son's finished his tea. Where are you?'

'Oh, let me bring it back, it's no problem,' she says. It's a soft voice, a little hesitant-sounding.

'Gosh, how kind, are you sure?' I say, and she says she'll be over in ten. She's only around the corner, in Pakenham Gardens. As she says it I see the street, its clipped hedges and crisp pointing, its doors painted olive and lavender. The black and white chessboard tiling on the front paths, the coloured glass in the top panels of the windows: pink, green, gold. 'Well, if you're sure,' I say, as Christopher drums his beaker on the tabletop, demanding milk rather as Tudor kings requested malmsey.

Of course, she turns out to be exactly the sort of person I

don't want to meet; exactly the sort of person I'd choose not to find my wallet on the street. I stand there in the doorway, with a stained tea towel over my shoulder, ketchup on my jeans, and (though I don't find this out till later) flour in my hair, and I look at her and just for a second I recognise her, her life; and I want it so much, really, that it hurts.

When I see her waiting there on the step, I know pretty much everything about her. At one level, I'm seeing someone about my age, small and dark, in black cotton and ballet slippers: slim brown limbs, a simple rather boyish haircut which is a little damp, as if she has just had a shower or a swim. At another level, I read her as one woman reads another, and I can tell, in that instant, that she is *free*. How do I know this? It's something to do with how slow and unhurried she is. There, on the doorstep, I feel she's waiting for something. Just for a fraction of a moment, she waits to smile, she waits to speak, and I rush to fill the gaps, sounding like an idiot. Only then does she start to look for the wallet, somewhere in her big straw shopper.

She looks like a person who can afford to take her time. Nothing, right now, seems more exotic to me than this. My whole life runs to a schedule: the headlong conscientious dawn-to-dusk rush to feed and entertain and bathe and rest Christopher (my own needs, necessarily, come somewhat further down the line, if at all). There's always the next thing to think about, or the thing after that.

And if I have the audacity to forget the timetable, or attempt to improvise, I know I'll pay for it, sooner rather than later. Christopher's margins are ribbon-narrow; if I allow him to get hungry or tired, he'll punish me. And those punishments are hard to bear. I'm already someone else, but the person I turn into at these low points is someone I never imagined I could be a few years ago: someone with a hot knot of fury where her heart used to be.

I spent my old life meeting people's needs, anticipating unreasonable demands and worst-case scenarios; I built a career on that sensitivity, that apprehension. It's my particular tragedy that I'm still programmed with a desire to solve all problems, even now, when the authority I'm answerable to is a tiny illogical tyrant. Managing him, his whims and caprices, his passions and hatreds, requires every scrap of my energy, every ounce of patience. And usually even that isn't enough.

So I open the door, and I see her, and in that moment I also see myself, my shortcomings. All the many things I now lack.

'Nina Bremner,' she says, holding out her hand.

'I'm Emma. I really can't thank you enough... You're a lifesaver.'

Her hand in mine is dry and cool. I release it hurriedly.

'Not a problem,' she's saying, starting to rummage vaguely in her bag. 'It was just lying on the pavement by the postbox. Outside the greengrocers'.'

'Oh – yes, I had that thing to post. Christ. Some days I think I'm going mad.'

'Well, at least you've got a good excuse,' she says, nodding at my belly. 'When's it due? I remember what that's like.'

'November. You've got children?' I ask, and somehow I'm disappointed by this. She looks so *other*. I don't want her to turn out to be like me, only better at it.

'One. But she's seventeen. Another species.'

'You don't look old enough, you must have been a child bride?' I say, and she laughs.

Behind me, down the corridor, in the kitchen, there's a crash. And then a roar.

'Ah, OK, you've already got one. How old?' she asks, dipping her head over her bag again. 'Sorry, it's here somewhere, I just...'

'Two and a half. I'd better – Do you want to come in

for a cup of tea?' I don't suppose she will. Why should she? But she seems amused. 'Sure,' she says. And then she's in the hall, stepping neatly round the bulk of the all-terrain buggy, bringing a faint clinging fragrance with her, pulling the front door shut as I hurry away, towards the kitchen and Christopher, who is pinned into his highchair and surveying the mess on the floor with lordly vengeful satisfaction.

Some visitors spectate. They stand there at the edge of the room, smiling and chatting as I rush around with carrot sticks and J-cloths, and I know deep down they're enjoying seeing me reduced to this. Of course, Nina didn't know me before, doesn't know the real me, but she notices what needs doing, and she does it: quietly, without ostentation or apology. While I'm flapping about, scooping houmous off the floor and wiping up the spilled milk, she fills the kettle and drops the dirty plates in the dishwasher. 'What a pretty house,' she says, finding mugs. 'How long have you lived here?'

'We bought it just after Christopher was born,' I say. 'We lived in Atwell Street for a bit after we got married, and it was a nice flat, but we wanted a garden. Of course there's loads to do, we haven't got around to any of it, we can't really afford to do anything now. Sorry about the mess. I never seem to be able to get things straight.' I hear myself saying these things, and I know what I sound like.

With deft small movements she lifts the kettle and pours the boiling water into cups, and as she does so the kitchen is wreathed with shimmering skeins of steam, catching on the sunlight slanting through the windows. 'I remember what that's like,' she says. 'Some days you feel like you're running the wrong way on a conveyor belt, never getting anywhere.'

'I never realised how much mess is involved in just living,' I say, with a little laugh, giving Christopher a matchbox of raisins and lifting him out of the chair. 'You know: just making him a meal is the act with a thousand consequences: all the peeling and cooking and cooling down and cutting, and then afterwards all the scraping and rinsing and wiping and sweeping. One stone, all these bloody ripples. Just the act of tidying up the chaos seems to generate more chaos. I open the cupboard to get out the mop, and when my back is turned he scatters clothes pegs all over the house, or hides the Hoover attachments in the recycling box. Or I find him wandering around clutching the bottle of bleach . . .'

I stop. I've said more than I meant to. It just came out in a rush. I'm glad I didn't tell her about the line I stumbled across in a dictionary of quotations, the eighteenth-century suicide note: 'All this buttoning and unbuttoning.' It's a phrase that I hear over and over, as if it's playing on a loop, as I move through the days.

She looks at me. She looks at me as if she recognises me, the real me. It's a shocking moment. For a second I'm scared I'm going to cry with the relief and horror of it.

'Sit down,' she says, pushing a chair forward a little. 'Drink your tea.'

I stare out at the small battered rectangle of grass littered with coloured plastic, the defeated unloved shrubs, the shed door that Ben promised to fix but which for now continues to list on its hinges, a reminder of our joint paralysis. Over the overgrown hedge, the Callaghans' washing sags on the laundry line.

Christopher is hunkered down on an upturned plant pot, eating his raisins, the ones he's not dropping. I see him bend over, pushing through the grass, searching them out with careful fingers. I think: *cat shit*. But then I think: *sod it*. So I sit. She pulls up another chair.

'Sorry,' I say, and I don't want the moment to linger, it's too painful, so I say, 'God, listen to me! I'm not always like this. Post-holiday crash. You know what it's like.' The cup, when I pick it up, is hot in my hands. The tea is too weak, but so what, there's a novelty in not having made it myself.

When she asks me where we went, I tell her about the agriturismo near Lucca, using the approved techniques for describing summer holidays (imply it was heaven, without going into too much tedious detail; make a joke out of the noisy humourless Belgians in the next apartment, the lack of mixer taps, and the dread anticipation of the next credit-card statement).

She says she hasn't been away. Her daughter Sophie spent most of the summer in the States with the father and the stepmother. (Not at all, it's all very cordial.) She missed Sophie, of course, but looking on the bright side, it turned into a fairly productive summer workwise. 'I hit a rich seam,' she says. 'So I stayed put, made the most of it.' She's a painter. Landscapes, mostly. Abstract. She has a studio in Kentish Town, in the old piano factory, and a show coming up at a gallery I've heard of in Fitzrovia. 'You should come to the opening,' she says, almost shyly. 'If you fancy it.'

I say I'd love to, which is true. I don't say that it'll never happen. 'Can't think of anything nicer,' I say. And now I'm seized with wistfulness, a desire that she should see me in a different context, so I add, 'Gallery openings! That's the sort of thing I used to do, when I worked in TV.' And as I say it, I feel the burn of humiliation, as if I'm claiming kinship with someone I barely know, someone infinitely more glamorous and sought-after. As if I'm trying to ride on the coattails of a person I was once introduced to a long time ago. *God, you sound pathetic,* I think.

'I'll drop an invite round,' she says. 'It would be great if you could come.'

There's a noise from outside: Christopher, bashing the hedge with his stick, frightening the cats. I step outside to tell him to stop while she finishes her tea, looks around for her bag. 'I'd better get going, Sophie's got a friend round and I said I'd make paella. Oh, I almost forgot.' She reaches into her shopper, pulls out my wallet and pushes it over the table towards me: a shamefully practical thing in jolly patterned oilcloth, its clasp straining against an undisciplined mess of receipts and loyalty cards.

I see her out into the early evening: a clear sky, full of chance and opportunity, the people coming home from work and walking along the street, heading for a jasmine-scented pub garden or a game of tennis in the park.

Christopher's calling for me. Has he hurt himself? It's not always possible to tell the difference between injury and indignation. I stand there in the hall, among the boots and the coats, the toys and the clothing catalogues I can't bring myself to deal with, listening to him. There's a broken rice cake underneath the radiator, and while I'm stooping to retrieve it I find a single red sock patterned with robots. When I pick it up it's firm and knobbly, oddly jointed: filled with a pebble, a clump of Lego bricks and a ring of dried apple.

If she remembers, I think, *I'll bloody go*.

Nina

In the end, it's ridiculously easy. I'm coming back from a run when I see her going into the greengrocers', manoeuvring the enormous unwieldy buggy between the straw-filled trays of plums and avocados, the sunny upturned faces of the gerberas. The greengrocer wears a patient smile as Emma moves around, blocking the aisles while she tries to interest Christopher in purple or green grapes. An elderly gentleman has to climb over the heirloom tomatoes – oh my God, the terminology – in order to reach the till.

As if anyone would steal your bloody toddler, I think. Just park him outside for a moment or two. What could possibly happen? But these women, they all live in fear of being the unlucky one. *Oh, I couldn't take the risk*, they say. All that anxiety. So many things to worry about. Parabens, E-numbers, UV rays. I wonder how they stand it.

I wait under the awning, in front of the boxes of yellow and scarlet fruit, turning towards the bookshop window as she selects a lettuce and pays for it. Then there's the business of edging the buggy out again, sending a shiver through the cherries. When the buggy bumps down onto the pavement something falls out: Christopher's shoe, a soft little fabric sandal. As she bends to retrieve it, as I squeeze past her to pay for my apple, I find it's the work of a moment to dip my fingers into the yawning mouth of her bag.

'Sorry to keep you waiting,' says the greengrocer, putting down a pallet of lemons, and I know what he's really saying: *Sorry about that dozy mare.* Outside, she's lifting Christopher up to the postbox as he pushes some envelopes into the slot. I can see the little grimace at his weight against her bump, his unhelpful vitality.

'That's OK,' I say, handing over the coins, her wallet snug between my arm and my ribcage.

At home, I spread the contents out over the kitchen table, assembling the clues. She's Emma Nash now. She lives on Carmody Street, in the little line of workers' cottages between the park and the main road. The usual credit cards, library passes, loyalty schemes. Receipts: organic milk from M&S, flour and cereal from Iceland. A recipe from the *Guardian* supplement for chicken curry. A green prescription form, scrawled over with a GP's hurried initials, for an entry-level antidepressant. Tucked behind the book of stamps there's a small tired-looking snapshot, a picture of a man, the husband, the Mr Nash, smiling into the sun, arms folded, leaning against a bike on a country lane. Quite attractive, I suppose.

I have a quick shower and then I make the call.

'Is that Emma Nash? I've found your wallet, you dropped it on the high street.'

She gushes a bit. I've saved her life, she seems to be going mad, she'd forget her head if it wasn't, etc.

'It's no trouble,' I say.

She's so relieved. She asks if I live nearby, offers to pop over once her son has finished his tea.

'Oh, let me bring it back, it's no problem,' I say quickly. I'm no longer nervous; I want to get inside her house. I want to see how she lives.

I anticipate that she'll be more flustered on her own

territory, less likely to recognise me, though the chances of that are really very slim. Still, I've got my line ready, just in case it's needed. 'I'm in Pakenham Gardens,' I say. 'It's only around the corner. I'll be with you in ten.'

I put everything back in the wallet and leave the house. It's a beautiful evening. Monica Prewitt is out in her front garden, trimming the lavender bush, filling a trug with the spent straws, and the fragrance of it drifts down the street. Someone in number 34 is practising Chopin in front of an open window, going over the same few bars, making the same mistakes: a pleasant, mildly melancholy sound. The pavements are warm and dappled with sunshine.

I slow down when I get to Carmody Street. The houses here are two-storey, rather than three-, and the façades are narrower, less ornate, set back behind cramped front gardens that barely merit the term. Not all the houses have been gentrified: several still have net curtains. One is pebble-dashed. There's a bit of double-glazing. Some ugly leggy climber roses. The noise of the main road at the end of the street changes as the traffic lights on the roundabout click through their sequences.

Emma's is a halfway house. There's a potted bay tree on the front step and a powder-blue front door, but the gloss paint is chipped, and some of the slats on the plantation shutters are broken, hanging off at an angle, giving the impression of a mouthful of bad teeth. *At full stretch*, I think, as I unlatch the little gate and walk up the short path. Then, *Here we are. Here we go.*

Standing on the step, I'm aware, when I swallow, of the dryness of my throat. I run a hand through my hair, still a little damp from my shower. Then I put my finger on the bell.

There she is, standing in front of me, a distracted smile, glancing over her shoulder – waiting for the bomb to go off in the back room – while she's talking: 'idiotic' and 'feel so stupid' and 'incredibly kind'.

Close to, it's quite overwhelming, the wholesome golden quality of her presence only partially dimmed by domesticity, pregnancy and the exhaustion particular to mothers of small children. The sheer height and health and strength and competence of her. I can see the dark roots of her hair and the streak of white at the temple where she has pushed it back impatiently with a floury hand. Ketchup on her jeans, the tea towel over her shoulder. She's still beautiful.

'Nina Bremner,' I say, and we shake hands.

'I'm Emma. I really can't thank you enough . . . You're a lifesaver.'

I say it's not a problem, and then I open my bag, look down into it. The wallet's right there, of course, underneath my cardigan, but I leave it, making vague noises – *Oh God where is it, it's in here somewhere* – knowing she'll have to ask me in. 'It was just lying on the pavement by the postbox,' I say, fumbling. 'Outside the greengrocers'.'

'Oh – yes, I had that thing to post. Christ. Some days I think I'm going mad.'

I look at her, smiling, nodding at her bump. 'Well, at least you've got a good excuse. When's it due?'

November, she says. When I tell her how old Sophie is, she says I must have been a child bride. And with this comment I remember her old impulsiveness, that reckless inability to pass on an opportunity to charm a stranger. It's a character flaw, I know that now.

Behind her, in the darkness of the house, there's the sound of the child throwing something or falling over. He calls for her. Flustered, she glances over her shoulder.

'Sorry,' I say, dipping my head again. 'It's here somewhere, I just . . .'

So she asks if I'd like to come in for a cup of tea.

Yes.

It's all pretty much as I'd expected. The white-painted hall, the scuffed skirting and the varnished wooden boards, the buggy and small wellingtons painted with beetles tumbled against bigger ones, a hobby horse lolling out of the umbrella stand. A wad of unopened post balanced on top of the radiator. A wooden heart on a string dangling over the gilt-framed mirror. A china dish of shells and keys. A ball made from those red rubber bands postmen drop on the pavements. All the quirky bits of individuality echoing prevailing tastes. *This is us. This is who we are.*

Beneath the chaos of crumbs and dirty pots, the kitchen is pleasant, unremarkable: pale blue units, enamel lampshade over the wooden table, a string of fairy lights looped over the Angie Lewin print of seed heads. The door is open to the small garden. Sun lies over the tangled grass, the tossed-aside watering can, the length of yellow hose. Someone's trying to grow some tomatoes out there, I see.

The boy, Christopher, has scattered the end of his tea on the floor. As his mother comes towards him he looks at her with a satisfied expression, as if he has brought some righteous punishment to bear. I hear her mutter, 'Oh, you—' and then she's at the sink, running hot water into a cloth. When she's wiping the table and the floor, I fill the kettle and switch it on, and then I collect the plates and stack them in the dishwasher. Christopher watches me without curiosity. 'And what's your name?' I ask him, and then I ruffle his hair, and I have the pleasure of feeling him twist away from my hand, objecting to my gesture. 'Oh, isn't he a poppet? They're so delicious when they're this age.'

We talk a little about how long they've lived here. I can tell she's half-proud, half-ashamed of the house and its humdrum dishevelment: the enamel milk pans in pink and pistachio green dangling from hooks, the chipped china jug stuffed with sweet williams on the sill, the finger paintings moored to the fridge with magnets (crowns, beach balls, tiny tins of Italian beer). The way these small choices reflect upon her.

Christopher is removed from his highchair and makes his way out into the sunshine while I pour the boiling water into mugs.

'Sorry about the mess,' she says. 'I never seem to be able to get things straight.'

I say something about knowing how hard it is.

'I never realised how much mess is involved in just living,' she says, trying to laugh. Incredulously, as if she can't quite believe it, as if it's nearly a joke, she describes all the small tedious steps involved in preparing a meal for her child and serving it to him and cleaning up afterwards: 'One stone, all these bloody ripples.'

She goes on for a little longer, the housewife's lament, and then abruptly stops, pressing her lips together as if to keep the words back. Her cheeks are bright with the novelty, the excitement of telling someone how she really feels. Or maybe it's shame. I watch her as she rinses the cloth in the sink, hangs it over the tap. There's something else in her expression that I can't quite read; it frightens me. Maybe she has caught the edge of some ancient memory. But then her face clears and I realise I'm safe. She won't remember. It meant nothing to her, after all.

'Sit down,' I say, 'Drink your tea.'

So she sits, and we talk a little about safer things, her Italian summer, Sophie, my painting. I can see how exotic the private view sounds to her, and I say she should come, if she fancies it. The look on her face makes me realise I mustn't follow through. *Hold back for now. See how it goes.*

Perhaps sensing I've retreated a little, she mentions – she can't help herself – that she used to work in TV. *I'm more than all this*, she's signalling. *Look, I really am*. Then, with a little moue at the effort, she rises to her feet and goes outside to remonstrate with Christopher, who is whacking the hedge with a stick; and while this is going on I rinse out my mug in the sink and halt in front of the fridge, picking off the little plastic letters, rearranging them to make a phrase, a private joke, just for my own amusement. When she comes back, I surrender the wallet and say goodbye, promising to drop off an invite when I'm passing, and as I walk off into the scented evening, I wonder whether she will notice it, or if Ben will: the orange and blue and yellow letters spelling out b-a-d-p-e-n-n-y.

Emma

Nina forgets the invitation. She must have other things on her mind, and in any case I find I'm slightly relieved she hasn't remembered: Christopher's a nightmare with baby-sitters; and once I've got him settled in his cot I can't really face the Northern Line. Easier to go downstairs and have a glass of wine while listening to people on the radio discussing movies and plays I'll never see.

Ben comes home and finds me chopping vegetables like a person in a sitcom. I hear his key in the lock, the sound of my release. But he doesn't know that's how I feel, and I can't put it into words. He comes home with his tales of incompetent floor managers and outside broadcasts gone haywire, and I feel nothing but envy.

'So, how was your day?' he might ask, sitting down at the table to eat the meal I have prepared for him.

I have to think hard to remember what we did. Did we see the GP today? Did I take Christopher to Monkey Music? Was this the day we went to the supermarket, or to Regent's Park to meet Amy and Dulcie? Sometimes I make it up, so I have something to say, and I find he can't tell the difference. 'Sounds nice,' he says, putting his knife and fork together, not really listening.

The business of getting out of bed and low chairs is now

accompanied by sighs and grunts. I wait on the stairs to catch my breath and grip the banister in the dark. In the evenings I'm taken captive by Braxton Hicks. My stomach is tight as a drum, and something is revolving slowly inside it, something purposeful with elbows and knees as definite as coat hangers. I can no longer lie back on the sofa; I have to prop myself sideways to watch TV. Sometimes I grab Ben's hand and place it just so, to show him what I have to put up with. 'Amazing!' he says happily, resting his hand there for a moment, then giving me a pat and taking it away.

We keep the back door closed now. The days are getting shorter. The grass silts up with fallen leaves. Christopher starts at playgroup a few mornings a week. He hates it at first, and I spend the first three or four sessions crouched on a low bench in the cloakroom, my back pressed into a chorus line of tiny coats, wondering if I dare leave. I'd planned to use the time constructively – go for a swim, tidy the garden – but once he finally settles in, I just head home and sit in an armchair by the window and don't move until I'm due to collect him.

I cannot get enough of the silence.

My older sister Lucy visits for a few days and we cloister ourselves in the tiny room that Ben and I called the study, the room that will be the baby's, sorting through the bin liners of winter clothing that various friends have donated. I don't really need any more sleep suits or miniature white mittens, but Christopher does quite well: some jerseys, lots of vests, plaid shirts, corduroy trousers, a decent waterproof coat. The washing machine processes all these diminutive manly outfits. We pair up the dinky socks. We fold the tiny pants. It feels as if we are preparing for some imminent catastrophe.

In the park I sit on a bench, watching Lucy pushing Christopher on the swings. 'Higher!' he shouts. 'Higher!'

Jane, an old colleague, sends me a chatty email. She's

researching a new show, a fly-on-the-wall documentary about au pairs. At first I think she's being friendly, just keeping in touch, possibly sounding me out for future collaborations, and then I grasp the subtext: she wonders if I know anyone interesting, or mad, who might work for a case study. *What about lunch?* she says.

Ah, I remember lunch: something Lebanese or Thai at a table overlooking the wet reflective pavements of Goodge Street, picking over the latest management cock-up. For a moment I allow myself to consider it, the journey in on the bus; waiting in the lobby for Jane to appear, smiling at people I used to know, *yes, this is my little boy, say hello, Christopher! Yes, the next one's due soon – I know, I must be nuts*; then the corner table, the unbearable frustration of trying to listen or speak while Christopher knocks cutlery to the floor, spills his drink and pulls my elbow, saying he needs a wee.

The look on her face.

No.

I email back saying it's all a bit crazy, due date looming and all that, I'll be in touch in the new year.

'You should have said yes,' Ben says one Saturday, as we're finishing lunch.

'What about Christopher?' I ask.

'Oh, there must be someone who could have looked after him for a few hours,' he says, as if it might be that easy. 'You need to keep your hand in, stay in contact. You'll want to go back one day.'

I know I will, but I also know (as does he, secretly) it'll be impossible. My professional life, at least in TV, is over.

In the old days, it wasn't a disaster if I had three months on and two months off; it was nerve-wracking, for sure, but doable, just part of the game. When people rang, I could always make it work. Overnighters, 5 a.m. starts, last-minute dashes to catch the red-eye, unreasonable bosses making unreasonable demands: the price you paid for a job that rarely bored you. It seemed a fair deal at the time.

But now I know what happened to all those women I looked up to, the producers and directors who fell over the edge of the world just as their reputations began to take shape. It's near-impossible to reconcile an only moderately successful freelance career like mine with family life. As we can't afford childcare on retainer, we've decided that it makes more sense for me to stay at home – here, with the baskets of dirty laundry, the shopping lists, the appointments pencilled into the kitchen calendar – while Ben profits from the plum spots vacated by female colleagues. So this is my lot now. It was always going to come down to this, if only I'd thought about it hard enough. If I'd thought about it hard enough, would I have made the same choices? Yes, yes, of course. But still.

Christopher has been lifted out of his chair and comes over, putting his plump little hands out to me, as if he knows I'm feeling sad. I lift him on my knee and put my nose in his hair. It smells clean and dirty at the same time: like damp straw, like an animal that has been out in the rain. His hand in mine is sticky with vinaigrette and grainy with bits of shortbread. I try not to mind. I don't mind, really. I blow in his ears, making him laugh and twitch, and then I whisper, very quietly, 'You're lovely, aren't you?' He puts his thumb in his mouth and leans back against me and when I glance up, Ben's smiling at us both, and then he starts to clear away the lunch things.

'You're doing OK, aren't you?' Ben asks later, as we wait for the BBC4 procedural to start. 'You'd tell me, wouldn't you, if you felt . . .'

'Of course I would,' I say as the screen goes white.

I'm fine. I'm fine. There's nothing to tell.

Nina

Atsuko comes back into the room. I hear her moving around quietly, the careful noises as she places my shoes by the door, washes her hand at the shallow basin, and opens her wooden box of bottles, which rattle as she selects the few she needs. All the little rituals. Like casting a spell.

She knows I don't like to talk. Just the basics. 'Is this OK for you?'

'It's great,' I say, into the aperture. I'm facedown on the upholstered gurney, my cheeks and forehead pressed against the protective tissue shield. I close my eyes. The iPod soundtrack starts: the familiar loop of pebbles dropping into pools, wind chimes, sitars, Tibetan bowls, Bedouin drums, the noise of birds and surf and the rustling of leaves. Ersatz nature, the contemporary shorthand for relaxation.

The smooth heat of Atsuko's palms and fingers as she sets to work on my shoulders, the diligent firmness which is almost, but not quite, painful.

I let my mind empty. I don't think about Sophie, who comes home from school and swiftly leaves again, telling me she's going round to Eva's to work on an English project; or holes herself up in her room with her laptop, communicating (I imagine) with strangers in LA and Kuala Lumpur and Brisbane, who might be seventeen or twenty-seven or fifty-three. I don't think about Charles, who is in Bristol overnight. I don't think about the fact that my father's in town, demanding some attention.

Cicadas, the drone of ethnic chanting. Atsuko's fingers are steadily working towards the point I'm always conscious of, the tender spot just below my right shoulder blade. Knowing it's coming – dreading it, but needing it too – I frown down into the aperture, bracing myself, tensing up. I can't help it. 'It's too much?' asks Atsuko, easing off. 'Is it too painful?'

When I'm dressed, walking home in the dark, feeling the new chill in the air and the warm film of oil on my skin, my phone rings. *Paul.*

'You are being elusive,' my father says.

'Am I?' I say, turning into Pakenham Gardens. All along the street the bay windows are lighting up, displaying similar domestic scenes: the unpacking of groceries, table-laying, clarinet practice. I catch a glimpse of Monica and Tim Prewitt, evening newspaper and novel angled into the light, sherry glasses on the ottoman.

'I've got a table at Marcy's. I hear the fruits de mer is fabulous,' my father is saying. 'I was hoping I could persuade you and Charles to join me.'

'Oh, tonight's no good,' I say, pressing the mobile into my shoulder, twisting the key in the lock and letting myself into the hall. The lights are off but Sophie's coat is slung over the banister: she must be upstairs. 'Charles is away and I've got plans, Bridget's coming over for supper. I could do Thursday, if you're still here then.'

'I'm not in town for long,' he says. 'Bring Bridget too. Who is Bridget anyway? She sounds great. I'm sure I'd like her.'

I can tell he's demob happy: off the leash, expansive, wanting an audience.

'Oh, I don't think . . .' I say, but he has made up his mind:

he's summoning up all his relentlessly twinkly charisma. Just listening to him makes me feel tired. You have to be in the right frame of mind to spend time with my father, and I'm not in the right frame of mind tonight. Charles (who is, after all, closer in age to my father than to me) knows how to play him, and finds him moderately amusing. I'm not so sure.

'You know we'd have fun,' he's saying. 'Go on, ring her, see if she likes the sound of a very good table at Marcy's and my undivided attention.'

I say I'll see. And I don't sell it to her. But Bridget, a friend since art school, thinks it's a wonderful idea, certainly more wonderful than a Thai takeaway on the tall stools in my kitchen. She has always wanted to meet Paul. The other night she was about to go to bed when she realised *Crazy Paving* was on TV; she turned over to catch the backgammon scene, and the next thing she knew it was 2 a.m. Plus, you know: Marcy's. Hel-*lo?*

In the shower, I scour away Atsuko's almond oil, my eyes shut against the deluge. *See the old man, get it over with. It might be fun.*

While I'm waiting for the cab, I knock on Sophie's door. 'Not in,' she shouts, so I push the door open a little and say, 'I'm going out to dinner with Paul. He's in town for a few days. You can come if you like.'

'I'm good, thanks.'

'I'll put a pizza in the oven, it'll be ready at half past. Don't forget.'

She slouches over her desk, moving her arm so I can't see what's on the screen. 'Homework,' she says, heading me off.

I'm the last to arrive at the restaurant. My father rises up behind the stiff immaculate fall of tablecloth, palming back his hair, showing his teeth. The go-faster stripe of white at his temple; the shirred weft of the narrow silk tie gleaming like fish scales. His cheek, when it presses against mine, is smooth, cool, smelling distinctly of his particular scents: black pepper and lemon, the interior of expensive cars, the ministrations of a laundry service that returns linen banded in yellow ribbon.

Bridget reaches over to kiss me, mindful of her champagne glass and the candle in its smoked glass holder. 'Paul's just been telling me all about Jessica Lange and Robert Redford,' she says. *Here we go,* I think.

'Just making up a few stories,' he says, signalling for a glass for me.

I wouldn't put it past him. My father lives on the margins of reality, the magical shimmering point at which fantasy becomes fact. His whole life, when glanced at, looks rather like a dream: the talent, the lucky break, the success, the money, the houses. The wives.

From my perspective, that of the child at the edge of the room, it often appeared messy, wasteful, destructive; but my father was sustained by the excitement. Perhaps he felt it was no less than his due. Once, in my early twenties, I sat at the back of a private screening room in Soho – the insulated hush of the red velvet and the thick carpet, people juggling wine glasses and notebooks as they took their seats – and Paul came in, and stood for a moment, talking with the director, and the two young women in the row in front of me bent their heads towards each other and whispered, and then one of them laughed, a small mirthless sound. Listening to that, I felt the familiar twist of pride and shame. There was a story there that I did not want to hear.

Bridget rotates her glass, catching the condensation with a finger. 'But you're still composing, aren't you?' she asks.

'Oh, when something interesting comes along. If Vincent – Vincent Usher – asks, for example. Good friends. I'm too old to learn any new tricks.' One of my father's few failures, a decade or so ago, came when he wrote the score for a much-admired indie director making his mainstream debut. 'He didn't know what he was doing,' my father complained privately. 'He had too many choices, and he couldn't see a way through them.'

He keeps himself out of mischief, he reassures Bridget: he's still working on his choral symphony (he's been working on his choral symphony for as long as I can remember, and occasionally when we've overlapped there I've seen the sheet music left out by the piano in his house by the sea: a sharpened pencil laid decisively across the workings, as if it's all in hand), 'and of course I have the little one to keep me busy. Nina's half sister,' he adds.

Bridget nods (*of course*!) and then they both look at me, smiling conspiratorially, as if I'm somehow responsible for this small person I barely know. I smile back. 'How is Clara?' I ask, obediently.

My father's second shot at parenthood suits him. He has more leisure and patience this time around, and fewer distractions. Also, Delphine is more assertive than my mother was. She demands (as one senses she always has done, throughout her short and privileged life) and he obliges, indulgently, with pleasure.

He talks about Clara, and in between we place our orders, and the waiter brings us wine and bread and lays out the implements for taking apart lobsters, a surgeon's arsenal, and the little finger bowls containing warm water and thin translucent wheels of lemon. My father describes the swimming, the reading, the pictures she draws, great sprawling panoramas unfurled over the kitchen floor like carpets of febrile hallucination: fishes with eyelashes, skyscrapers fitted with rocket boosters, gigantic spiders wearing high-heeled shoes.

Bridget finds all this charming at first, but she has children of her own, and he senses the exact point at which she starts to lose interest. 'We were sorry you and Charles couldn't visit us this summer,' he says to me, setting to work on his fritto misto, crisp golden langoustines and whitebait and scallops heaped on utilitarian sheets of cheap grey greaseproof, the restaurant's little joke at its customers' expense. 'You really should make more use of the house.'

'Maybe in the spring,' I say. For a moment, I think of the wooden louvres angled against the sun as it spins remorselessly over the series of white boxes. The pale gravel that hurts your eyes, the smell of rosemary and pine, and the sound of the sprinklers in the late evening, water pattering onto the floodlit lawn. The perpetual striving for that impossible extravagant green.

'It would be nice there now,' he's saying. 'All the tourists have gone, the light is fantastic in the autumn, you can get into any restaurant you like. Why don't you fly down there for a week, take your sketchbooks?'

'It's a lovely idea, Dad,' I say, 'But Sophie's at school. I can't just take off like that.'

He supposes not. He asks after Sophie, now she has been mentioned, but he doesn't have much grasp of teenagers. 'Oh, Sophie,' sighs Bridget, loyally. 'So pretty, so together! I was never like that when I was seventeen, were you, Nina?'

'No,' I say. 'Although I'm not sure *together*'s the right word, exactly. Sophie's a bit of a mystery to me at the moment.'

'And how is Charles?' my father continues, not really listening. 'I saw the practice got a bit of attention somewhere or other a few weeks ago. One of the supps, Delphine pointed it out.'

'There was a nice piece in the *Wall Street Journal*,' I say.

'That's right. New museum in Chicago, somewhere like that. Looked like a packet of chewing gum to me.' He makes an I-am-awful face at Bridget. 'Charles is terribly serious,' he says, raising his eyebrows for a new bottle. 'It's quite *fun* seeing Nina off the leash like this. Girl's got to let her hair down sometimes.'

I smile in the way I've always smiled at my father's remarks. He can't help competing with my husband. He tried it with Arnold, too, but Arnold minded more, made more of it, came close to disliking him. Charles finds Paul funny, harmless. My father senses this, and hates it. So he's always keen to get a poke in, when he can.

Now he asks how Bridget and I know each other. Naturally, he has forgotten what I told him on the phone. Bridget, who used to paint large disconcerting oils of bus shelters and underpasses and municipal roundabouts, and who was once shortlisted for a prestigious prize, talks sheepishly about her new venture: she's trying to get a business together, drawing quirky portraits of people's houses viewed from the street. Fanlights, window boxes, cats on steps, clouds reflected in dark glass. 'They make a lovely gift when they're properly framed up,' she says. 'I've got a few commissions. People at school, mainly. Money's rubbish, of course, but, well, you have to keep your hand in.' The embarrassment of this confession makes her anxious to change the subject. 'But you must be so proud of Nina, really keeping it all going. Did you get to the show?'

Ah no, he couldn't make it, sadly, there was a reason, some visitors passing through on their way to Cannes. The usual line: he heard it was a tremendous success.

'I sold quite a few,' I say, tricked into defensiveness. 'The gallery was really pleased! A French collector bought a series of three, the three biggest works in fact. Michael didn't know the buyer, said he was new to the gallery. Walked in, picked out the yews sequence, all very decisive. New apartment in Knightsbridge, by all accounts, near Prince of Wales Gate. Bit of a break, really.'

My father squeezes his muslin-sheathed lemon over a last

scallop. 'Oh, perhaps that was Pierre Geroux. I sent him in your direction. You remember Pierre?'

A flare of disappointment, hearing him say it. Dimly, I remember a wet evening in the Place des Vosges, my father's friend grinding out a cigarette underfoot, tight curls threaded with raindrops, a camel scarf tucked inside a loden collar. 'Oh yes, I think that was the name. How nice. I hope he enjoys the paintings.'

'Are you still doing those landscapes?' he asks, fastidiously dabbing his fingers on his napkin, turning to Bridget as she says I've still got it, she thinks I'm heading in a new direction which is both beautiful and strange. 'They feel like paintings from the edge of the world,' she says, and I'm struck that she has picked up on this, and pleased; and then I remember it was on the print-out which Michael distributed at the opening.

'Quite fabulous, aren't they?' my father is agreeing. 'Great *big* things.'

'I've had a good summer,' I say. 'When Sophie was away with Arnold, I just got my head down and it went really well.' I look him in the eye: 'You might recognise some of the locations. Do you remember Jassop? For some reason, I've been thinking about Jassop recently. Bits of it are in there, I think.'

'Ah,' he says, restless, not interested. 'Well, I'd love to see the studio sometime.'

We talk a little about my mother. He doesn't always ask about her, especially when Delphine is around – though Delphine plainly couldn't care less about this ghostly failure, this person who still calls herself Mrs Storey, who lives in the country where she makes jam and bread and pots, and – when she has had too much to drink – becomes morose and spiteful, calling me up to pick over the hand life has dealt her. These things I keep to myself while I tell him (feeling vaguely disloyal) about the pottery class she is teaching at the local institute, the excitement with the chickens. 'Chickens!' he says, stirred almost to surprise. 'And yet of course, I can quite see Helen with chickens.'

Later, we stand on the pavement outside Marcy's for a few moments, saying our goodbyes, moving aside as people weave in and out of the heavy doors leaving little incomplete jokes hanging in the air behind them like smoke. I glance in the window, into the room which is full of a buttery low light pricked out with candles and silverware, and see the waiter clearing our table, whisking away the wine glasses and the coffee cups, the plate of petits fours, and lowering on a new white cloth with easy dramatic precision. A couple approaches, fresh from an opening night or a concert; the waiter adjusts a knife and swings to greet them. A swift reinvention, the final movement of someone else's evening.

Bridget spots a taxi and hails it, and while she's leaning over to tell the driver our addresses, I kiss my father goodbye. 'I'm in town till Thursday,' he says, 'So I'll ring you and we'll fix a time to meet at the studio. If you'd like that?'

'That would be fun,' I say, but we're both aware that something else will come up, or he'll forget. 'I'll look forward to it.'

'He must have been quite a handful when he was younger,' sighs Bridget as the taxi pulls off. 'Still is, I'll bet.' Hastily, she glances at me, worried she has gone too far, but I wave a hand, dismissing the concern. 'Oh, relax,' I say. 'I'm over all that. He was never like the other fathers.'

'No . . . I can't imagine him *mending* anything. Fixing a tap. Oiling a mower.' She's a bit pissed.

'He was always hopeless,' I say. 'Takes a pride in his hopelessness. Maybe he needed to find people who would deal with all the dull stuff for him. I've often wondered if that's why he wanted to marry my mother.'

I can see Bridget's a bit shocked; she's fond of Helen. When we were at college I took Bridget to Sussex a few times, and even now my mother inquires after her, putting the questions that would never occur to my father. I guess Bridget is thinking of my mother's wild hair tethered with tortoiseshell combs, the postcards stuck up in the downstairs loo, the milk bottles full of dusty pussy willow. 'Oh, but she must have been beautiful!' she says, then, more doubtfully, 'They must have had *something* in common.'

'Who knows,' I say. Perhaps if I had a sibling, we'd be able to make sense of it together, find the connection between the self-absorbed composer with magpie tastes, and the distracted hippy with clay under her fingernails. 'Whatever it was that initially brought them together – and I'd rather not dwell on *that* – I can't imagine how they lasted as long as they did.'

'Do you know what really happened?' Bridget asks, and I say oh, it's all a bit foggy, and my mother's version – which is still aired regularly – is unhelpful, as she deals in a general sense of grievance rather than specifics. They held it together until I was round about seventeen, although by that point even I could tell the interesting parts of my father's life were happening elsewhere; and then one day, just before the autumn term began, my father left the house in Jassop for an appointment in London and never came back.

I say I don't remember him leaving us (that's a lie), but I'm able to describe for Bridget the sudden change in the atmosphere at home: a sort of desperate gaiety as the house filled up with the people my father had been unable to stand. Penny, who ran the local riding stables; Philip and Malcolm, bridge-playing antique dealers; Gillian, the reflexologist with bad teeth and a nervous laugh, who said 'et cetera, et cetera' when she had nothing to say (which was, as my father had noted, often). On her own, my mother slumped; she needed to bolster herself with company, to lose herself in pursuits. Her diary filled with distractions: French classes, am dram, creative writing clubs, volunteer work. For a while, she and Gillian toured the south coast, going to séances and hypnotism shows in tarnished ballrooms that smelled of Jeyes fluid and hopelessness, pretending not to take them seriously.

Shortly after I went to study in London she sold the house in Jassop and moved to the next county, and I hoped she would leave the story of her great sadness behind. But it didn't quite work out like that.

The taxi clicks steadily through the pounds. The Magic Tree swings and twists over the jaywalkers, the Belisha beacons, the people leaving 24-hour stores carrying blue plastic bags. Under the fake scent, the cab smells the usual way: damp, too warm, vaguely metallic, like the inside of a mouth. I lean closer to Bridget, the sugary suggestion of face powder. Orange bands of light march steadily across her trench coat.

'How's Fred?' I ask, because I really should. A nice enough man, but deathly dull. He's in compliance, a word which sounded rather evocative – almost suggestive – when I first heard it, but which I now understand, though not from anything Bridget tells me, to be as boring and precarious as anything else in the City. I listen, playing Fred bingo, as Bridget checks off the key words: Singapore, bonus, Emirates season ticket. 'We must have you round for supper soon,' she says as the cab pulls up outside her house, a double-fronted Victorian that used to be a dentists' before Bridget took it on, tearing out the partitions and fire doors, painting the large rooms a very pale grey and filling them with a range cooker the size of a small car, Italian slate flagstones and cornicing as white as icing, figured with oak leaves and acorns.

Perhaps I'm too hard on Fred, I think, as the taxi bears

me away up the hill. He's a decent enough man. Somewhere along the line, he just stopped being fun. He must have made jokes once; he must have been able to laugh at himself not so very long ago. When do people change? When do their imaginations ossify? I picture him standing on the touch-line at Paddy's rugby matches, shouting encouragement and clapping his leather-gloved palms together as his breath mists the cold blue air and the boys knot around the ball, gathering and dispersing like microbes or sheep; and for a moment my own father leaps in my memory from long ago, arriving at my degree show just as everyone else was starting to leave, accompanied by a new girlfriend, a pretty creature whose name I've now forgotten (though I recall a very tight dress and heels that got caught in the steel stairs), and how he couldn't keep his hands off her, turning her round as if she were an ornament on display, unable to conceal his pleasure.

Emma

We can't agree what to call her.

'She doesn't look much like a Madeleine,' Ben whispers.

'Well, suck it up, she doesn't look much like a Cecily, either,' I whisper back. 'She looks like a Norma. Maybe a Belinda or a Pam.'

We laugh silently, aghast. The baby lies there in the car seat, her face as crumpled and jaundice-yellowed as a windfall apple, asleep and yet still inexorably stirring. I'd forgotten this animatronic stage, when they move in jerks, when they click and whirr and spasm abruptly into terrible tiny piercing alarm-screams that make the sweat pop out in beads along my hairline.

'She's not so bad, is she?' Ben breathes. He bends down, examining her in a way one never can when she's awake. 'She's rather lovely. Jesus, those fingernails . . . look, she's cut herself, look at her cheek.'

When he says this, I hear the reproach. *You should cut her nails before she does herself an injury.*

'You could trim them,' I say. 'Do it when she wakes up. Or maybe it would be easier to do it now, while she's asleep. Although it might disturb her nap.'

'Where are the nail scissors?' he asks, and I know I'll end up doing it, because it's easier than telling him what he already knows: *they're in the bathroom cabinet* (which he will go and stand in front of, vaguely scanning the jumbled shelves, unable to see them, though they are right there, between the box of Elastoplast and the arnica gel).

The baby's sleeping, I think. What on earth am I doing here, wasting time like this, staring at her? I should be washing my hair. I should be sitting down, or lying on the bed with my eyes shut. I should be returning a phone call or doing an internet grocery shop or replying to emails or finding the library books which I never finished but which are now very overdue. I should be spending quality time with Christopher, who is downstairs on the sofa, zombie-eyed in front of *Balamory*, where he has spent the last few weeks, more or less.

'I'm going to jump in the shower,' I whisper, starting to move away, and sure enough as I do so the baby's arms whip out wildly as if she's falling, the startle reflex kicking in; payback for allowing her to fall asleep unswaddled. As swiftly as a shadow on a hillside, her complexion switches from yellow to maroon. The thin scratchy punishing noise begins.

'Shall I . . .' says Ben, but we both know this is my job: to sit in an empty room holding this small unhappy thing close to me, allowing it to fasten on to my flesh, my milk pumping in, displacing the toxic silt which is waiting there in the plumbing. Dealing with that will fall to me, too.

I unbutton my shirt and move to the chair, kicking it so it angles towards the window, aware now of just how much my shoulders and back ache. Ben picks the baby from the harness, lowering her into my lap. She's hot and damp and firm and squealing, an animated bag of dough smelling of farmyards. The urgency of her hunger makes me feel slightly sick. There's the usual wailing desperation as she tugs and strains, goldfish mouth flapping, fists flailing, her eyes screwed shut in fury: *where is it, where is it, I want it.*

Then, thankfully, silence, though she's tense as a tripwire until the let-down.

It hurts a bit, I've still not got the latch quite right, but it's not as bad as it was. *Relax.* I make myself sit back, push my head against the chair, cup my hand over her skull, and breathe out. I'm almost not uncomfortable, as long as I don't move at all.

'I'll go and start Christopher's supper,' Ben says, edging towards the door. 'Do you want anything?'

'A cup of tea would be great. And a biscuit,' I say. The moment he leaves the room, I realise that I should have asked him to turn on the radio, which is on the bookshelf, just out of reach. It must be about five thirty, or six. I wouldn't mind listening to the news. I've no idea what is happening out there, in the world, where people go to work and meet friends, and have conversations. I'll ask him to move the radio when he brings the tea. So for now, I listen to the sound of her swallowing, great greedy gasping gulps, and feel her sigh and relax against me, as if she's abandoning a grievance.

Ben's bedside lamp is on behind me, and when he comes back I'll ask him to turn it off, because its reflection makes it hard for me to look out of the window. For now I must sit here, trapped by my reflection and the reflection of the room behind me: the rumpled bed with its Welsh blanket tossed over the white duvet, Ben's box of earplugs and the stack of news magazines on his bedside table, the muslins and tissues and glasses of water on mine. The changing table with its hygienic paraphernalia. The books and, out of reach, the radio.

Though I can't quite see them, I can hear the people out there on the dark street, coming and going. I listen to the purposeful or desultory nature of their steps on the pavement, the bicycles and car doors, the jingle of keys.

Children's raised voices. I press my socked feet against the lukewarm radiator, willing the evening boost to start.

I sit here in the yellow chair, in the room where she was conceived, and I'm aware that I'm wishing my life away. *Where the fuck's that tea?* I think. The sound of the television drifts up the stairs. Ben bangs some pots in the kitchen. 'Fishfingers and peas OK? Or would you rather have pesto pasta?' he calls. *Don't give him a choice,* I think. Christopher, locked into cartoons, doesn't answer.

Far below me, low in the ground, there's the distant hum of the Northern Line, a vibration conducted through the layers of ancient compacted earth – layers of sand and mud and clay studded with bones, oyster shells and fragments of pottery, things that people once held precious – before it shivers up into the matchstick foundations of our house, its joists and floorboards, its window frames and door jambs. Feeling the vibration, I think of the illuminated metal cylinders speeding through the tunnels carved into the dirt, the travellers inside them, pushed up against each other, gently swaying together as the blind tracks curve.

Ben hates this, when he notices it. I love it. It reminds me we're still part of something.

I could shout. I could call for him, and when he came, I could ask him to switch on the radio and turn off the light. I could say, 'Any chance of that tea?'

She wriggles a little, flinging out her arm, brushing my jaw with her fingers. I feel the tiny laceration of her nails on my neck.

Nina

As the pumpkins and the glass baubles come and go in the shop windows, as we sink deeper into the dark wet winter, I see her in the distance from time to time: toiling behind the double buggy in the drizzle, hood pulled over her hair; being expelled from the park as the gates are locked at dusk. Sometimes I toy with the idea of catching up with her and saying hello, inspecting her at closer range, but I never do. Watching her is enough, for now. I can see how she's feeling: the tiredness, the loneliness. I almost feel sorry for her.

Despite the plug-in heater and the fingerless gloves and the paint-spattered kettle, the studio is so cold by mid-afternoon that I'm not very productive. Bright mornings, when the sun falls on this side of the building, are better, more stimulating: dazzling air inside and out. I'm still working on the Jassop paintings. Charles, who comes to the studio every few weeks for a companionable inspection, is very struck by them. 'So this is Kent, is it?' he asks one Sunday morning, moving around in front of the canvases, examining them, one by one. 'The place where you lived in your teens? How odd that you've started thinking about it now.'

'Maybe it's something to do with Sophie,' I say, easily. 'When we lived there, I was around the same age as she is now. Maybe that's why. But it's only an idea of Jassop, really.

A fragment of a memory. I can't really remember that much about it. We weren't there for very long.'

'Was that before or after Oxfordshire?' he asks, and I say *after*, it was the house my father bought with the proceeds of *Crazy Paving*, when my mother was on her self-sufficiency jag, when she wanted a garden full of sweetpeas and redcurrant bushes, some space for her looms.

There was another reason why we moved away from Oxfordshire and though I've never felt any particular need to share this with Charles I doubt whether he'd be surprised by it. That was the house that my father began to leave. Before long, he was always away, in London and Los Angeles; sometimes when I asked where he was this week, my mother didn't seem to be entirely sure; and then there were the times when I'd answer the phone in the hall and no one would speak, and the silence would build and accumulate, an avid sort of silence caught in the tight coils of cord. Someone listening quite patiently while I said again and again, 'Hello? Hello, who's there?' And then after a few seconds, the connection would be cut. 'Who was that?' my mother would call, and – unsure of why I was lying, but knowing a lie was necessary – I'd call back, 'Wrong number.'

Sometimes my mother must have taken these calls, though she never mentioned them to me. Standing in the hall, the receiver grasped like a duty, a punishment. 'Hello? Who's that? Is anyone there?'

When my father eventually came home, with carrier bags full of Duty Free scent and cigarettes, and packs of Hershey's Kisses for me, there would be a few days' grace, and then I would start to catch hold of the edge of arguments, arguments taking place behind closed doors when I was meant to be asleep or out or doing my homework. Mostly I would hear my mother's wild emotional indiscipline, but if I listened for long enough I would hear the sore, sour sound of my father.

And then the house was put up for sale, and we moved to Jassop, and the phone calls stopped, for a while at least.

'She kept her spinning wheel and her looms in the attic,' I tell Charles, 'and when he was at home he was always in the drawing room, on the piano, or the telephone – so it wasn't exactly a surprise when they split up. It was a lovely house, though, the oldest bit of it was in the Domesday Book. Or at least, that's what they told me.'

As I say it, I remember stepping from the hot garden into the little porch, its pegs hung with mildewy macs, and then passing down into the thankful chill of the kitchen, the soft cold flagstones underfoot, the striped roller-towel on the range rail, the china sink capillaried with pale blue, the paper bags of sugar and flour leaning into each other on the pantry shelves. One particularly deep cupboard had mesh panels in the door: the meat safe, where not so long before game birds and joints of beef and lamb were stored.

'We could go and have a look around one weekend,' he suggests. 'Book a hotel. See the marsh churches. What do you think?'

'Might be fun,' I say, but I don't want to go back. I never have. This is as close as I want to get: the thick streaks and smears and beads of paint, bands of colour, the sky, the light. Nothing too specific. I remember long afternoons – always hot, always indolent with heat – spent in the garden at Jassop, making the snapdragons snap while the pansies ('kitten faces', my mother called them) trembled in the breeze, and I remember that feeling of waiting for something to happen. Something exciting or marvellous. I knew it was on its way. I didn't know what form it would take, but I knew it was coming.

My bedroom was under the eaves, with a low sloping

ceiling. No door handle, just a wooden latch. Pale yellow walls, a blue coverlet on the bed. When I was little I'd made a family of clay owls which my mother had helped me to glaze and fire (five or six of them, in waistcoats and aprons and spectacles), and even as a teenager I liked to see them there on the windowsill, set out in order of size, looking out owlishly towards the sea.

I wonder what happened to the owl family. Probably my mother has them still, in a shoebox at the back of a cupboard. The arrowheads of their sculpted feathers. The sharp little nibs of their beaks.

'Let's walk over to Hampstead for a coffee,' Charles is saying, so I tidy up, putting some sketches in the plan chest, and as I do so I pause for a moment as the manila envelope slides into view. My hand goes out to it, and then I put the papers on top of it and close the drawer.

We leave the studio, passing Casey – who runs an internet operation from a unit on the same floor, selling imported Japanese sports drinks and energy bars – in the dim concrete stairwell. The noise of our footsteps chases us down into the cold street. I do not think of the envelope, nor the white-bordered Instamatic snaps it contains; inexpertly and pretentiously composed, speckled with the leaky bleached stars of accidental exposure. The blacks bleeding into the reds.

Emma

Ben's father Dirk comes out to greet us, his mustard corduroy trousers a beacon in the dusk, his mouth opening and shutting as the headlights sweep over him and the naked lady in the hostas before coming to rest on the double garage. There's a moment of silence when Ben switches off the engine, and then the baby wakes up and I reach out for the handle.

'Emma, splendid, how was the traffic?' he's saying, striding towards me, his hands flapping out to seize my waist. I intercept them just in time, grabbing his fingers, glad I remembered. Here's Christopher, shyly stumbling up behind me, Blue Bunny dangling by one ear. Dirk greets him rather perfunctorily, then turns with more enthusiasm to Ben, wanting to know about the sat-nav and the bypass.

Ben brandishes the car seat containing Dirk's granddaughter. This is their second meeting; Dirk and Peggy came to see me in hospital, bringing yellow flowers. But Dirk has other things on his mind. 'Yes, it's new,' he says, gesturing expansively at the silver Audi estate parked in its own special spotlight on the gravel, as if we've all been clustering around, clamouring questions. 'Trade-in. John Brethwick made me an offer I couldn't refuse. Miles to the gallon, it makes sense, had it a fortnight, haven't had to fill it up once.'

Dirk was in shipping insurance and claims to be retained, in some capacity, as an ad-hoc consultant. Secretly I find it hard to believe that his firm is a willing participant in this arrangement: I imagine the smoke-signals from the front desk on the days when he drops in to the huge redbrick HQ off Holborn, the PAs on high alert, the bigwigs suddenly remembering critical meetings on the fifth floor. Dirk buttonholing clerks by the water-cooler, passing on the benefit of his wisdom and experience. He's a man of infinite butterfly interests: opinions on everything, though they vary from day to day, and sometimes from hour to hour, depending on whether he has been absorbing data from the *Spectator* or the *Today* programme or a copy of Peggy's *Daily Mail.* For Dirk, the important thing is having an opinion. Its particular flavour matters less.

'You'll see we've had a new alarm system put in,' he says, indicating a box on the wall under the eaves, but at this Cecily starts to twist and whimper in her harness so I say, 'I think I'd better—' and almost reluctantly he says of course, come on into the warm, Peggy's getting tea ready, there's still some Christmas cake left.

I wouldn't mind feeding Cecily in the sitting room, just to get up his nose, but when I say she's hungry Peggy tells me she has popped us in the Blue Bedroom, it's all set up, I should find everything I need up there. So I put Cecily over my shoulder and go upstairs, along an acre of olive carpet illuminated by dim glazed wall sconces in the shape of scallops, and lie down with her on the bed, on the slippery periwinkle bedspread, because the chair by the window has no armrests.

While Cecily feeds, I work through the pile of Christmas round robins that have been left out for us (although the pond-water illumination cast by the squat little ceramic bedside lamp, with its pleated shade, does not make this easy). For all the wrong reasons I love these letters. I love the ludicrous spectacle of strangers' lives artlessly set out for my delectation: the foreign holidays, the house extensions ('we finally got rid of the builders!'), the silver-wedding celebrations and theatre trips to Stratford-upon-Avon. Cynthia and Derek are learning Portuguese! Kathy and Malcolm have bought a camper van! Berenice has moved to Wales!

And yet, beneath it all, it's clear that a displacement is taking place. Peggy and Dirk's friends are now defining themselves through their grandchildren's achievements: the art prizes and choral scholarships, the A-stars and Russell Group offers. *Something is pushing them to the side of their own lives.* I put down the letters and feel the chord reverberating, and I resolve to be kinder this visit. More patient, more understanding. Nicer.

Sated, Cecily rolls off me, her cheek flushed and shiny with milk. *I will be good,* I think.

Downstairs, Dirk is showing off his new electric curtains (gizmo was a special offer at the back of the *Telegraph* magazine, he couldn't resist), zapping them with a remote control, revealing and then hiding the spotlit lawn, the bare trees and birdbath, the topiary hens – themselves an excuse, I've always suspected, for the chainsaw.

'What do you make of that, eh, Christopher?' he says, over the high-pitched whine of the motor, making the sprigged curtains dance and sway: open, shut, open. 'Clever, isn't it?'

Christopher, hypnotised, transfixed with longing, puts out his hand.

'Better not, old chum,' Dirk says breezily. 'Delicate mechanism. Not a toy, I'm afraid.' He zaps the curtains so the view vanishes, and pops the remote on the highest bookshelf, next to the row of military history. *That's that.* Peggy hands me my tea and admires Cecily in a rudimentary fashion: all very arms' length. 'What an absolute dear she is,' she calls as she returns to the kitchen. 'Would you like some Christmas cake, Emma?'

I would, and I deserve it, but I can't cope with Cecily, hot tea and tiny plate (nor, indeed, the uncontrollable look of disapproval that would cross her face if I accepted: Peggy does three spin classes a week, plus a Friday Zumba, and views sugar as the enemy, though she seems bent on giving her menfolk type-two diabetes), so I say I'll pass. Christopher returns his attention to the dish of chocolate fingers on the ankle-high coffee table. He won't eat any supper after this, I know; but fuck it, that's not my problem tonight. 'Dirty hands!' cries Peggy, rushing in with a damp cloth as he lunges for the ornamental chess set.

I close my eyes, feeling the baby's solid dampish weight against me, imprisoned by it. But I need do nothing here: it's all out of my hands, beyond my control. My life is such that these visits, which I used to dread, which are still full of uncomfortable moments, are now beginning to qualify as relaxation. In the kitchen, Dirk is showing Ben the pop-up plug socket on the central island, and the special bin system under the sink for separating wet waste from dry. 'We saw that programme of yours, that one on the GCSE marking scandal,' Dirk says as they come through. 'Very good. Shame you couldn't get the Secretary of State to comment.'

This is typical Dirk: many things go over his head, but he is always able to identify his son's disappointments or weaknesses, eager to bring these failures out into the light. I catch Ben's eye, and he glances away, at the Nordic pine in the corner.

'Lovely tree, Dirk,' I say, and – as I knew he would – he gives me its full provenance: it's a bit of a tradition, Mike Caxton rings him when the delivery comes in so he gets first pick; of course they need a bit of a monster with ceilings this high.

The fairy lights wink on the tree, threaded between the coordinated balls and birds and angels. This year, everything is either silver or white. 'Shall we do presents now, or after we've eaten?' says Peggy.

Later that evening, as Cecily rustles sleepily in the travel cot at the foot of the bed, Ben and I undress in low light. At moments like these, I long for a proper therapeutic debrief, a bit of a giggle, as well as some sort of vaguely appreciative apology, but I won't get either from him and I know it's wrong, *mean*, to want them so much; just as I know it's wrong, *mean*, to wish Dirk and Peggy might offer us a little financial help while we're going through this tight spot (though of course Ben would never solicit or accept a handout, even as the shed door lists on its hinges, the brown stain on the ceiling of Christopher's bedroom grows larger, and the mortgage repayments and credit-card bills stalk our dreams).

'They seem very well,' I murmur, finding a clean babygro and putting it next to the wipes and nappies, ready for the morning. 'Your mother's really into this gym thing.'

Ben, climbing into bed, grunts. The slippery blue bedspread whispers as he pushes it down towards the foot, and then it slides off altogether, pooling on the carpet, a lake of static. 'I expect she spends a lot of time in the salad bar,' he says, 'gassing with Angela Sinclair.'

I look down at Cecily, whose dark eyelashes are fanned out on her round cheeks, her fists curled on either side of her head. Her chest rises and falls in her moon-patterned sleeping bag: in, out, in. I visualise Peggy on the treadmill in pink velour joggers and a light sweat glaze, eyes locked onto *Cash in the Attic* or *Homes Under the Hammer*.

I rub moisturiser into my face, my neck. When I pull back the duvet, there's a dark smear of chocolate and a flattened foil wrapper on the pillow: one of Peggy's thoughtful touches.

I must have melted my guest orange cream unwittingly, when I was feeding the baby this afternoon.

The visit unfurls as these visits always do. We gather for chilli con carne and baked gammon and rissoles made with leftover turkey. We attend the Sinclairs' New Year drinks where Ben becomes rather animated because one of the other guests was once a formative crush. We go for wet walks along the bridleway, Cecily in the backpack, Christopher managing to get water in his beetle wellingtons, necessitating an early return. In the evenings, with the children in bed, we watch period dramas and play competitive games of Scrabble and listen to Dirk talking about a new ride-on mower he's thinking of buying, to Peggy havering over where to go in February (Cape Verde islands? Madeira?).

At regular intervals during the day, Peggy does a ground-floor sweep after which bossy little cairns of our possessions – jumpers, Blue Bunny, bibs, wipes, the tube of Christopher's eczema cream – are left for our attention at the bottom of the stairs. It's a silent scream of protest. And, as things are never where I left them, it makes my life just that little bit harder.

We spend a lot of time saying, 'Put that down, Christopher,' or 'That's Grandma's special china bell, it's not for playing with,' or 'The curtains aren't a toy.'

'He's a livewire, isn't he?' says Dirk admonishingly as we return the Scrabble tiles to their rightful place. The chess set is missing a queen and two pawns but no one has yet commented; with luck, we'll find them before we leave. 'Bright as a button, I expect?' There's an edge of doubt in his voice. It's just before lunch, a time for peanuts and sherry. I never have sherry anywhere else. Here, it's a bit of a highlight.

'That reminds me, Dirk,' says Peggy, over the scream of

the electric carving knife, 'Jemima's been put in the top sets for maths and literacy, did Tom mention that?'

Dirk did know. 'And of course the standard at The Chase is terribly high,' he adds, for our benefit.

Jemima is their other granddaughter, precious firstborn of Ben's brother Tom. Tom was going great guns in corporate finance – Dirk was always keen to tell us that he was nailing targets, collecting scalps, being showered with bonuses – until about three years ago when it emerged, in a roundabout fashion, that he had been made redundant. Since then, Tom has been 'regrouping', 'working on something very hush-hush', although he and his matchy-matchy wife Carolyn, who does something in 'comms', don't seem to have pulled in their horns: they're still a two-car household, they're still going to Verbier and Dubai, and the porridge-faced Jemima continues to put on her blazer with the green piping every morning. Is there a boater? I think there might be a boater.

We sit there, waiting to be called for lunch, and suddenly Dirk rocks forward in his chair, barking, 'Oh, stop fiddling!' and Christopher is looking down at the coffee table, at the upended bowl and the spilled peanuts, a salty finger in his mouth. *Uh-oh.*

On the last morning we come down and find that Christopher has risen early and balanced two cushions on the sofa, giving him access to the holy grail on the top shelf. The curtain mechanism is broken, the curtains jammed at half-mast. Dirk puts a brave face on it. 'Not to worry,' he says, taking the back off the remote to see if new batteries will do the trick. They don't.

We escort Christopher to the naughty step, out in the cold hall, next to a balled-up pair of walking socks and a copy of *Peepo*. He sits there mute, bearing his punishment, almost noble in his acceptance of it.

Back in London, unpacking the children's bag, stuffing

the dirty clothes into the washing machine, I find the little green drawstring sack from the Scrabble set, and inside it the queen and the pawns.

Nina

Sophie's face, I think, is like the moon, cold, mysterious, remote. I look at my child now, standing there in the hall in martyred resignation – slightly knock-kneed as the fashion has it, her hair pulled in a slippery fall over one shoulder – and I'm not sure who she is.

She puts her tongue in her cheek, turns the rope of her hair around, twisting it, tugging it, bored, waiting for the moment to pass.

The inflections of Arnold that I notice at these moments, when Sophie's busy hating me, are hard to bear. The weary inhalations. The lip-pressing. The holding back from saying things that I can, in any case, imagine. When she speaks, I smell Wrigley's first, and then cigarettes.

'My phone ran out of juice,' she's saying, 'So I didn't get your message.'

'Well, you should have remembered to charge it up properly,' I say, hearing my voice, shrill, reverberative, appalling. My power, already compromised, dwindling further. 'And you could have borrowed a friend's phone. It's a school night! How many times do we have to go through this?'

She stifles a yawn, the phone in her hand suddenly illuminating as a text or email arrives. 'I just forgot. I won't do it again,' she says, moving her hand quickly to hide the light that confirms her deceit.

'I've heard that before,' I say, deciding not to take her on about the phone right now: *pick your battles, first things first.* 'I was worried! Anything could have happened.'

'Well, it didn't,' she says, and then, more quietly, 'For God's sake. It was only an hour.'

I check my watch. 'Two, nearly three, actually. Where were you, anyway?'

'At Tasha's. She asked me for supper.'

'I'll talk to her mother tomorrow,' I say, but she interrupts: 'Oh, don't make a fuss, Tasha had to keep an eye on Tilly, their parents were going out. I said it would be OK.'

'Oh.' I feel my anger slackening slightly, my desire to believe.

'Look, I won't do it again,' she's saying, and as I say, 'You're running out of chances,' she shrugs off her school blazer in an attempt to delineate the end of the episode. Her head lowered over the phone as she walks away, up the stairs. 'Yup, yup, yup.'

Charles has tidied up the kitchen after supper and is in the sitting room, socked feet on the footstool, reading the *Evening Standard*. He raises an eyebrow as I come in, nods at his single malt. 'Can I get you one?'

'No, thanks.' I can't sit down quite yet. I move around the room, between the white sofas, putting another log in the wood burner, collecting the *Economist* and adding it to the pile of last weekend's supplements. Rain hits the window in fits and starts, as if it's being flung in handfuls. I pull the curtains against the black night.

'She's fine,' he says in a low comforting voice. 'It's normal. It's what they do, teenagers. School's OK, isn't it?'

'As far as I know. No, nothing to worry about there. All on track.' I find it hard to put it into words, this sense that

I'm losing her, that she's moving away from me, into a room that I can't see clearly, as it's badly lit or full of smoke. A place where anything might happen.

What am I scared of? Perhaps it's a car. A dark street. A drink briefly left unattended. A careless boy or an older man. The usual horrors. Or it could be something more prosaic, more everyday. Perhaps I'm frightened that she no longer needs me in quite the same way. That my authority is being diminished, and I can do nothing about it.

'She's a sensible girl, more sensible than Jess was at her age,' Charles says, as he always does, and thinking of Jess – the fast druggy crowd I've been told she fell in with at school, her job at English Heritage, her window boxes and stew-making – I laugh a little and switch on the TV and watch the last half-hour of a spy thriller.

Upstairs, Sophie moves from her bedroom to the bathroom and back again, and finally shuts her door for the night.

Emma

It could have happened to anyone. So easily done, it doesn't bear thinking about. Anyway, it's all fine, people behaved as you hope they will, with kindness and decency – after all, the world is full of good people, we need to remember this – and Christopher has already forgotten about it. He hasn't mentioned it since.

Just one of those things.

Everyone agrees it's not my fault: Ben, Lucy, the Monkey Music mothers, as we sit cross-legged on the carpet in between 'Wheels on the Bus' and 'Mary Mary', the children's raincoats piled on a chair at the edge of the community hall. The other mothers make offerings of their own stories: Ruth's Max ran off at London Zoo; Miranda came *this* close to leaving Jimmy in Sainsbury's car park; when Fran was away for an uncle's funeral, Luke forgot to pick up Ruby from the childminder ('I came out of the wake and there were six messages from her on the phone. It was seven-thirty!').

People couldn't be sweeter, more understanding, more sympathetic. But I know what they're thinking. I don't blame them. I'd be thinking the same thing, in their shoes.

During the very earliest weeks of my first pregnancy I had a dream about motherhood. I dreamed that I had a newborn baby of my own, the size of a thimble or a larva, a tiny mewing scrap of dependency that I kept in a walnut-shell cradle. I can't remember if it was a boy or a girl, blond, dark or a redhead: the key thing was, I was forever losing it. The dream was one long desperate ransacking of cutlery drawers and recycling boxes and laundry baskets. When I woke up I told Ben the dream, gratefully turning it into a joke, a riff on my own entirely appropriate anxieties (the phrase 'elderly primagravida', boldly scrawled across my hospital notes, did not fill me with confidence); but even as we laughed, I was still feeling the cold sickening buzz of panic in my blood. I'm not sure that sensation has ever really left me.

An afternoon in the park. Early spring, the long wet paths gleaming in thrilling bursts of sunshine, buds punctuating the chestnut branches to mark the end of winter. I have lifted Cecily out of the buggy and I've wedged her into the little swing in the babies' playground. It's the first time I've bothered to do this, and at first she's terrified, hating it, her mittened fists flailing, unable to fathom the pendulum rhythm; and then suddenly the penny drops, and she starts to enjoy herself, her mouth open in a great astonished O of delight. Christopher is on his Christmas micro scooter, racing up and down along the flat stretch between the playground and the park gate, sailing through and around puddles bright as mirrors.

After a few minutes I look at my watch, and then I glance around. I can't see him.

I turn my head, checking the paths. A woman jogs past, earphones in, lost in her own secret soundtrack. A man bends down for a stick and throws it for his spaniel.

I scan the shrubbery, the battered huddled outline of the ornamental walk, the view over to the kitchen garden, and then I turn in the other direction, towards the pond, the boardwalk around it, the disused drinking fountain and the line of empty benches leading to the adventure playground.

Two women walk past with pushchairs, chatting and laughing. The sun slides into cloud.

He's wearing a bright green anorak and a knitted wasp-striped bobble hat. I search for that acid flare of yellow, and I can't see it anywhere.

I pull Cecily out of the swing, ignoring her complaint, the crumple of her face, and I clip her into the buggy. Which way? I come out of the playground, the weighted safety gate knocking my thigh. I turn right, to the pond. 'Christopher!' I shout, and then I shout it again, hurrying the buggy along, my eyes on the black water through the iron railings, snarled with leaves and twigs; and, hearing me, two fifty-something women glance up out of their conversation and come towards me.

'He's nearly three, he's wearing a green jacket and a yellow striped hat,' I tell them. 'His name is Christopher, he was just there, on his scooter,' and I point, and they say they didn't see him by the pond, he didn't come in their direction, they're fairly sure of that, but they'll do a quick circuit and they'll check the adventure playground as they go past. 'Thank you so much,' I say, for something to say, and then I'm off again, hurrying in the other direction this time, towards the kitchen garden and the shrubbery.

It's dark under the trees, and as I pass, calling for him, heavy fat drops of water slide from the overhanging foliage and fall on me, little detonations on my cheek and hands, spilling through my hair.

I'm calling for him, and Cecily has stopped crying, maybe it's the motion of the buggy or maybe she can tell from my voice that something's wrong.

A few people hear me shouting and approach, concerned, wanting to help, and then they join the search, but it's all hopeless, I know it, he's not here. 'Thanks, that would be great,' I say to them, and then I run off, heading uphill to the little café, the terrace deserted, chairs tilted to the tabletops, the windows opaque with breath and steam from the Gaggia, and there's no sign of him, and I can't see him on the lawn, and – oh Jesus – he's not near the fountain either, though it's a source of endless fascination. I run up to the fountain, and I look in, and then I turn on my heel and bump the buggy down the broad steps, between the broken stone urns, heading downhill again, taking the path that comes out by the compost bins and the lower gate.

When I reach the road I stand there for a moment, looking up and down, my chest rising and falling, the air scouring my dry throat. The road's quiet as dusk begins to settle, the jolly lollipop flash of the Belisha beacon starting to assert itself in the fading light. I realise a Fiat Punto has halted to let me cross. I wave it on. 'Christopher?' I shout, into the trees, and it's a pathetic sound, weak and insubstantial, nothing like it feels.

This isn't happening.

I need to call the police?

'There she is.' A voice behind me. I turn around, electrified by hope. The two women from the pond are hurrying along the path towards me, and a park attendant is with them, a man with a radio, but no child in a green anorak. The park attendant sees the expression on my face and puts the radio to his mouth.

It has only been five or ten minutes, I realise. It doesn't sound like much. Anything could happen in five or ten minutes.

No.

I describe Christopher to the park keeper, who bends his head into the crackle, passing on the information to the police: Christopher Nash, nearly three ('No, it's Christopher, not Chris,' and I nod dumbly, confirming this again, horrified by the contrast with the normal circumstances in which an explanation is required: *We always expected we'd abbreviate it, but he doesn't look like a Chris. He just looks like a Christopher)*. Blond hair, blue eyes. Green quilted jacket, yellow-and-black bobble hat, navy trousers and wellingtons painted with beetles. Purple micro scooter.

This high, I say, showing him, not sure how to quantify it.

Someone says my name, and it's Fran from Monkey Music, with Ruby on her balance bike, heading for the gates and home. I see Fran's face change as she comes closer and sees the look on mine. I start to cry then, and the park keeper, whose name is Gareth or Gary, says, 'The police will be here any minute,' and moves away, letting Fran get closer. As she hugs me, Ruby looking up at me with huge curious eyes, I see that Cecily has nodded off in the buggy. Part of me is still stuck in that old, safe life, because for a moment I feel the echo of that tinpot panic: *too late for a nap, she won't go down easily at seven*. Then, contemptuously, I let the thought go, because it means nothing.

The dark is racing across the park now. The two ladies who have been standing around talking in low voices shuffle off apologetically, muttering reassurances. Then we hear the siren. A moment later I'm being helped into a police car while Fran takes the buggy. 'Thank you, I'll call you,' I mouth as the car pulls off, and I see her face as I go, strobing in the light.

They've switched off the siren, I don't know why.

There are two youngish police officers in the car, they tell me their first names, John and Lauren, and they do their best: they seem organised, reassuringly invoking protocols, but I can sense the undercurrent beneath what they say. 'We've got another car out locally and two foot patrols doing the park,' Lauren tells me, leaning back so I can hear what she says as John takes a right towards the cemetery, 'And the chances are, he has just wandered off, got lost somewhere.

We'll just drive around the neighbourhood and see if we can spot him anywhere. Chances are, he hasn't gone very far.' She asks if I wouldn't mind buckling up.

The radio hisses and whistles, another unit reporting from higher up the hill. My heart soars and then plummets. 'Just keep your eyes peeled,' John says. 'We'll go nice and slow, so we don't miss anything.'

We're driving along the edge of the estate, the white stepped terraces chalky under the sodium lights. Behind the little balconies, windows are lighting up. The aquarium flicker of TVs, the snub as people pull curtains.

By the wheelie bins, six or seven kids kick a football against a wall. They scatter when the police car slows to a halt alongside, but John rolls down his window and calls, 'We're looking for a lost toddler,' and the boys come closer, interested, possibly even concerned, despite themselves. They haven't seen anything. *Thanks. If you do*... Window up, drive on.

This is it, this is really happening.

A bus sails by, full of light, people inside reading books, checking their phones, looking bored.

'Is there anyone you need to call?' Lauren asks, and I say no, though I know I must ring Ben. But I'm trying to put that off for as long as I can. Telling him, like telling Fran, requires a vocabulary that I don't possess. I keep my eyes on the pavements, the deep dark patches of shadow at the edges of things: buildings, bushes, stairwells.

We turn left at the library and slowly work back towards the hospital, which rises up in front of us, huge and illuminated, like an ocean liner. As we drive past the entrance, I see the shuttered florist's kiosk, the empty escalators endlessly rolling up and down. Three smokers in wheelchairs are spaced out in the concrete plaza, one trailing an IV stand.

Here the streets are a little busier, people coming home

from the tube or changing buses. Pizza-delivery signs, the cold white of cyclists' LEDs. Up the hill, a snaking impatient chain of ember-red brake lights.

It has been several years since I've been out alone at this time of day, able to notice such things. These are sights I seldom see.

The radio crackles now and again, officers checking in, nothing to report.

'You're in Carmody Street, aren't you,' says Lauren, consulting her notes. 'So we could just head down there, just to make sure.'

My face is wet with tears, and the sensation makes other tears come faster. *He's not quite three. Last week, I forgot the bananas in Sainsbury's, so I left him in the checkout queue with the basket, I said I'd only be a minute, but he came to find me. 'I was scared,' he said, 'I was scared you wouldn't come back,' and even as I picked him up and hugged him, I felt a rush of irritation. Just thirty seconds, is that too much to ask?* I squeeze my eyes shut; and then, quickly, I open them again, because I might miss something, and I mustn't miss anything.

Bus stop. Railings. Postbox. All the familiar things.

The tick of indicators as the police car pulls out, crossing the main road and taking the first right down Carmody Street. Sunil Faradosa lifts his bike through the front door, Kay Callaghan is hauling Morrison's bags out of the boot. 'Nothing,' I say, as the front step of our house comes into view. 'Can we go back to the park?'

'I think we should probably go down to the station,' Lauren says, and I close my eyes, just for a second, unable to bear the implications, assailed by an overwhelming sense of him – the softness of his skin, his hand sticky in mine, the way he smells when he is asleep, Blue Bunny tucked under his cheek – and I think I'm going to be sick. I open my window and inhale. *In, out. In, out.* I see John stretching up to check me in the rear-view mirror. 'Just hold on,' he says, switching on the siren.

The radio crackles again, and a man's voice says something very quickly, I can't quite understand what, but Lauren has picked up and says, 'Ten-four, that's good news,' and I can hardly accept it, not at first, it feels like the sort of luck I'm not in any way entitled to; but when she leans back towards me, the handset still held close to her mouth, I see the expression on her face.

They keep the siren on so we get to the police station in maybe four or five minutes. But I won't believe it. I won't believe it when we're pulling up in the car park, and I won't believe it when Lauren stands back so I can run on ahead, into the bleak illumination of the reception area, where Christopher is sitting with a woman in uniform who is placing a little plastic cup of hot chocolate on the table in front of him. He glances up eagerly when I call his name, and he looks fine: exactly the same, as if nothing has happened. Behind him, the clock on the wall says it's not quite six. He has been missing for just under an hour. Fifty minutes, maybe.

I kneel down in front of him and wrap him in my arms, and he lets me, for a moment, and then he starts to struggle, and he says, 'Look, hot chocolate,' and I allow him to wriggle away from me, just for a moment, so he can take a sip, and then he looks up, distressed, *It's too hot*, and Lauren laughs and says she'll go and top it up with some milk from the fridge. So I sit down and pull him onto my knee and press my head against him while he eats another biscuit, and I can feel the detonations as he crunches through the Bourbon Cream.

When she comes back with the cup, Lauren tells me he was found just outside the park at the top of the hill, about ten or fifteen minutes ago. He was on the street, sitting on someone's front step, playing with their cat. Lady was on her way out, so she called the station and dropped him off on the way.

'These things happen,' Lauren says.

I guess so, I say. Thank God.

'Where did you go?' I ask him some time later. I've read the story (*Goodnight room and the red balloon, Goodnight kittens, goodnight mittens*), and I'm lying next to him on his low bed. He's in his flannel sheep pyjamas, his hair still a little damp, the emerald-green towel hanging on the doorknob, a beaker of water on his bedside table next to his Moomin collection and the Playmobil guinea pig pen. Fran has dropped Cecily back, I've fed her, and now Ben is putting her down in our room.

'Where did you go? You know, you mustn't wander off like that, darling. I missed you.'

He picks up Blue Bunny, presses one long velvety ear to his top lip: something he does when ready for sleep. 'Don't go away again,' he says.

'I won't. It's easy to get lost, isn't it. It was a bit scary. You need to stay with Mummy.'

'I want my scooter,' he says.

'I wonder where it is,' I say. 'Never mind, we'll get you another one.'

He looks sad. 'Poor scooter,' he says, 'All alone. The lady said to leave it.'

'What lady?' I say, but he's yawning, and I pull the duvet up to his chin. 'Maybe another child found it,' I say. 'A little boy who always wanted a purple scooter, but didn't get one for Christmas. He'll look after it.'

He rolls over and I lean across to switch off the lamp. On the chest of drawers his toadstool nightlight glows: the china mice silhouetted in the open doorway, the cosy little golden windows. I remember Christopher's bitter disappointment when we presented it to him, when he first peered in those windows, and at first I didn't know what was wrong, and then I realised – some distant echo from my own childhood – that he was expecting to see beds and a little stove in there rather than electrics and a low-voltage bulb. 'It's just pretend,' I explained. 'It's to look at. It's not real.'

'Mama,' he murmurs into Blue Bunny, and I kiss him, inhaling his smell, toothpaste and camomile shampoo, feeling the sturdy compact warmth of him, telling myself, *He's fine. Nothing happened. One of those things. Everything's fine.*

Nina

Walking back from the studio, I decide to go the long way home, through the park. The air still feels damp after the quick flurry of rain, but there's a sense that we're on the cusp of a new season, that something's about to change. The sun's a little higher in the sky than it was this time yesterday. If you half-close your eyes, a promise of green is just starting to declare itself, quite tentatively, on the trees.

I come round the corner, the sun on my back, and see a small boy. He's on a scooter, coasting along the flat bit of path by the compost bins, one foot casually held out to the side, demonstrating the absolute effortlessness of the activity. A slow graceful loop and a push, and he's off again, coming towards me, squinting a little in the sun.

I walk along the hedge towards him, thinking about popping into the café for a cup of tea before going home, and then I recognise him, even though he's wearing a striped knitted cap over his bright hair. There's a flash of yellow and black as he goes past. I turn to look after him, and then I see her in the playground, a little way off: angled away, bending over the swing, talking to the baby who is bundled up in a pale blue snowsuit – one of her brother's castoffs. 'Do you want to go higher?' I hear Emma say, quite clearly. 'Do you want to go over the top?'

The hum of the scooter's wheels as Christopher comes past me again, swooping busily towards the line of yews. I can see the pleasure he takes in his mastery of the movement.

I was going this way, anyway. So it's not really following. I keep to the route I'd planned, under the trees, heading in the direction of the café. It's dark here, and the foliage is full of the afternoon's brief rain shower. He's a little ahead of me, and then he's slowing down, turning. But the path is too narrow here, and the scooter runs into the hedge. He steps off it, tugs it round. I know no one can see us. 'Hello Christopher!' I say cheerfully, coming closer.

He looks up at me, puzzled, one foot on the scooter board. Those beetle-patterned wellingtons, splashed with mud.

'Do you remember me?' I bend down in front of him, smiling. 'Where's your mummy? I know your mummy. She's called Emma, isn't she? And you're Christopher.'

One hand rests on the scooter, the other has gone swiftly to his mouth.

'Have you lost her? Are you lost?'

He won't say anything. I know I don't have much time.

'Oh well, never mind, I'll help you find her. Come on.' I hold out my hand and straighten up. 'Don't worry. She won't be far away. We'll find her.'

I can see he doesn't really want to come with me, but the pull of convention – the desire to do the right, the expected thing – is strong, even in children this young. No one wants to look the fool. 'Come on,' I say, jollily. 'Let's find her. I'll bet she hasn't gone far.' And I take his hand, and I tug it, just a little, so he moves off with me, dragging the scooter with him. 'Oh, let's leave that,' I say, because I imagine it'll be one of the things she'll tell people to look out for, like the yellow knitted cap. 'Look, I'll just put it behind this bush, just here, for safekeeping. No one will see it there. We can come and fetch it once we've found her. How about that?

And, oh dear, look, your hat, it's all wet. Let me put it in my bag for now. Pop your hood up. That's right.

'How naughty of her to wander off like that! Still, I'm sure she hasn't gone far. Do you know, this reminds me of something.' And I start to chant it, quite quietly, as we walk through the shadowy shrubbery, though I haven't thought of this poem for years and years – not since Sophie was tiny.

James James
Morrison Morrison
Weatherby George Dupree
Took great
Care of his mother
Though he was only three,
James James said to his mother,
'Mother,' he said, said he;
'You must never go down to the end of the town
If you don't go down with me.'

James James
Morrison's mother
Put on her golden gown,
James James Morrison's mother
Drove to the end of the town,
James James Morrison's mother
She said to herself, said she:
'I can get right down to the end of the town
And be back in time for tea.'

He's wondering whether to cry now. I can feel him slowing down, wanting to protest, knowing this feels wrong, so I say, 'Look, I've got some chocolate, would you like some?' and when I say this I see him brighten slightly, rallied by greed, and I think: *OK, good*, and we keep walking uphill, along the dark enclosing avenue of trees, away from the playground, while I say, 'I'm sure it's in here,' and make a big show of reaching down and rummaging in my bag. 'I know it's in here somewhere! Oh goodness, where have I put it? Silly old me! Do you like chocolate? What sort of sweeties do you like best?'

'Jelly snakes,' he says, finally. I'm not sure if it's shyness that took him so long, or an inability to decide, to commit.

'I bet I've got some jelly snakes at home,' I say. 'Strawberry ones. Lemony ones. Which are your favourite? I tell you what, let's go and get you some jelly snakes first, and then we'll find your mummy.'

He's looking over his shoulder now, back the way we've come, in the direction of the abandoned scooter and the playground, knowing something odd is happening; but again it's such a weak instinct, overpowered by greed and that courteous impulse not to offend.

'I think the purple ones are the best,' I say, taking a firmer hold on his mittened hand, pulling him along, quite gently. 'They taste like blackberries. Do you like those ones?'

On we go, along the secret perimeter of the park, as the dusk rises and the temperature drops. As we come out into the open and pass the huge rhododendron bushes by the top gate, an old man steps into view – but he's facing away from us, watching as his dog rolls and tumbles after a ball, so we're safe.

As we pass through the gate, I hear someone shouting far away on the other side of the park – a high voice, strident, frightened, quite carrying – so I carry on talking, chattering away, keeping him busy. 'Not far now. This is my street. I wonder if my cat will be at home. Do you like cats? He's called Henry. He's very friendly, as long as you don't pull his tail. I'm sure you wouldn't pull his tail, would you?

'Ah, here we are. Home!' I say, glancing up and down the street, checking to see if anyone's sitting in a car, about to hop out or drive off, and wondering if anyone's watching me from a bay window. 'Up here, come in,' I say, and he's holding back a little, so I take his hand again, firmly, and lift it, half-dragging him up the stone steps. I get him inside, and then I shut the door.

Sophie's out at orchestra so the place is empty. All dark. I switch on some lights and zip off his coat, tugging it down his arms while he stands there, unsure. The mittens come off with it, dangling on their greying elastic: open beseeching palms. I hang the coat over the newel post at the bottom of the staircase. 'OK, let's get you those sweets,' I say. And then, quickly, before he can say it, 'And then we'll find your mummy. How careless of her to get lost like that! Never mind, she won't be far away. Don't worry, we'll find her. I'll help you.'

When I've performed the pantomime of banging through drawers and cupboards and have told him that I can't find the jelly snakes, he's disappointed; but accepts the consolation prize of Smarties, on standby for Sophie's emergency cupcakes. He sits on the floor working his way solemnly through the tube, his fingertips colouring up like bruises, quite silent and apparently content, while I have a cup of tea and check my emails. Henry appears at the kitchen window and Christopher goes very still as I let him in, as I pick him up and carry him over, giving instructions: 'Always start at the head, nice and gentle, don't be scared, he won't bite, yes, that's right, look, he loves that, he loves being tickled under his chin.' After a while, I can see Christopher is enjoying himself. I look at this little boy in his cords and tractor sweatshirt, sitting on my kitchen floor, with an empty glass of milk at his side, playing with my cat, and it's a lovely sight. It does me good.

I check my watch. Half an hour. Long enough. I put my mug and Christopher's glass in the dishwasher, and wipe Christopher's hands and face, then I call the local police station. 'A little boy, he says his name is Christopher and he says he's almost three, I just found him on the front steps of my house in Pakenham Gardens, just above the park. No idea how long he'd been there, he was playing with my cat.' I give my name and contact details, and I listen and make a suggestion, and we agree I'll drop him off at the station: 'No, that would be best for me, I've got to go out anyway,' and then I tell Christopher to say goodbye to Henry, and he's quite reluctant, until I say that his mummy is worried, she's waiting for him.

Someone's standing in the car park in front of the police station as I pull up, but it isn't her, she can't be here yet, though I imagine she's on her way. I help Christopher out, and pop his yellow cap back on his head, and I confirm my details, and then I say, 'Goodbye Christopher! Don't go wandering off again, will you?' and he shakes his head, obediently, a little chagrined. 'Glad to help,' I say. 'God, I'm late. Of course, just let me know if you need anything else.'

Then I get back in the car and drive off, and as I accelerate onto the main road I pass a police car – siren screaming, blue lights flashing – going in the opposite direction. Just for a moment, I think about what she'll be feeling, what she will have felt. Just for a moment. It's enough.

I couldn't remember the end of the poem earlier this afternoon, but it comes back to me now:

James James Morrison's mother
Hasn't been heard of since,
King John said he was sorry,
So did the queen and the prince.
King John (somebody told me)
Said to a man he knew:
'If people go down to the end of the town, well,
What can anyone do?'

Emma

There's some routine follow-up with the police, of course; and while Lauren is filling in the forms, I say, 'I've been meaning to ask, who found him? I'd like to thank them, if that's possible.'

'Let me check,' she says. 'I'll find out if they're up for that.'

A few days later, she rings and tells me the name.

'Nina Bremner,' I repeat, turning the name over, sensing its familiarity. And then, 'Oh, I know Nina!' I say, and somehow it doesn't come as a surprise. It feels right; as it is meant to be. While I take down the number, I'm remembering the precise shock in that long-ago moment of recognition, when she stood in my kitchen and I told her the truth – 'One stone, all these bloody ripples' – and I could see from her expression how well she understood me. So long ago, and so much has happened since then, and yet that exchange remains sharp and crystalline, a moment of absolution.

Sit down, she'd said, pushing a chair forward for me. *Drink your tea.*

I don't call her immediately. I realise that in some strange way I'm looking forward to speaking to her, and I want to extend this, the curiously pleasurable anticipation.

Of course, I'm turning Nina (with her neat cap of dark

hair, her slim tanned wrists, her deft birdlike movements, her stillness) into something she is not, someone she cannot possibly be. But the thought of contact with her is exciting, a novelty, a bright prospect. I have things to say to her, as well as questions I want to ask about Christopher and that terrible afternoon.

The obstacles of real life play their part in the delay. I take Cecily to the GP for a round of jabs, and her temperature spikes; and then Christopher picks up a bug from playgroup. For days I'm flat out, racing from floor to floor and room to room with sick bowls and damp flannels and sippy-cups of water, changing bed linen, hanging up laundry, making soup, which Christopher refuses to taste.

Sitting in the kitchen one lunchtime with Cecily on my lap, Christopher scowling as I hold out the plastic spoon, I experience one of those moments when one's life comes into appalling focus: *this is it, this is me, there is nothing else.* I haven't washed my hair for three days, I have mouth ulcers and a stye, I'm wearing yesterday's clothes pulled off the bottom of the bed in a hurry, we have run out of milk, teabags, apples and loo roll. I think of Ben, out in the world, making phone calls and flicking through the papers, having a sandwich at his desk or making his way through Soho to a meeting, and I put the spoon back in the bowl and say, 'I don't know why I bloody bother,' and the anger in my voice shocks me as much as the thing I've said.

Christopher looks at me, his cold-rheumed eyes filling.

Guiltily, I let him loose on Ritz crackers and Cheese Strings.

After lunch, I ready them for their naps. Murmuring, I move through the rooms, pulling curtains and straightening blankets, fetching soft toys and propping them against pillows. Then I gently shut the doors and stand alone on the half-landing for a moment, listening to the click of the radiator and watching the rain trickling down the windowpane, looking out over the backs of the empty houses, the stretches of stock brick obscured by long waving arms of bindweed and runaway thickets of bamboo. The pale grey sky races by in a hurry.

The house fills with the particular atmosphere that accompanies peacefully sleeping children: a rich narcotic silence that creeps down the stairs and twines itself around the table legs. If I'm not careful, I'll fall asleep myself, on the sofa, with my palm under my cheek and my socked feet tucked under the Welsh rug, and the afternoon will vanish, and the evening will go to pot. So I keep myself busy: I put on another wash, unload the tumble dryer, fold a mountain of laundry, wipe down the kitchen table and restore the sitting room to some sort of order. Then I electrify myself with a cup of espresso, made with the little stainless steel percolator we brought back from our summer holiday, and find the note with Nina's number on it.

It's a mobile number, and I'm preparing myself to leave a message – will 'unknown caller' tantalise or inconvenience? Will she be a pessimist or an optimist? – when she answers.

'You won't remember me,' I say, 'Emma Nash. The police gave me your number. You found my little boy, Christopher, when he'd wandered off in the park.'

'Christopher!' she says, 'Of course I remember! He was so sweet . . . I'm just glad I could help, the police told me it all ended well. You must have been out of your mind.'

'Yes – I was – but I think we've met before,' I say, and then I remind her of the dropped wallet, her kindness all those months ago.

'So that was you!' she says. 'Yes, of course, Emma, *Emma Nash.* I should have recognised Christopher, I suppose, but they change so quickly – and, you know, one toddler looks pretty much like another once your own kid is past that stage . . . How are you doing, have you had the baby?'

'The baby's six months old now,' I say. 'I was with her in the playground when Christopher wandered off. I guess I took my eyes off him for a moment or two.'

'It happens,' she says. 'You mustn't beat yourself up.'

'Well, I do,' I say. 'But I really wanted to thank you. It's mad, isn't it: that's twice you've basically saved my life.'

'Oh, for heaven's sake,' she says, laughing, but I can tell she feels this isn't an inappropriate thing to say. 'It would be good to catch up. Look, why don't you come round for lunch one day?'

'I've got the kids,' I say, but she's not bothered. 'I'd like to see Christopher again, and meet the baby. You said it was a girl?'

'Cecily,' I say. 'If you're sure?'

So we fix a date for the following week. I tell Ben about it that evening, but he's distracted and doesn't pay much attention. He finished work unusually early and came home via the mini-Waitrose on Tottenham Court Road. Now he's stationed at the hob, being spattered with fat. Man cookery. It's a dangerous, absorbing activity.

Ben's cooking nights are a mixed blessing. On the one hand, he's adventurous, tempted by Sunday supplements and the fish counter, by voguish or intimidating ingredients like goat's curd, za'atar and chicken livers. On the other, he's profligate with equipment, as if the challenge is to employ every single pot and utensil that we own, so by the time he's finished the sink will be stacked chin-high (the washing up is my responsibility. That's the house rule. One cooks; the other washes up).

Tonight, as it's a Friday, he's really pushing the boat out: a warm salad with scallops, followed by duck with celeriac purée. I'm sure the purée will come in dainty TV-inspired blobs and smears at the side of the plate. Like little speech marks. *'Isn't Ben good?'*

'Mmm,' he says, when I tell him about Nina's invitation (though I don't tell him that I already know her, that she's the person who found my wallet on the pavement all those months ago, because where would that get me? Best not to remind him of that other fuck-up), 'That'll be nice,' and then he puts the tongs down next to the sink, so the dark grease drips and pools on the counter.

I sit there, not saying anything, not reaching for the J-cloth.

'Isn't Ben *good*?' his mother will say to me in a low admiring voice when she and Dirk visit, after Ben has carved his roast, a plate of meat that will have been marinading in its bath of liquor and herbs for twenty-four hours, and which will have kept him busy all morning while I was changing nappies and popping out for emergency garlic and laying the table and filling the water glasses. And I think of all the little meals that fall to me, which are eaten without anyone really noticing the crispness of the potatoes or the bite of the green beans: the modest everyday dishes that pass entirely without comment, competently executed and palatable. *Isn't Ben good?* I suppose he is.

The scallops are a bit overdone and the duck is too bloody, but I compliment both dishes, bearing in mind how lucky I am. Then Ben tops up his glass and goes into the sitting room, and I fill the sink with bubbles while listening to a radio programme about farming subsidies.

Later that evening, I'm on the very edge of sleep when Ben comes to bed. My mind is just turning elastic, fantastical – I'm at the gorgeous point at which thoughts turn into dreams – when the light from the landing hits the bed, and I hear the water running in the bathroom basin. The water and the light are switched off. Then he slides into bed and I feel him reach for me, hear him whisper, conscious of Cecily asleep in the cot by the window.

I go along with it without enthusiasm or, to be fair, apparent reluctance, though secretly I resent – of course I do! – being stolen away from that glorious golden realm of possibility, just as it was within my grasp. The moment just before I go to sleep is often the highlight of my day: the letting go, the sense of becoming unreachable.

It's an illusion, of course, as Cecily's 3 a.m. teething cries demonstrate. I get out of bed. The room is chilly, but I'm already bathed in sweat triggered by that familiar hopeless panic: *Baby's crying. Fix it.* She hasn't got a temperature, but she won't settle for a feed, and then she does, and I sit there in the yellow chair in the darkness, feeling hot and cold. Tired, wired. Lonely and yet never ever alone.

She reaches out, her arm in its soft flannel sleeve, her perfect fingers flexing, a pale star. She puts her hand on my arm and rests it there, warm, firm, exactly where it wants to be. *Happy, sad*, I think.

Over the next few days, the children throw off their illnesses. By the time Wednesday comes around, they're fully restored, so much so that I am tempted to cancel. Twice I summon Nina's number on my phone, and only a small-scale domestic catastrophe (custard boiling over in the microwave, Christopher poking post through the floorboards) stops me from calling her up and making an excuse.

What on earth was I thinking? Without seeing it, I know the sort of house Nina lives in: linen upholstery, delicate bowls and sets of *things* left out on low tables. She'll prepare a meal that Christopher will refuse to eat. Cecily, overtired, won't nap in the buggy, and all attempts at conversation will falter at the two-sentence mark. I brace for failure.

When she opens the door, I feel my disadvantages sharp as knives as I lug the buggy up the steps and coax Christopher

– clinging doggedly to my thigh – into the hall. I'm sweating by the time I get everyone indoors; my face feels damp and shiny. 'So good to see you,' I'm saying, but I'm not seeing her, I'm only conscious of the chaos that I'm bringing to her house, the dirty-fingered toddler, the red-faced, ripe-smelling baby.

'Look, Christopher,' I say, once the front door is closed. 'It's Nina. The kind lady who found you when you got lost in the park. Do you remember?'

He pushes his face into my leg and mumbles something indistinctly.

'Yes, well,' I say, unzipping his coat. 'It's very kind of you to ask us round.'

She takes the coat, hangs it up, and then steps forward and puts her hands on my elbows and kisses me. Her hair brushes my face. A smoky sort of scent, figs and spices, sweet and complex and insistent. I'm not sure I entirely like it, but I imagine that's the point. 'It's a pleasure,' she says. 'It's nice to see Christopher again. Do you remember Henry, Christopher? He's in the kitchen. He's excited about seeing you again.'

Who's Henry? Christopher pulls his head away from my leg and glances down the hallway. 'He's waiting for you,' she says, and he looks up, doubtfully, so I say, 'Yes, go,' and then miraculously he's releasing my thigh and inching away.

'Cat,' Nina explains. 'You probably heard, Christopher was sitting outside my house when I found him, with Henry, the two of them just sitting on the step. So of course I stopped and asked him his name and rang the police straightaway. I can't begin to imagine what you must have been going through.'

I can't think of anything to say to that, so we stand around the buggy in silence for a moment; and then I say, 'I'm sorry, I really must change her, her timing's terrible,' and Nina laughs and shows me into the loo, which has one of those wanky yet also somehow desirable overhead china cisterns with a long chain flush (probably reclaimed at vast expense from a boarding-school refurb), and an antique blue-patterned sink, and a row of huge chemists' bottles on the windowsill. Cecily lies on the dresser, bathed in the red and green light cast by the giant flagons, staring up at them as I attend to her. I lean forward and we rub noses and she giggles, and then I pop her on the floor and wash my hands, using the French soap in a proper soap dish, a chunky white bar carved with a little sailor boy. While I'm rinsing my hands, I look at myself in the mirror, and see how flushed I am, and so I dab some loo paper over my face and into my armpits, blotting the evaporating sweat. It's not just the humiliation of arrival; the house feels a little too hot. Then I fit Cecily on my hip and go down the corridor.

It's huge, the kitchen, but more welcoming than I'd expected. Not quite so pared-back. Not quite as oppressively tasteful as I'd feared. Old tawny floorboards dimpled with the imprints of furniture scrapes and dropped pots, and blackly freckled with ancient woodworm. A rather beautiful modern rug in greens and golds. A linen press full of antique etched glassware. A pale grey jug filled with white freesias, petals translucent in the sunlight spilling over the table. A glass dome on a dish of decorated cupcakes: sugar flowers, hundreds-and-thousands, edible glitter. Radio Three, down low: Liszt or Chopin, maybe.

A large painting – a dim-coloured landscape of some sort – hangs over the fireplace at the far end, probably one of Nina's, but I can't get a good look at it from here. Christopher is on the floor, carefully stroking a black and white cat, who is reclining there like an emperor, just about tolerating the attention for now.

'And this is Sophie,' Nina says, 'My daughter.'

Glancing up from the iPad, she half-rises from the table, politely lifts a hand, says, 'Hi.' Tall, loose-limbed, in skinny jeans and stripy socks, a hoodie with lettering on the front: I recognise the logo of a store that I'd be too intimidated to enter.

'Do they let you out for lunch?' I say, and she looks at me blankly, and Nina says, 'Oh, it's half term.'

Of course, she goes to the private school further up the hill. I've seen the kids streaming in and out of the wrought-iron gates in their yellow-trimmed blazers, in intimate confiding pairs and trios, or in larger, more febrile packs. Clumsily, because girls this age frighten me – I remember how unwaveringly assuredly judgemental I was at seventeen, how mercilessly I judged my mother and her friends – I ask the usual questions. She's taking English, French and history. Applying to do modern languages. Year out, she thinks, au pairing in Paris.

'You should tap Sophie for babysitting,' Nina says. She's busy at the kitchen counter, cutting and rinsing lettuces, drying them in a tea towel and throwing them into a large flat wooden bowl. 'She's quite experienced, aren't you, Soph?'

Sophie tells me that she spends quite a lot of time in the holidays with her American half-siblings, Otto and Astrid. In London, she sometimes looks after a neighbour's three-year-old. Also, her friend Tasha's younger sister, who's eight. She makes smiley faces at Cecily, who wriggles and gurgles in response.

'I'm not sure, Cecily's so tiny,' I say, but even as I'm saying it, I'm thinking about how wonderful it would be, getting the pair of them down and then darting out with Ben for a few hours: to the cinema, or even just the Italian place by the tube station. Just walking there would feel like a novelty. Out in the dark, the winking lights.

'Well, bear it in mind,' says Nina, pushing back the sleeves of her jersey. The white cuffs of her shirt flash as she pours oil and vinegar into a jar, adds salt and sugar, screws on the lid and gives it a shake. Now she's pouring the vinaigrette over the salad, reaching in, turning the lettuce leaves over and over with her bare hands, coating them. There's something so careless and easy and straightforward about this; and – very distantly – familiar too, though I can't remember who else does it. Perhaps a character in a book.

'Can I help?' I say, as one does, as if I'd be any assistance with Cecily on my hip, grabbing at my neckline. I fed her just before we left, and now she's beginning to shade into nap-time irritability. *Oh, don't be silly, it's all under control, have a glass of wine.* I'd love one, I say, but first I'll try my luck, see if she'll go down to sleep in the buggy for a bit. Chances are she won't, but.

Nina says I'm welcome to put her in Charles's study, at the end of the hall, it'll be quieter in there.

The study is muted, as plain and perfect as an egg. There's nothing stray or random in here, nothing out of place: no paper drifting over the desk, no pens in pots, no pictures on the walls. Its asceticism is full of purpose. A plan chest, shelves of architecture books, a slimline silver laptop, a 60s recliner by the window overlooking the magnolia tree. I walk around the room with her for a bit, patting her back while looking at the architectural models in the Perspex boxes: a university campus, a museum in Vienna. I don't know how to analyse the buildings, so my eye goes quickly to the tiny little people animating them, the students and tourists gathering for scale in the covered walkways and around the fountains, casting their miniature shadows. Cecily has gone quite still, so I release the blind, filling the room with a sub-aquatic dimness, and lower her in, fastening the straps and tucking the blanket around her. In the half-light, she tilts her face to one side and gazes at the wall: a hopeful sign. *Maybe it'll work. That'd be a first.*

Back in the kitchen, lunch is waiting. The dishes on the table are not, at first glance, Christopher-friendly – it's all Middle Eastern-inspired, lots of aubergine and flatbreads and pomegranate seeds scattered on the salads – and I anticipate an embarrassing scene, but he is tempted by the little meatballs studded with pine nuts, and the herb-flecked couscous also goes down well, so I think: *that's one less thing to worry about.* Well-rested and well-fed, Christopher is not bad company; the problems start when he's running low.

We go back over that awful afternoon. Nina tells me about coming back to the house in the late afternoon, and finding Christopher and Henry on the step. 'He seemed quite happy, he wasn't distressed at all.'

Hearing his name, Christopher has cocked his head. 'Do you remember, Christopher?' Nina asks, 'Do you remember, that afternoon you came here?' and I hold my breath, not sure what I hope.

'Jelly snakes,' he says. 'You said you had purple jelly snakes. But you didn't.'

Nina laughs, tickled by the detail. 'You're quite right,' she says. 'I didn't.'

'And,' he adds, 'you said to leave the scooter. You put it in the trees.'

'Scooter?' she says. 'In the *trees*? I don't think you had a scooter, did you? I don't remember that. Maybe it was someone else. But I do remember the jelly snakes.' She tears a flatbread in two, reaches for the aubergine. 'I wanted to get him into the house,' she says to me. 'It was getting cold, I had to ring the police. So I promised him jelly snakes and lured him indoors. What did I give you in the end?'

'Smarties,' he says. 'A whole packet!'

'Lucky,' I say, and he wriggles in his seat, wanting to get down. 'Can we go to the swings?' he asks.

'Not now. Maybe when I'm finished,' I say, my fork poised, but Sophie pushes back her plate and says, 'Oh, I could take him, if you like. Just for half an hour or so?'

'Really?' I say, unsure if she means it, unsure if Christopher will agree; but he does.

The offer is made so casually, it's barely even a kindness. And yet at this moment, at this point in my life, there's nothing more appealing than being excused some of the endless responsibility. Five minutes, half an hour of not being in charge: it's hard to explain how wonderful this can be.

I guess I wouldn't mind being alone with Nina, so cool, so together, so inexplicably interested in me. Just for a bit.

Once Sophie and Christopher have left the house with their cupcakes, I let Nina top up my glass. I never touch alcohol at lunchtime. I drink and experience that pleasant slippage, the exuberant, dangerous sense that in ten minutes, or twenty, I might say almost anything.

As women must, we talk a little about partners: I tell her about Ben, TV, the gloom of the freelancing landscape, and I hint at the gnawing anxieties that accompany the drying-up of my earnings; and she says things aren't great for Charles and herself either, though I sense she's being tactful. This house and its location on this particular street don't suggest financial insecurity. Anyway, it is somehow obvious that she makes, or has, her own money.

Out in the garden – as orderly and disciplined as the study – the sun comes and goes behind thin whipping clouds. The stone bench shines and darkens and shines again. Henry picks his way over the lawn, and vanishes into the shrubbery. There's a patter of applause from the radio as the lunchtime concert comes to an end.

'How was your show?' I say.

'I thought you were going to come to the opening,' Nina says, reminded of some old half-forgotten surprise. 'I told Marnie at the gallery to send you an invite. Didn't it get to you? God, she's hopeless . . . or maybe I got the address wrong. It went pretty well, thanks. I sold a few. That always helps.'

'I'd love to see your work,' I say. 'I've googled you, I couldn't find anything. I was thinking you must work under your maiden name, is that right?'

'No – I use Nina Setting. My first husband's surname, Sophie's father. We were very young, I was just starting out. One of those rash idealistic decisions you come to regret quite quickly.'

I'm not sure if she means the marriage, or taking his name, or both, but it's too soon to ask that sort of question.

'That's one of mine,' she says, collecting plates and nodding at the canvas over the fireplace. I pick up my glass and walk down the room towards it. I'm anticipating the same blank nonplussed sensation that I experienced when I looked at her husband's architectural models, but standing in front of Nina's painting isn't like that at all. I see it, but mainly I feel it: the slow endless friction between sea and sand and wind, the snap of salt in the air, the crooked stunted trees and the cracked earth of the track. 'Wow,' I say, leaning in to examine the lines and beads and planes of paint, scored with brushes and something else, something flatter and smoother: a finger, perhaps, or a knife. The painting dissolves into its structure the closer you get to it. I pull back, and it changes again. Eventually, I say, 'It's incredible. I love it.'

I'm thinking about how wonderful it must feel to make something like that, how satisfying; and to my horror I find my eyes are filling with tears. Partly it's amazement, I realise, and partly it's because the landscape seems somehow immediate and familiar, personal in the way that good art can be; but mostly it's envy. An incredulity that she is free to do this. And that she can.

She comes and stands next to me. 'It's quite old,' she says, 'I think I painted it five or six years ago—' and then she sees the expression on my face. 'Emma,' she says. 'Are you OK? What's wrong?'

'I'm fine,' I say, rubbing at my face, incoherent with embarrassment. 'That's what happens when you get no sleep and drink wine at lunchtime. But, you know, it just sort of took me by surprise. I love it. The atmosphere. The sense of the weather. I think it's wonderful. I wish . . .'

But what do I wish? I'm not sure I can put it into words for her. I wish I was as free as she is.

'Where is it?' I ask. 'Or is that a stupid question?'

'I paint the sea a lot,' she says. 'Bits of East Anglia and the south coast. The bleak bits, mainly. Mudflats, estuaries. Sometimes I use old photographs. I don't like it when the sun comes out.' She turns from the painting to me. 'You alright? I remember what we talked about last time. You seemed a little low. You doing OK?'

'Oh, that,' I say. 'I'm fine! Yes, it's OK. Knackering, of course. But it's OK.'

There's a beat of silence, while I wonder what I'm going to say next, and then I hear – with a mixture of relief and disappointment – a wail from down the hall: Cecily, waking up. I look at my watch. Bang on forty-five minutes. My clockwork baby.

As we walk home a little while later – the usual stop/start progress with the buggy, as Christopher hunkers down to inspect ants on the pavement or clambers up onto low walls, trailing yellow crumbs from a going-home cupcake – I say, 'That was fun, wasn't it? Lucky you, having Sophie to yourself. Did you have a nice time in the park?'

'I showed her the Hollow Tree,' he says. 'And we went to the café for an ice lolly.'

He's gassing away excitedly – after the swings and the café, they went and had another look for the scooter – but I tune out: *I must order him another one,* I think. *Bound to be on sale somewhere.* The disparity in our heights – his snorkel hood and his habit of directing all his chatter towards the pavement – makes conversation almost impossible, so he talks, I pretend to listen. I'm not missing much. I return to the painting, its subtle insistent presence in the room. I wonder what it would be like to live with it.

Christopher is still going on about the scooter; something about it not being where she said to leave it. It's all a muddle, as usual. 'Never mind,' I say, as we turn off Pakenham Gardens, onto the high street, the trays of rhubarb and oranges set out under the greengrocers' awning. 'We'll see if I can find you another one.'

'Purple?' he asks. Yes, I say. Purple, if I can find it. I'll do my best.

Nina

It's after eleven when the phone rings. It can only be my mother. Charles hands me the receiver and goes off to brush his teeth. I put down my book and sit straighter against the pillow, bracing myself.

'I left a message,' she says. 'You're avoiding me.' Beneath the complaint, I hear the assertiveness of the alcohol. A rustle on the line as she adjusts her grip on the handset. I picture her in the kitchen, elbows on the table, the remains of supper in a pan on the stove, a plate pushed away; less appealing than the glass. Her hands, the silver band and the garnets, the clay half-moons scraped away from under her fingernails. She was always fastidious about that.

'I didn't check,' I say, but she isn't listening, she wants to say things. Just the usual, the stuff that needs to be said every few months. 'No, of course I know how *busy* you are,' she says, with a punchy little laugh. 'Of course, it's hard to find the time to fit me in. I know exactly where I come on your list of priorities.'

'Oh, that's not fair,' I say, and then I give up. There's never any point in taking her on when she's like this, all booze and bitterness, carefully enunciated. I hold the receiver to my ear and let her talk for a while, two minutes, three, now and then saying, 'Really,' and, 'I'm sorry you feel like that,' while she rolls on, occasionally breaking for what I assume is a mouthful of wine or brandy, getting wilder and wilder in her accusations. I've never made the time for her, all the sacrifices she made, who cares if she lives or dies. All the turned backs.

'Look, I'll come down,' I say eventually, as Charles moves around the bedroom, putting his shirt and balled-up socks in the laundry hamper, briefly placing a hand on my shoulder. 'Tomorrow, if you're free.'

'Suit yourself,' she says, but I can hear she's running out of steam; she's prepared, finally, to be mollified. I say I'll be there just before lunch and we end the conversation almost conventionally, with goodnights and sleep wells. I hand the receiver back to Charles. 'One of those,' he says, slotting it back into its cradle. 'I suppose she was due another.'

In the dark, I lie there, grateful for the kindly weight of his arm over mine. After a while, the rhythm of his breath slackens and deepens, and he rolls away, towards the ghostly hands of his alarm clock. I wait, I wait, and it's no good: the boat is sailing, and I'm not on it.

I don't want to think about what I'm thinking about, so I find the earphones in my bedside drawer and plug them into the radio, pressing the illuminated buttons until I catch the signal of a phone-in station: crazies and wasters and security guards on nightshifts. Little bursts of animation: humour and prejudice and loneliness in the dark city. At some point, I fall asleep, and my dreams are knotted ones, unrestful, full of mislaid bags and taxis that won't stop when I hail them. Handwriting that turns into spiders. Rooms full of people who take no notice of me, and when I open my mouth no words come out, just a sort of dry whistle. Or I'm hurrying up that dark twisty staircase, and – as ever – it's unclear whether I'm chasing someone, or whether I'm the one being chased.

This last dream is always the one that comes back to me, and I can feel its persistence the next morning, as I buy my ticket and find my seat in the half-empty train to Sussex. The sound of echoing footsteps, the close dim atmosphere of the stairwell. The sense of something closing in, or slipping away, always just out of sight.

I turn my face to the window as the train starts to move. Charles suggested I take the car, but I prefer this strange elevated route out of town, the rooftop tour of south London as the carriages rattle between spires and old smokestacks and the tips of poplars; the sudden glimpses into school playgrounds and street markets and quiet litter-strewn alleys, narrow avenues of blackened brick. Little by little the city falls away, like something giving up, and then the acoustics of the carriage change, and we're out in the open: meadows riven with streams, the fast blue shadows of clouds on the hills.

I drink my coffee and wait for the familiar landmarks: the three trees dotted with crows, the Theobald farm, the scout hut, the roundabout with the fussy municipal planting. The level crossing, bells ringing, lights flashing.

Two other people leave the train with me: an elderly man and a boy in his late teens or early twenties, who walks moodily over the footbridge, eyes fixed on his phone. Since the sun is trying to come out, I decide not to wait for the bus, but to walk to my mother's house: I'll go the long way round as it's quieter, more bosky. Once I've passed the half-hearted industrial estate, with its mail-order party shop and garden centre offering OAP lunch specials, I turn into the bridleway. It's rutted and muddy after the winter, the steep banks on either side pocked with foxholes and snaking with roots.

I always like the idea of the bridleway more than the reality, a fact I only remember as I plunge deeper into it. *Murder Lane,* I think, as I hurry along, slipping and sliding a little in the red mud, suddenly wanting and not wanting to look over my shoulder. I can't remember what its real name is now. That's what we always called it, my mother and I. Some awful story about an abduction, a body discovered down here, long ago, while my mother was house-hunting in the area. Probably the story scared off other buyers; perhaps that's why she could afford it. *All places have these legends*, I tell myself. *Buck up*.

The bridleway broadens into an unmade road and as I pass a barn and some outbuildings and allotments, I feel the sun strong on my back, and the ordeal falls away, although I may be about to walk into another one.

My mother lives on the edge of the village. When she first moved here from Jassop, it was because she wanted a change, to feel part of something: how handy it would be, to pop out to the butcher, the bakery, the post office and the little tearoom. Over the years, those signs of life have gone, eroded by the retail parks and supermarkets. The general store run by Rajesh, who commutes down from Orpington, clings on; of the three pubs, only The Half Moon survives (laminated A4 menu, too-large portions of freezer food, biker fights in the car park on Saturday night).

The cottage is long and half-timbered, set back behind a charming garden full of ferns and brick paths and long unruly grasses. The hens are picking their way over the lawn, gathering under the apple trees. Raindrops hang like glass beads on the washing line as I unlatch the gate, unsure of what I'll find here today. These meetings can go in two directions: ugly and confrontational, her breath still hot with spirits; or amnesiacally pleasant, no one referring to the conversation that prompted the visit.

She's at the kitchen window, washing up, watching for me. She waves merrily through the glass and comes to the door wiping her hand on a tea towel. 'I'm just making some coffee,' she says as we kiss hello. 'How lovely to see you.' *OK, so it's going to be like this, is it?* I think, a little wearily, but also relieved, as she shakes ground coffee into a pot. I take one of the rush-bottomed chairs and unlace my boots, which are clotted with mud from the bridleway. 'Easy journey? How's Sophie?'

We sit at the kitchen table drinking out of the glazed aquamarine mugs, the Kilner jars on the shelf above us full of green lentils and split peas and dried cannellini beans, white and curled like embryos. The door is open to the garden and the murmur of the hens, so it's a little chilly for my liking. My mother never feels the cold. She flings open the windows in early spring, and they stay like that well into autumn. She believes in vests and layers of jerseys, thick socks and bracing walks. When she visits us in London, she gripes about the central heating, like a memsahib incapacitated by the tropics.

So, lightly, I tell her about Sophie, just the easy fathomable stuff: grades, clubs, the orchestra. I don't say that my daughter is edging away from me. I don't share my fear that one big argument might cause her to detach, to float off towards the people in the background, the people with cars and money and places to go late at night. I don't want my mother to tell me this is entirely natural.

'Sophie's an angel,' my mother says, in a tone of mild complaint. 'Now: you at seventeen. That was a handful.'

'Oh, please,' I say, because we both know I was a good girl, quiet, shy, busy with my sketchbooks and clay sculptures and camera, taking the train up to London at weekends to visit the Tate, sitting for hours in front of the Turners, while Gillian and my newly separated mother went foraging in the hedgerows for elderflower, cobnuts and sloes.

But my mother, with a laugh, is off: the clouds of hair-spray, liquid eyeliner smeared on the towels, the endless whispered phone calls. 'What do teenage girls find to tell each other?' she asks, pouring me more coffee, coaxing the beak from a milk carton, and I shrug, mildly. I don't know, I can't recall, and I no longer have enough access to any of Sophie's conversations, real or virtual, to refresh my memory. We sit quietly for a moment: I'm thinking of Sophie through the ages, her hair in pigtails or curling down to round little shoulders, and then leaping up in a blunt line along her jawline; the appearance and disappearances of fringes and freckles; her mouth filling with small pearls and emptying and filling again with Scrabble tiles. The still point: her watchful, solemn eyes.

Maybe my mother is thinking about me; maybe she's thinking about herself. Sometimes it's hard to know where one of us ends and the other ones start.

'And Charles? How is Charles?' My mother likes my second husband, as most people do, particularly those who were intimidated by spiky impatient Arnold with his ragbag of grudges. She approves of Charles's creativity, and also his geniality. I tell her about the Austrian job, the interview he has in Newcastle next week. We discuss my painting, some pots she has just sold through a gallery in Brighton. And when we've finished our coffee, while she pegs sheets on the line, certain now of the weather, I scrub the cups and leave them in the draining rack, and put the empty milk carton in the recycling box alongside the wine bottles and the bottle of own-brand vodka, the other things I will not mention to her.

She makes me lunch: soup, a few cheeses on a wooden board, a salad tossed by hand in the way she taught me: sleeves pushed up over her forearms, the square-nailed fingers coated with oil raking through the leaves. We drink water from the tap. The house creaks and settles around us, as it always does: the wood expanding and contracting with the seasons. In high summer, the front door sticks in its frame, warped and misshapen by the heat. 'Did I tell you, I had a brush with the police last week?' I say, because I want to try the story out, see how it sounds. *Poor woman, she took her eye off her little boy in the park, distracted by the baby, could happen to any of us. Glad I could help.*

'Actually, the mother turned out to be someone I sort of knew,' I add, and for a moment I wonder if I could tell her, if I'd dare. She would remember. I'm sure of that. And then I think of the empty bottles in the big green box, and I say, 'I've bumped into her a few times. She has that desperate look. Don't really know what came over me, but I asked her over for lunch during half term. I thought I might offer Sophie up for some babysitting.'

On the washing line, the sheets and nightdress catch the sun like flags, rippling in the breeze. She said it would brighten up, and it looks as if she was right.

That evening, I make omelettes using the eggs my mother gave me, the orange-yolked eggs from her hens. 'Oh, she was fine,' I tell Charles. 'She was perfectly normal, as if that phone call never happened.'

'What phone call?' asks Sophie, coming in from the hall. I didn't know she was at home. It's a choir night.

'Oh, she was just in a grump about something,' I improvise. 'Anyway, she seemed fine today. On good form. She said you'd be very welcome if you wanted to go down and visit next week during half term.'

'I'll think about it,' says Sophie, fibbing back. 'But I've got a stack of revision.'

'Have you got plans for next Wednesday?' I ask, tilting the pan so the egg hits the hot butter and foams into lace. 'Someone called Emma's coming to lunch, she's after a babysitter, I thought you might be interested.' Yes, she'll make sure she's around. Hastily, she eats an omelette and pulls on her boots and her beanie and goes off to choir, leaving a particular sort of emptiness behind.

When the day comes, I open the door to Emma, and as usual, she's incapacitated by motherhood, like a Victorian morality print: Christopher attached to her leg, the burden of the enormous unwieldy buggy. Smilingly, I stand aside and let her lug it all up the steps. Bump, bump, bump. She's perspiring by the time she backs into the hall. I feel the embarrassment coming off her as she unwinds her jolly candy-striped scarf and gives it to me, along with her waxed jacket and Christopher's green coat. The ungainliness of her life sharpens for us both in this setting: the high ceilings and pale walls, the heart-lifting scent of freesias. The order.

I feel a need to touch her, to experience the heat of her humiliation, so I put my hands on her elbows, holding her still for a moment, and press my cheek against hers. I inhale. Sweat and washing powder, apple shampoo, the sweet sour faraway smell of breastmilk. I turn my head to let my hair fall across her face for a moment, and then I step back, saying how lovely it is to see Christopher again. He's gazing up at me doubtfully, two grey beads of snot on his upper lip. My fingers itch for a tissue, but instead I tell him the cat's waiting for him in the kitchen. Unsure for a moment, he weighs it all up, but I can see he remembers this house, he had a nice time here, with his milk and his Smarties, and a cat is a cat; and eventually he peels himself from Emma's leg and cautiously makes his way down the corridor, away from us.

I'm aware of Emma noticing it all, seeing the little things. I give her a glass of mineral water, and she turns the glass around in her hand, examining it. Her fingers trace the grain of the table. Taking stock, taking comfort. There's no envy in her: she's too tired for that. She's just comforted to be here, surrounded by it.

And yet she finds Sophie intimidating. I observe Emma tensing up, asking too many questions, reminded of being on the very edge of things. Left out. It's a good moment to float the idea of Sophie doing some babysitting. Even though Sophie scares her, just a little, I see the flare of hope in Emma's eyes: an evening out, every so often. Surely she's entitled to this?

As she's putting the baby down for a sleep, while Christopher lies on the floor, talking to the cat and crayoning on a pad of paper, I tell Sophie – lowering my voice – that I'll give her a fiver if she'll take him to the park after lunch. 'Ten,' she says, experimentally. 'OK,' I say, hearing footsteps coming back down the hall.

For various reasons I've been uneasy about introducing them, but I needn't have worried. As an adolescent, I was short on the confidence which is – miraculously, horrifyingly – Sophie's defining characteristic. Sophie always deserves to be in the room. And so, despite the other things that might link that distant faraway me to my daughter (colouring, build, the shape of our eyes and necks and hands), the connection passes unnoticed. It's not so surprising. At seventeen, I lacked – or believed I lacked, which came to the same thing – those qualities that make an impression, the qualities Emma then so amply possessed, and which she now perhaps recognises in me.

Of course it's also possible that the moment itself had had no significance for her.

Over time, I've come to see that so much of a personality boils down to confidence: whether you have it, or not. In many cases, it's really all that counts. All there is. I started with very little, but found it as an adult, through painting, and through Arnold, through motherhood and all those years when Sophie needed me so passionately. I'd guess Emma, having started with plenty of confidence, has gradually lost it. You couldn't say we complement each other, exactly; but perhaps in some strange way she complements me. It's a thought which amuses me as I make the salad – mixing it by hand, as my mother does, so the vinaigrette is evenly distributed – and passing her the wooden servers.

I can tell Emma is apprehensively anticipating Christopher's reaction to the dishes I've prepared, which are full of spices and herbs, and I've resolved, if he objects, to smile brightly and say *oh dear, there's nothing else, would he like some more bread.* But as it turns out, he has a sense of adventure, and doesn't do too badly. We talk briefly about that afternoon in the park and there's only one threat of awkwardness, when Christopher refers to the loss of his scooter ('You said to leave it. You put it in the trees'), but I gloss over this quickly, with good humour, conveying my bafflement, and the tension is quickly forgotten, ascribed to a child's muddle or fancy.

When he has finished, I catch Sophie's eye. *Park.*

I'm not sure whether Emma will accept my suggestion. These women are so twitchy, so fearful, so superstitious about the threats lurking out there, lying in wait for their children. To be fair, after the park incident, no one could blame Emma for caution. But no, she thinks it's a wonderful idea. She wants, I can see, to be alone with me. I listen so attentively, so sympathetically. And Sophie's very enthusiastic, so pleasant.

Once Sophie has taken Christopher away, I fill Emma's glass with wine. *Go on, be a devil. Where's the harm.* She's pinking up, flushed with the novelty and intimacy of it all. I picture her eating her usual lunch in her little kitchen: the plastic plates and bibs, the ludicrous cartoon cutlery, peas rolling around on the floor. *You really don't get out much, do you?* I think, as I make her tell me about her husband, a freelance TV director, and the touch-and-go nature of their finances since her own career ground to a halt. She doesn't go into details but I sense real financial anxiety here, so

I say what I'm meant to say at this point, hinting at our own difficulties, but I'm fairly sure that she knows it's just a courtesy: tact, more than anything else.

When she asks how my show went I let her believe that I was puzzled, maybe even a little bit hurt, that she didn't come.

She'd love to see my work. She googled me, but drew a blank, nothing came up for Nina Bremner. Ah, but I use Setting, I explain. No, it's not my maiden name. My first husband's surname, Sophie's father. It's not a lie, the explanation I give her: 'We were very young, I was just starting out. One of those rash idealistic decisions you come to regret quite quickly.' But there's more to it than this, of course. I continue to sign Arnold's name on the back of my paintings in tribute to him. I will always be grateful that he took me on, extricating me from everything I wanted to leave behind: the shadow of my father's success, lengthening year by year; my mother's sense of failure and resentment, rarely articulated but always present, like the sad tired ghosts you sense just round the bend of the stairs in very old houses, or waiting in the far corners of the quietest, darkest rooms.

'That's one of mine,' I say as I collect up the plates, indicating – just a little shyly – the landscape over the fireplace. Wanting to test her.

She rises and walks down the room to look at it.

As I lift my tumbler and hold it to my mouth, I see the water trembling slightly, a shimmer on the surface, a reverberation. *Sip. Swallow.* I put down the glass, watching as she pauses in front of the mantelpiece (the papier mâché apple Sophie made in primary school, the wooden bowl filled with worry beads).

What will she see? Will she say something stupid? I'm almost certain she will.

But her response is one I hadn't anticipated. She makes a

noise and leans in, examining the brushwork. She's staring at it so intently, I feel a hot rush of panic. What was I playing at, showing her this? What did I think would happen? In a sort of terror, I draw closer, conjuring up a lie, a rather wild and useless lie, anything to distract her from the truth, which is that I painted this shortly after returning her wallet, and brought it to the house in preparation for this lunch. *It's an old painting*, I tell her. *I painted it five or six years ago.* I summon up the courage to look her in the face. Her eyes are full of tears.

She's fine, she says, swiping at her face with fingers, saying she really shouldn't drink at lunchtime. Again, a moment when I experience the heat of her humiliation, close-up. But she loves the painting, she really does, it took her by surprise. 'The atmosphere. The sense of the weather. I think it's wonderful. I wish . . .'

She trails off, thinking. 'Where is it?' she asks. 'Or is that a stupid question?'

As I tell her that I like to paint the sea, mudflats and estuaries around East Anglia and the south coast, I'm aware that I'm saying too much. Rabbiting on nervously. *Turn the tables.* I put on my most cow-like expression, very patient and understanding, and I bend towards her as she bends towards the painting, and I ask if she's OK. I say I remember that last time we talked, she seemed a little low.

'Oh, that,' she says. 'I'm fine! Yes, it's OK. Knackering, of course. But it's OK.'

I think she's about to say something else, but then we hear the baby crying at the end of the hall, a wail of bewilderment at finding herself abandoned and alone in a strange room, and Emma hurries away from the painting, and from me; and the moment when we both might have spoken the truth is lost. But when they've gone home, taking their noise and mess with them, I remember the look on Emma's face as she looked at the painting of Jassop, and I wonder what it was that she saw there.

Did she recognise the trees, the sky? Did she know where the path was leading? Again, I remember walking down the track: taking care where I stepped, afraid of twisting my ankle. My shoes moving in and out of that small bobbing shadow, over the cracked uneven earth.

Emma

So we fix a date and I'm glad it's in the distance because this gives me more time to think about it, to look forward to it. Of course, I'm full of doubts; that's only to be expected. Entirely natural. What will we do if Cecily doesn't go down like a stone at 7 p.m.? Will Sophie cope if she wakes up? What if Christopher cries and begs me not to go, not to leave him with this girl he doesn't really know at all?

I voice these fears to Fran after Monkey Music, and she gives me a pep talk, as I hoped she would.

'God, you lucky *lucky* thing,' she says, trying to interest Ruby in a Babybel. It's a mild day, we've filled Tupperware boxes with egg sandwiches and dried apricots and Jammy Dodgers, and we're chancing a picnic, the first of the year. The recreation ground stretches out ahead of us, the grass marked here and there with the scars and gouges of winter football. At the little Tyrolean cuckoo-clock café, a short queue snakes to the hatch: people wanting salted caramel or lemon curd ice-cream. Above the line of trees the sky is suddenly clear and blue, and for a moment, sitting here on the bench while Cecily sleeps and Christopher and Ruby collect twigs, it all seems within my grasp. Maybe I'm over the worst. Maybe it gets easier now.

'It's a step in the right direction,' I say.

'I can't remember the last time Luke and I went out for dinner,' sighs Fran. 'Jesus. Six months?'

'We haven't been out together since Cecily was born,' I say. 'If someone had told me . . .'

'Well, quite.'

I'm reminded of a day a few weeks after Cecily's birth: an emergency appointment with the GP. I remember the pain of the mastitis, but I also remember the wild shocked relief of stepping out of the house by myself in the late afternoon, the first time I'd been properly alone since she'd been born. Leaving the children with Ben; making my way, unfettered, through the underpass and along the main road; giving my name to the receptionist and sitting quietly in the waiting room, waiting to be called. I could have waited there forever, watching the fish in the tank, the bubbles popping out of the treasure chest, the water weeds twisting and flexing in the invisible currents.

Yet the prospect of this night out with Ben is not uncomplicated. As well as the anxieties relating to leaving the children, I'm daunted by the scale of the project: finding something to wear, putting on mascara, making conversation and staying up late.

So, it's good it's some weeks off. I'll be up for it when the day finally comes.

'Where shall we go?' I ask Ben one breakfast time. It's the busiest time of day: everyone in one room, the dishwasher needing emptying, a load of laundry already in, the kettle whistling gouts of steam. I've mashed up a banana, and Cecily is tasting it with concentration. Many emotions crowd her face in rapid succession: disgust, cautious optimism, greedy delight, and fury when it's all gone. On the radio, someone is saying that a bumblebee is only ever forty minutes away from starving to death. I scrape a damp flannel over Cecily's cheeks and mouth, and, in an attempt to distract her, cut her a crust off the toast I'm buttering for Christopher. 'Shall we go into town? Anything you fancy at the theatre?'

'Not sure I can face the West End on a Friday night,' he says, making himself a tea, not bothering to see if I'd like one too.

It's not deliberate, I tell myself. *He just isn't thinking*. Somehow asking if he could pour me a cup would make it worse, more of an event, so I don't. Christopher wants jam on his toast. I get the jar from the fridge.

'What about the cinema? I quite fancy the cinema . . .'

'Maybe,' he says doubtfully. I turn my back so he can't see my expression. He has no idea how much energy I've put into arranging this. Finding Sophie, sorting logistics with Nina, nailing down a date and a fee. 'Who's this girl again?' he's saying. 'How old did you say she was?'

Don't you dare, I think. *Don't you fucking dare.*

'God, how many times?' I say quietly into the open fridge as I replace the milk on the shelf. Then I turn round and say, 'Nice sixth-former, her mother's that painter who found Christopher, that time he – you know. You liked Sophie, didn't you, darling?'

Christopher's licking the jam off the toast, carefully, attentively. He doesn't respond.

'And Nina's only up the road if Sophie needs any help. Which she won't,' I add.

Ben presses his lips together, judiciously, as if he has the casting vote. *Fuck's sake*, I think. All my doubts about the evening scatter. *I'm going out, I'm going out if it bloody kills me.* I need something to look forward to, something more than takeaway Indian in front of another boxset.

I think of people taking my coat, pulling out my chair and pouring wine so cold it frosts the glass. Someone placing a plate in front of me, and then, some time later, unobtrusively removing it. Occasionally I used to go to restaurants where waiters would attend to the table after the main course with fairy-sized silver brushes and dustpans, scrupulously sweeping up the crumbs and spiriting them away, making everything wonderful again. I look at the mess on the floor, the mess on everyone's hands and faces. Cecily has had enough of her high chair, and is beginning to twist and wail, waving buttery fists in the air.

Ben backs off, citing his clean shirt, looking at his watch.

I'm standing in the sitting room with Cecily on my hip, trying to find the overdue picture books, when he leaves the house. 'Look, there's Daddy,' I say, going over to the window, lifting her up so she can see as he steps onto the street. 'Wave at Daddy!' Ben doesn't look up. We watch as he pauses by the post box, reaching into his jacket pocket, pulling out two white cords, fitting them into his ears, then walking on, nicely sealed in.

The waste of it amazes me. Imagine having so much of it that you'd choose to shut some of it out.

Sophie babysitting. It's on the kitchen calendar, but we don't speak of it again. Ben has robbed the prospect of some of its appeal. As the date approaches and I still haven't decided how to make use of the evening, I catch myself wondering if it's worth all the hassle. I can't find a film I want to see. We'll be knackered anyway. Perhaps I should cancel.

I send Nina a text, half-hoping she'll do it for me: *S still OK for Friday?*

Absolutely! She'll be with you 6.30.

I remind Ben on the Friday morning. 'I could meet you somewhere,' I suggest.

'I'll come back and pick you up, we might as well drive,' he says. A duty date, then. Just the one glass for him.

I decide I'm bloody well going to enjoy myself, if it kills me.

When Christopher is at playgroup and Cecily has gone down for a nap, I pick up the phone, and it's a pitiful business: the people who answer heave little sighs, communicating their disappointment in me: such a shame to leave something like this to the last minute, to spoil my own evening by not thinking ahead. I'm offered a few tables here and there at 6 or 10; alas, there's nothing else available. 'Thank you so much,' I say, and put the phone down, imagining a young woman in black crêpe pursing her lips and closing the ledger with a sorrowful snap. Then I dial another number.

I get six or seven knockbacks, and it's beginning to take its toll. I'm on the point of calling The Headless Woman down the hill to see if they can fit us in at the bar (maybe Ben'll be in the mood for black-pudding scotch eggs or mackerel with beetroot) when I think, *Oh, just one more throw for luck, and then I'll give up*. So for the hell of it – because, really, we can't afford it – I call Marcy's, trying to keep the apology out of my voice as I tell the girl what I want. A table for two, at a decent time, in your restaurant.

'Oh, but you're in luck, I just had a cancellation,' says the girl, sounding pleased for me.

Maybe it's meant to be.

After that, Friday runs smoothly, finding its own structure: I pick up Christopher, make lunch, haul everyone round the supermarket, pop out to the park. Fran's there; she asks us over for tea. By half past six, we're back home, Cecily's in the bath, chewing on a rubber duck, and Christopher is sitting on the bathmat, plucking off his socks, his forehead furrowed with the effort. His Schleich horses are lined up on the floor beside him, ears pricked through thick tumbling manes, daintily lifting their hooves: Arthur, Chocolate Cake, Broken Whitey.

I hear the sound of Ben coming home, the key in the lock and the door slamming, his coat sliding – with a percussive jangle of change and keys – from its peg onto the floor. Then he's coming up the stairs, two at a time, a happy sort of noise.

'Daddy!' shouts Christopher, one sock off, and Ben comes in, rubbing his hands, saying: Thank God it's the weekend, well done for nabbing Marcy's, of course we can't really afford it, but oh well what the hell, it's not as if we do this very often.

The doorbell rings just as I'm lifting Cecily out into her orange towel, while he's lowering Christopher in, calling him Monkey Boy. 'That'll be Sophie,' I say, topping up with the hot tap and reaching for a nappy. 'Would you let her in?'

As I pull Cecily's sleep suit on and fasten the poppers, I hear the door opening, a grumble of traffic from the street drowning out the greeting, the door shutting, and then in the quiet I hear a woman laugh. It isn't Sophie.

'Will you be OK in here?' I say to Christopher, spinning the tap off, but he's not listening, he's marching his horses over the elephant flannel, the soap boulder, the glacier of his knee. I get to my feet and put Cecily on my hip, and then I go to the top of the stairs. I look down, and I see the two of them, their dark heads shining in the light, standing together in front of the mirror. She lifts her face and laughs again, and then catches sight of me. 'Hello Emma,' she calls. 'Hello Cecily.'

'Nina!' I say, and my first instinct is disappointment and a lack of surprise that this thing I've made happen has, in the end, come to nothing: Sophie has flu or has broken her leg, *poor her, never mind, of course it doesn't matter, how sweet of you to come round to tell us in person, you shouldn't have bothered.*

Nina's taking off her coat and Ben's reaching out for it, then bending down to pick up his own, and then he's hanging the two of them side by side, next to Christopher's green anorak. While he's doing this, he's saying, 'Really? Are you sure?' and then he turns to me, hands open – helpless, accepting – and says, 'Sophie's not feeling very well, but Nina has very kindly offered to step into the breach.'

She pulls off her boots and comes up the stairs towards me, wrinkling her nose at Cecily, who lunges forward, drawn to the glittering black beads on her necklace. 'You need a night out,' she says, holding out her arms. Obediently, I find myself handing her Cecily, who is usually so clingy, so reluctant to go to strangers. But perhaps she remembers Nina. Perhaps her scent – that strange complicated scent, the perfume I'm not sure I entirely like – is familiar. 'I saw the look on your face when we talked about it at lunch,' Nina's saying. 'It's important. You need a night off, every so often.'

'Wow,' I say. Cecily has her hands on the black beads, faceted to catch the light. She grips them in her fists, rattles them. Nina edges her neck away, tucks the necklace into her jersey. 'Oh, you darling,' she says to Cecily, pressing past me, heading to the bathroom. 'Now, where is your delicious brother?'

I was planning to give Cecily the bottle myself, but Nina insists. She'll do it. Look, here it is, all ready. They'll be fine. She has it all sorted out: I can put Cecily down for the night just before we leave, while she and Christopher have a story. Or two. What's your favourite bedtime story, Christopher? *Goodnight Moon*? Good choice! *Goodnight stars, goodnight air, goodnight noises everywhere.* Go ahead, she says to me, standing there in the doorway, my baby in her arms. Hop in the shower! Have a quick G&T! Seriously. It's your night off.

I tell her the only other crucial piece of information that comes to mind – please don't let Christopher, just out of nappies, have anything else to drink; as long as he has a wee after the story, he'll stay dry overnight – and retreat, with

Ben, to our bedroom. We shut the door and laugh quietly, both a little humiliated, but elated too, already demob-happy. 'Isn't it sweet of her?' I say, pulling off my jumper, hoiking the wrap dress off its hanger, looking for tights. 'Do you think we should have refused?'

'I'm sure she has better things to do on a Friday night,' says Ben. 'She looks the type. Still: gift horse, mouth.' While he's ringing a taxi – I don't comment, but this already feels like fun – he inspects himself in the mirror, pulls a jacket out of the wardrobe.

It all goes to plan. When we leave twenty minutes later, Cecily is silent in her dark room, the blackout blind pulled down to the radiator, door shut. In the pool of light cast by Christopher's yellow-shaded lamp, Nina is curled up on the bottom of his bed, admiring his horses. I go in, picking through the channels of toys, and kiss him, and back away onto the landing, not looking at the brown stain on the corner of his ceiling, which I'm aware has grown a little larger since I last inspected it. 'This one looks a fine fellow,' Nina says, smiling at us over his bent head. 'Have you thought about entering him for the Grand National?' Busily arranging them on his duvet, basking in her attention, he barely notices our departure.

Thank you so much, I signal from the doorway. *We'll be back some time around eleven, I imagine.*

It's nothing, she mouths back, waving a hand, encouraging us to go. *You look great! Have fun!*

The minicab's there, waiting for us, the radio cranking out elderly power ballads, people with big hair and raspy voices singing about true love, cheating hearts and the one who got away. It all sounds fine to me. The city is lit up for us tonight, the street lamps like golden balls floating down the hill, the cheap gritty sparkle of north London, with its kebab shops and Irish pubs, giving way to the immaculate terraces of Regent's Park: the shimmering windows of the Danish church, the flesh-coloured stucco villas with their staff entrances and floodlit porticoes set back behind arrow-head railings. Every so often, the quick blue wink of a primed security system: on, off, on.

I tell Ben (and it's not the first time he's heard this story, but he listens to it without demur) about a party Nick took me to in one of these buildings after the first year at university: a second-floor flat full of people he knew from school, all chain-smoking and talking in some sort of code. I can't recall the name of the host, but I remember the impassive waiters in white jackets with brass buttons, the girl being sick in the loo, the aspect over Cumberland Green towards the Broadwalk.

The cab crosses Marylebone Road, sailing past the curved white cliff of Broadcasting House, tailing double-deckers down Regent Street. People swarm and cluster around bus stops and restaurant entrances, pausing to check their reflections in the plate-glass windows arranged with all the things people want us to want next: the New Sandal. The New Dress. In these displays, it's already high summer. Time, marching on, stopping for nothing. I feel its pulse beating beneath the trashy commercial tattoo, and I can't help it, I find it irresistible, intoxicating.

We step out of the cab onto the broad pavement, and pass into the pitch and yaw of the restaurant. The table we're shown to at Marcy's – we weave our way there between winks of candle flame – is at the edge of the room, with a good view. The thick gold carpet sucks up the clatter, the sound of rings on crystal and cutlery being laid to rest on china: all you hear is the low murmur of gossip and confidences, the soft pop of corks being pulled. This isn't a place for spectacle or showing off. Nothing as cheap as that. We order drinks and pretend to study the menu, surreptitiously alerting each other to the elderly Hollywood diva dining with her much-younger husband, both with matching facelifts; the food writer eating seafood with her teenage children; the disgraced former Cabinet minister, whose date appears to be a no-show.

The butter is unsalted, a pale primrose-coloured moon beaded with ice water, in its own white dish. My knife slices into it. Over to our left the Hollywood legend laughs, a light ribbon of noise, a sound she has often been told is musical, like bells.

I have my phone in my pocket, set to vibrate, just in case. I don't forget about it but I allow myself to become less conscious of it as we make our choices and drink the house wine and talk about a novel we've both read, the hope that one day we'll be able to afford to build into the side return, the industry scandal involving people I used to know, Fran's neighbours, the ones who let the budgerigars fly loose around the sitting room. We don't really talk about the children. It's something I become more aware of as the evening passes, and I'm a little proud of our achievement. *Look what we still have in common*, I think. *We're both still here, underneath it all.*

And yet at the back of my mind – while the courses succeed each other and the tide of diners ebbs and flows around us, thinning out a little, the room almost submerged by hush, and then filling up quickly as the theatres empty into it – there's the constant thought of Nina, sitting on my sofa, her feet tucked beneath her, flicking through the *Standard* or watching the ten o'clock news, maybe walking around, making some tea, looking at the kitchen calendar and running a finger along the books on our shelves. That thought is a peculiar, shameful one. *Oh God, the mess.*

'You're right,' says Ben, as we wait for the bill. 'We need to do this more often.'

'I could tell you weren't exactly looking forward to it,' I

say. The camomile flowerheads in the glass teapot slip and slide into the silver strainer as I top up my cup.

He admits he wasn't thinking straight. It has all been getting on top of him, he confesses. Cutbacks. The fear of where the next job will come from. The broken nights. Sometimes the prospect of stepping out of the rut is exhausting. 'But you were absolutely right to arrange this,' he says, 'We need to shake it up a bit from time to time. Sod the expense.' He manages not to wince at the bill.

We make lots of plans on the way home, giggling and leaning into each other as the tube rattles north, but the conversation evaporates as we step onto the platform and start the long ascent to the surface, the escalators grinding away beneath us.

By the time we're at the end of our street, we're almost sober, hauled back into the orbit of our usual preoccupations. My new shoes are starting to hurt, pinching a little at the heel. I look down at the red suede flaring as the street lamps come and go. Cats flee from a bin as we pass. Ben takes my hand. 'Thanks for organising this,' he says.

'Don't thank me, thank Nina,' I say.

We let ourselves in and I hurry into the sitting room, not taking off my coat, keen to release her as soon as possible, so she knows we haven't taken advantage. She rises from the sofa, a smile on her face, sliding her smartphone into a pocket. 'Did you have fun?' she asks. There's a mug on the floor by her feet. She bends to retrieve it. 'Let me,' I say.

'Oh, really, I . . .'

I take it from her and stand there, slightly dizzy. The wine. Or maybe I'm just tired. The room looks a little neater than when we left it. Oh God, she's tidied it up for us. Toys in the box, crayons in the Golden Syrup tin, a sharp-edged pile of old newspapers and magazines on the coffee table.

'Any problems? Did it all go OK?' I ask.

'Absolutely fine! Not a squeak out of her, she must have read the manual, and Christopher went off like a lamb after a few stories . . . well, three or four, plus some poems. I couldn't resist A. A. Milne.'

I carry the mug through to the kitchen, noticing that she has cleared the surfaces, put a few things back into the cupboards. The plates and cups that I'd left in the sink have been washed and left to drain on the side.

I remove my coat and hang it up in the hall, and then I kick off my shoes. Ben's coming down from checking on the children, suggesting wine or (silly voice) a wee dram, but Nina refuses, zipping up her boots, winding her thin dove-grey scarf around her throat.

'We can't thank you enough,' I say. 'Can we offer you—'

She frowns, reprovingly, and laughs. 'Of course not! It was my pleasure. No, just give poor old Sophie another shot when you want another evening out. She was so sorry to let you down.'

'How is she?' I ask, and Nina says that when she rang earlier, Sophie was heating up some chicken soup and looking forward to an early night.

No, Nina didn't have the M&S curry I'd defrosted: just a pear and a bit of cheese and a herbal tea. Honestly, it was no trouble, she was glad to help. Ben brings her coat, holds it out for her. She slides her arms into the sleeves, turns to smile up at him, pulls her thick dark hair free from the collar in one smooth gesture. Then she lifts a finger, points to a framed photograph on the bookshelf. 'Let me guess: your parents, Emma? I've been looking at it all evening. Such a strong resemblance! Christopher looks so like your father.'

I pick up the picture, angling it so the reflection slides off their faces. The pair of them at my grandparents' house one long-ago summer day: my father with a bit of a sandy summer beard, my mother in a smock with big buggy sunglasses pushed up on top of her head. The picture fades a little every year; at some point, I suppose, nothing will be left of it.

'Really?' I say, peering closer, and though of course I've occasionally seen my father in Christopher – mysterious flashes of familiarity during jokes or grumps – I never expected this from anyone else.

She says yes, absolutely. 'Don't you think?' she asks Ben, who has poured himself a little whisky and thrown himself down in the stained armchair, displacing a squeaking bear. 'You must have noticed it.' He says he doesn't really know; he never met them.

I explain that my mother died just after I left university; and that Dad had a heart attack six years ago, a few months before I met Ben.

She looks at me and says the usual things but I can see that she can feel it; she's able to imagine what that must be like. It means something to her. The room blurs suddenly. *Christ. Bloody booze.*

I turn away, replacing the photograph, straightening some junk on the mantelpiece, composing myself. I don't think she notices. She goes up to the frame, touches it briefly with a fingertip ('Fantastic sunglasses, aren't they?') and moves away, into the hall, and I'm fine then, right as rain.

'Really, thanks for this,' I say as she turns on the front step, the cold air flooding in. 'I don't know how to thank you. Would you and Charles come to dinner?'

'Well, you don't have to,' she says, darting in for a kiss. 'But that would be fun.'

When I've double-locked the front door and clipped on the security chain, I pick up my red shoes and wrap them in the pink tissue paper, and put them back in the black box, heel to toe. Sliding the box into the hallway cupboard, next to the walking boots and the tubes of tennis balls, I wonder when I'll wear them next.

'She's rather glamorous, your friend,' says Ben, yawning, his legs over the arm of the chair. There's a hole in his sock, which I won't be mending. 'Her coat was Prada, incidentally. I'm sure I've seen her in Caffè Nero first thing. Gassing away about the head of Latin.'

'God, those pulled-together women,' I say, catching the yawn off him. 'Their mani-pedis. Their coffee mornings and their 4x4s. All the time they spend at the facialist. When did beauticians become facialists, anyway?' I've made him laugh, but at some cost: I feel bad, disloyal, ungracious. 'Actually, you should see her paintings,' I add. 'She's pretty good. You know, she's not just one of those *wives*.'

'I'm sure she isn't,' he says. The house is getting cold, the evening boost long-gone from the radiators. I look at my watch. Christ, Cecily will be up in five hours. Six, if we're lucky.

'I can't imagine why she's being so nice to me,' I say, with a little more honesty. 'Maybe she's bored.'

'Or, maybe she just likes you,' says Ben, reaching for me. 'Maybe she just thinks you're *great*.'

Christopher wakes us at 3 a.m., having wet the bed. And Cecily is up at 6.30. Not a good night. But overall, it was worth it. Given the chance, we'd do it again.

Nina

A yellow envelope half-wedged through the letterbox. I open the flap and sequins tumble out – blue, green, gold – and twinkle to the floor. Irritated, I swing over to the wastepaper bin. The card is Christopher's handiwork. Glue, glitter and potato prints.

She has nice handwriting, the confident loping clarity of the top set. Greek Es and capital As crossed at the bottom to make elegant triangles. *Thanks so much for lunch, what a treat. And if Sophie's up for a bit of babysitting, tell her to get in touch.* Better if it all goes through me, I think, dropping the card in the recycling box.

'How much?' Sophie asks. She and Tasha are in the kitchen, leaning over the iPad, laughing about something on YouTube, raking back their hair with their fingers. Self-grooming, a sort of tic. The volume's down low, I've no idea what they're watching.

'I'm not sure, what's the going rate? You can sort that out with her,' I say.

She dips her head to the straw, sucks. The pink in the glass goes down an inch, like the temperature dropping. There's mess strewn all over the counter: banana skins, the hulls of strawberries, puddles of melted vanilla ice-cream. 'Oh. Fine, tell her I'll do it,' she says. To Tasha, she says, 'My mother's pimping me out as a babysitter.'

'You're so *awesome* with the little ones,' says Tasha, and they bend towards each other, quivering with the terrific effort of repressing laughter. If I asked what was so funny, they wouldn't say; they'd just look up at me, suddenly impassive, making their eyes round and cool, and then, when I left the room, I'd hear the stools creak as they pull oh-my-God faces at each other and mouth, Shut *up*!

I drill down and get some dates out of Sophie, and Emma picks one of them, and the whole thing is fixed.

In the studio, I'm trying to start a new painting, but it's not working. Things aren't right, haven't been right for a month or two. I can't find the right place, I'm lost.

One morning, Michael from the gallery rings to say he has just sold another, the shingle bank picture I wasn't sure about. 'Yes, it's all going well,' I tell him, and then I put the phone down and go back and stand in front of the canvas, looking at the colour whipped up on my palette, the choppy lines of the knife in the paint.

Stuck. The more I think about it, the worse it gets. I'm haunted as much by the time I'm wasting as by the lack of inspiration. I've been so close to something, and now it feels as if it's slipping through my fingers, ducking out of sight. I'm reminded of those dreams when I find myself with important news to deliver, entering a grand room full of people, a party or a ball, and no one bothers to look in my direction; and when I open my mouth to shout at them no words come out, just a thin reedy whistle which is easy to ignore. All those turned backs.

At a quarter past one, I lock up and go down the concrete stairwell to the street. At the sandwich bar, Mario nods at my stained fingers as I pass him the money and asks, 'All right? National Gallery bothering you yet?'

I walk north, passing the school gates, and veer into the Heath, the sudden verdant swell of Parliament Hill a customary surprise up ahead. There's a free bench by the tennis courts, the one I usually choose, donated in memory of a violinist who liked to sit here. Inside the wire box, a twenty-something coach is putting some trim PTA-types through their paces, patting balls relentlessly over the net, shouting instructions and reprimands. 'You took your eye off it!' he calls, and, 'Follow through!' Eager for his attention, the women line up at the side of the court, pivoting in their white shoes, practising phantom returns. The new foliage on the trees ripples and shivers, a searing translucent yellow in the sunshine.

When I've finished my sandwich, I fold the paper wrapping and hold it in my lap, and I close my eyes, seeing black and red, feeling the hesitant promise of the season on my face. Little by little, we're inching further into the year. I should take some comfort from this, but today I feel too bleak.

My phone vibrates in my pocket and when I pull it out, I see it's a message from Emma, checking whether Sophie is still OK for the babysitting. *Absolutely!* I text back, with a confidence I don't feel. The fantasy daughter I've loaned to Emma is looking forward to Friday, eager for the responsibility, full of jokes and rhymes and stories. She cannot wait to hold Christopher on her lap, to draw a finger over his palm while chanting 'Round and round the garden, like a teddy bear...'

My Sophie, the real one, is not so bothered.

When I remind her about the arrangements for Friday she says, 'Oh, right,' in a way that makes it clear she had forgotten all about it.

She comes back from school at the end of the week drooping with cold, scattering Kleenex over the stairs (white flowers, or Hansel and Gretel's breadcrumbs) as she goes up to change out of her uniform. Instead of staying in her room or going out to meet her friends at Costa, she lies on the sofa in sweatpants and bedsocks, watching quizzes and cookery shows, every so often requesting – in a baby voice – hot honey and lemon. She doesn't ask me to call Emma, she's too sharp for that. She just lets me know she really shouldn't be going out like this.

It's Arnold's fault for insisting on giving her such a lavish allowance, killing off any financial motivation she might otherwise have had.

For a while, I'm undecided. I think of Emma looking forward to her evening, excited but a little intimidated by all the effort involved in doing things differently, just this once: dressing up, leaving the kids, making conversation. Getting out into the world, seeing that it has all been ticking over happily, not missing her at all.

The thought of pulling the plug, robbing her of all this, is quite appealing.

And yet, and yet. There's an opportunity here for me. I feel the rightness of it. *Why not? Two birds, one stone.*

I mustn't give her advance warning, or she'll cry off. So I leave Sophie wrapped in her duvet in front of the telly, and I walk round to Emma's house. The lights are on in the sitting room, and the curtains are open: from the street, I can see the framed print slightly askew on the rear wall, the dented sofa cushions, the black handles of the buggy, curled like rams' horns, just edging out of the corridor.

I ring the bell. Ben opens the door. As I'm admitted to the hall, we feint through the carefully humorous business of introduction and explanation: *I've left her with plenty of water and paracetamol, right as rain by tomorrow. We couldn't let you down.*

Even after I've set him straight, he's puzzled by me: I'm not what he was led to expect: his wife's new friend, the person with all the answers, the person who keeps saving the day. Perhaps he was expecting someone heartier-looking.

He, on the other hand, is exactly as I'd anticipated.

I take it all in, quickly.

As we stand there, my eye catches a movement, and I glance over his shoulder and watch our reflections in the cloudy speckled mirror hanging behind him: the gleam and fall of my hair as I twist it behind an ear, the way he stoops towards me, making a self-conscious joke. The small gestures of embarrassment and courtesy and gratitude.

'Well, it's very kind of you,' he's saying, and I can hear he's not totally confident about this, but it's not his place to question it. 'If you're sure . . .'

Emma comes to the top of the stairs. She's holding the baby, Cecily, on her hip. Emma's top is splashed with water, and her face is pink, shiny, hot-looking, as if she has been boiled. Beneath the fluster of her greeting, she is (I can see) resigning herself, quickly, to failure: she thinks I've come round to cancel.

Ben has neglected to ask for my coat, so I pull it off and hand it to him, moving things along, and I let him explain the situation. 'Sophie's not feeling very well,' he says, 'But Nina's very kindly offered to step into the breach.'

Tugging off my boots, I prop them with the other shoes under the skirts of the coats and go up the stairs, advancing towards her, murmuring reassurances. 'You need a night out,' I say, reaching for Cecily, who in turn is reaching for me, drawn to the glitter of my long jet necklace. Emma surrenders the baby. I catch the surprise as Cecily goes to me without complaint. 'I saw the look on your face when we talked about it at lunch,' I say. 'It's important. You need a night off, every so often.'

Cecily's fingers, busy on the string of beads. I dip my head, cooing at her while pushing the necklace into my jersey, out of sight. *Hands off.* 'Now, where is your delicious brother?' I murmur, bearing her away.

He's having a bath: a small, rather poky bathroom, with a window facing onto the neighbours' side return. A whirring extractor fan and a few squares on the wall where little fingers have industriously worked away at the mosaic tiles. A bottle of formula has been placed on the counter, next to the folded pyjamas.

Christopher glances up – he's playing with a collection of toy horses, marching them through the foam, arranging them around the edge of the tub – and I say, 'It's me! You remember me, don't you? Mummy's friend, Nina? With Henry the cat? I get to put you to bed tonight. Sophie's not well, so I thought I'd do it. Do you want one story, Christopher? Or – as it's a special night – what about two?'

Almost reluctantly, he tells me the name of his favourite book. Oh, I remember *Goodnight Moon*: the comb and the brush and the bowl full of mush. The same scene revisited again and again. Everything just so; exactly as it should be. The inventory of reassurance. And yet Sophie never really liked *Goodnight Moon*. She was spooked by the quiet old lady whispering 'hush'.

'Goodnight stars, goodnight air,' I recite, from memory, 'Goodnight noises everywhere.'

Behind me, Emma is hovering, smiling, uncertain. Cheerfully I dismiss her. *Leave the bottle to me, go and get ready – have a shower! A G&T!*

She asks me to ensure Christopher doesn't drink anything else tonight – he has recently dropped the night nappy – and after that she and Ben retreat to their room while I pop the baby down on the carpet and help Christopher out of the bath. For a moment or two Cecily is content to sit there unsteadily, but then she starts to grizzle, looking for her mother, threatening to build up to something, so

I hurriedly help her brother into his pyjamas, biting my lip as the cotton jersey snags and wrinkles on his small damp limbs: an ancient just-remembered frustration. Now I'm under pressure to silence Cecily, to show them I can cope, so I scoop her up, lifting and then – as Christopher leads me to her room – jokingly half-dropping her, trying to distract her with excitement, needing to make her forget her tiredness and hunger and my unfamiliarity. She's not convinced at first, but then I feel it, a fat bubble of laughter rising up inside her, and I think, *bull's eye*.

While we sink into the chair – her soft head in the crook of my arm, her hands grasping the bottle in proprietary fashion – Christopher toils busily to and from the bathroom, collecting his horses and showing them to me, telling me their names, their favourite foods and particular talents. I can hear the tidal *whoosh* as Cecily sucks; a little muscle just below her ear pulses with every swallow. Her expression begins to glaze, her long dark lashes hover and flicker, lowering themselves onto her cheek.

'Broken Whitey, I can see how he got that name,' I say, tuning out of Christopher's chatter, looking around. It's a box room, barely big enough for its contents: a wooden cot, a chair, a white-painted chest of drawers, a changing mat on the floor. An alphabet frieze runs around the wall. A is for acrobat, B is for bear, C is for cloud.

Cecily chugs through the formula, a doughty trencher-woman, and then Ben comes and takes over for the last bit.

I'm sitting on Christopher's bed, legs tucked up on the spaceman duvet, when Emma appears in the doorway, slightly self-conscious, her hands in her hair. Waves of gardenia gust over me as she kneels to kiss Christopher goodnight. She's wearing a blackberry-coloured wrap dress, gaping a little at the bosom, and thick purple tights; gold eyeshadow and a bit of foundation have sharpened her up, given her definition.

There's a little splash of mascara above her left eye, but I don't say anything apart from how nice she looks. *It's nothing*, I mouth, waving a hand, encouraging her. *You look great! Have fun!*

Behind Christopher's chatter, I hear them going downstairs, opening cupboards, collecting coats and bags and keys, leaving the house.

When they've gone I make him put his horses in their stable and then I read him *Goodnight Moon* and a few A. A. Milne poems, including the one which has special significance for us both, and then I escort him for a last wee and run downstairs to fetch a creature he calls Blue Bunny and a sippy cup of milk. Just before I turn off the light, I hand this over and watch as he sinks half straightaway, enjoying the treat of milk in bed; and then I pull the duvet up over his shoulders, and I say, 'Well, goodnight then. Sweet dreams.'

'Where's Mummy?' he asks, sitting up suddenly.

'She's gone out to dinner with Daddy. Back when you're asleep.'

'She didn't kiss me goodnight,' he says, and I can see the horror in his eyes, the realisation that she's not here, she has left him.

'She certainly did, you little fibber,' I say, lightly, pressing him back down onto his pillow. 'I saw her do it! She came in, wearing her best dress, and kissed you goodnight.'

I watch him as he remembers this, and though it's not much of a consolation he knows from my expression that this is as far as it's going to get him.

'Goodnight, Christopher,' I say from the doorway, quite firmly.

'Don't close it!' he calls. So I leave the door open a little, and from the landing his room looks wonderfully cosy, the heaps of bears and blocks and trucks, the hobby horse propped up against the chest of drawers, the golden windows of the toadstool nightlight.

I tidy up the bathroom, draping the bathmat over the radiator rail, wringing out the flannels and rinsing the toothpaste off the basin. Someone has lugged a basket of wet laundry up from the machine in the kitchen but hasn't had time to hang it up, so I wrestle the clothes airer over the bath, pitting myself against its flimsy cantankerous gymnastics. Socks and pants and vests, the demoralised-looking bras in dishwater shades dangling there like pale bats.

Once that's done, I peep round Christopher's door and see he's already asleep, an arm thrown over his head, the blue bunny under his cheek. Not a squeak from Cecily.

I stand with my hand on the doorknob of the master bedroom, waiting, though I'm not sure what I'm waiting for. Then I turn the handle and go in. As I push the door shut behind me there's a scraping noise which alarms me, and then I realise it's her necklaces, strung over the hook: wooden discs and perspex baubles and cheap ethnic charms, swinging and clattering against each other. I put out a hand to still them.

They've closed the curtains and left the bedside lamps on. The room smells pressingly of her floral perfume, and underneath that there's the vague soupy scent of bodies and sleep. A wooden bedstead, a fringed blanket shaken across the duvet, belts and shirts and trousers slung over the foot. A Lloyd Loom chair painted duck-egg, heaped with jerseys. I pause in front of the chest of drawers, poking through her makeup bag, unscrewing the lids and clicking open the compacts, my eyes catching in her little flashing scraps of mirror. Dipping a finger in the round pots of shadow and blusher, smudging their gauzy golds and dream-coloured pinks over my wrist.

Next, I go to her side of the bed and look at the things on

her bedside table, the novel she's reading (the one everyone was reading last summer, or the summer before that), a book about raising boys. Eye serum and a tube of budget hand cream, last night's cold mug of herbal tea, the bottom black with sediment. The drawer contains paracetamol, a herbal sleeping remedy, antidepressants. No surprises there. And then there's a little orange jotter.

I sit down on the bed, turning the pages; and as the handwriting engages me I lie back, nudging the dented pillows up behind my head, lifting my feet onto the blanket. The handwriting is less elegant late at night or at the crack of dawn, and in other ways too it's a joyless sort of document, full of afterthoughts, panicked intentions and dreary ambitions.

Cecily's jabs
Library books
Cotton buds
GP re hydrocortisone cream
Lucy's birthday present
Cancel veg box
Ebay newborn stuff
Smear test
SHED DOOR
STAIN ON CHRISTOPHER'S CEILING

I turn a few more pages. Meal plans, ideas for Christopher's birthday party, a list of novels she has read or plans to read. There, that's all there is, apart from a single line: *All this buttoning and unbuttoning.*

I almost feel sorry for her now. So easy to feel sorry for someone whose life is full of such tasks and aspirations. Lying here, in her place, on her bed, my head on her pillow, it is all pitifully clear: Emma is the engine of this home, the person who propels it forwards, keeps everyone fed and clothed and healthy and happy – and yet she's entirely alone within it, and getting lonelier with every item ticked off her checklist. This is what it comes down to: the flat-out invisible drudgery of family maintenance, the vanishing of personality as everyone else's accrues. *You never asked for this, did you, Emma? You didn't know it would be quite like this.*

Ah, well. We all have our crosses to bear.

I swing my feet off the bed and shake out the duvet and blanket so the impression of my body is lost, and replace the jotter in the bedside drawer, underneath the blister packs of medication.

Downstairs in the kitchen, while I'm waiting for the kettle to boil, I rinse the crumbs off the plates left in the sink, and then I pull open a few cupboards, checking what's on the shelves and in the fridge, putting away the jam and the Marmite, running a cloth over the surfaces. Whistling a cheerful tune under my breath: 'Housewives' Choice', I realise.

It's strange to be here, alone, surrounded by the sense of her: all the little things she collects, the context she has carefully assembled for herself. The tortoiseshell reading glasses on top of yesterday's evening paper; the enamel pans in pistachio green and strawberry pink; the fridge magnets holding up the macaroni collages and the play-school newsletters (my little message is long gone. I wonder if anyone noticed it). There's a dish of pears on the table, so I help myself to one – it's slightly over-ripe, but I don't fancy the ready meal they've left out – and peel and eat it, with a stick of decent cheddar. Looking around, taking it all in.

Wholesome mess and order, a more confident display of self than the bedroom allowed.

I rinse the juice off my fingers and carry my mug through to the sitting room, a room I haven't been in before, placing the tea on the low table in front of the big baggy sofa, an object with pennies and crumbs and pens doubtlessly calcifying in its fissures. Its vast ugliness fills me with gloom.

Next, I draw the curtains. Better to have some privacy. Not that I'm doing anything wrong, of course; in fact, anyone glancing in from the street would see a person tidying up, setting the room to rights. Yet I'm keen not to be seen as I wander around, touching things, examining them and turning them over, lifting the lids of boxes and pulling open drawers, reading the notes and greetings cards left out on the mantelpiece, between the candlesticks and pebbles shaped like ghosts. *Lovely to see you on Sunday! Thought Christopher would enjoy this! Happy Mother's Day!* All the here and now.

The wooden marble run is set up on the coffee table. Absently, I set a few marbles rolling. *Click, click, clickety click.* The glass balls roll down tracks and over bridges, bowling along ramps and spiralling into chutes, triggering the motion of tiny seesaws and roundabouts. One thing leading to another. It's as restful to look at and listen to as a fountain. Idly, I collect another cold handful of marbles and start them off again. *Click, click, click.*

And then I see it, the thing I didn't know I was looking for. On the bookshelf, in a silver frame, a picture of two people. I recognise them, of course, though this picture must have been taken a few years before I knew them, a fact made obvious by her hairstyle, the cut and pattern of her tunic, the line of his collar. There they stand at the end of a long summer's day: a little self-conscious, smiling and squinting vaguely into the sun, a trug of something – broad beans? – at their feet. A long black shadow falls over the stony track towards them: the photographer's shadow, probably a child's, though it's impossible to know for sure. Lucy's shadow, or maybe Emma's.

Behind them, their shadows in turn fall on a wall, the

rough warm stone of the barn. It's the stone that has the effect, more than the man and the woman. Alone in Emma's sitting room with the picture in my hand, I'm taken by surprise, overwhelmed by the hot dry scent of that summer, grass and salt and strawberry-flavoured lipgloss; the snags and twists of dirty wool dancing on the miles of barbed wire. The boredom, the long days when nothing ever seemed to happen, and then the sudden unfurling sense of possibility.

Avid now, I put the frame back where I found it and start to hunt, running a finger along the books, craning up to look on high shelves and crouching down to check low cupboards. It'll be here somewhere, shoved behind the rolls of wrapping paper, forgotten under the Hungry Hippos box, the sewing kit and jigsaw puzzles.

I find it quite quickly, in the cupboard behind the TV. Cloth-bound, a navy blue album, each page masked in crisp yellow-tinted plastic. I know this is the right volume because I recognise some of the clothes: the tight green jeans with the zip at the ankle, the oversized grandpa shirt, collarless, in wafer-thin striped cotton. I sit on the floor flipping through the pages, the blood buzzing in my ears.

Here they are, all for me, the four of them, leading their busy interesting lives: in London, mostly, crowded around dining tables and lolling in deck chairs in narrow city gardens; and holidaying somewhere on the Mediterranean, to judge by the beaches and ruins and meals eaten overlooking the harbour. (Ah. Now I remember the legacy of that Greek holiday, taken at the start of that summer: the tan and the freckles, the blonde streaks she told me she had encouraged by combing lemon juice through her hair, the Stowe schoolboy who was sending her mix tapes.)

The Hall family archive, as artfully curated as these things always are: a painstaking construction of picnics and birthday cakes, white teeth and raised glasses, national landmarks and

Christmas tinsel. No room here for insults hurled upstairs and slammed doors, the moments when people lie on their bed wishing everyone else was dead, though surely the Halls had their share of these too. Looking through Emma's collection, I'm struck by how little these pictures have in common with the photographs people take now, the casual why-not off-the-cuff snaps of people yawning or laughing or mucking around. Emma's parents saved their film for shots that stood a good chance and that mattered. The times when the light was right and people were still and formal, conscious of the moment, already colluding in its artifice.

There's only one picture that I can confidently identify as coming from that August at Jassop: Emma and Lucy out in a field with Mrs Pugh's dog, a wire-haired terrier (I can't recall its name). Two tall healthy-looking girls in plimsolls, obediently maintaining their smiles. Tolerant of the attention, at ease with it. *Go on then, hurry up and take it before my face falls off.*

Frustrated by the coarse grain of the print, I look closely at Emma's expression. Was this at the beginning of the fortnight, or the end? How can I tell? But then I remember, and my eye goes to her wrist, and I see it isn't there, and I know it must have been taken that final afternoon, before their father drove them back to their real lives in London. That's how I can tell.

I lean over the photograph, summoning up the things I cannot see in it, the things it will not tell me, longing to steal it, to tear back the plastic film and rip the little square off the once-sticky ribs that held it in place all these years; and then I shut the pages and put the album back where I found it. Who will open it next? No one else will search for that picture. It will never mean as much to anyone else as it does to me.

I think of Christopher and Cecily as enormous sprawling

adolescents, mockingly paging through the album: *God, Mum, look at your hair.* A joke, a comical fragment from the unimportant past, the time before them.

I wonder if Emma ever stalks her younger self as I stalk mine, full of rage and pity.

I have an appetite for it now, and I go through the room with new zeal, sorting and lifting and turning over, peering into the china bowls and wooden boxes, and finding buttons and memory sticks and the key to the small filing cabinet. The bank statements suggest things are a little bleaker than Emma had indicated, but then it's just product warranties, utility bills, the wedding and birth certificates, the passports in their funky covers. Nothing more of interest there or in the hall cupboard or in the pile of recent post left out by the toaster.

Disconsolate, I stand in the hall, gazing into the badly lit aperture jumbled with the shadows of backpacks and trainers; and then, because there's nothing else, I pick out the black shoebox, its lid discarded to one side. It's from an expensive store, spilling layers of peony-pink tissue paper, proof that she's really trying tonight. The receipt is tucked into the tissue: an online purchase from last week, full price.

It's not much, this curl of paper, but it'll have to do. I walk around the house with it, deciding where to leave it, struck by how little room there is here for Emma's history: Ben, Christopher and Cecily demand her absolute commitment to the present, as if her past is somehow a threat to their future. All those busy, healthy, confident years, the Brownie badges and tennis coaching and swimming galas, the house captaincy, the university theatre productions and the column in the student rag, the work placements and rapid promotions. The boys and men, the dates and declarations. The sense that it all must be leading, inexorably, to something. And now this. Was it always leading here, I wonder: to teetering piles of laundry, to teaching yourself to joint a chicken, to never running out of milk? Was it?

When I've found a place to leave the receipt I go upstairs to check on the children, holding my breath as the door catches and drags on the carpet of Cecily's room; but she's deeply asleep, surrendered to it as only babies can be (a long-lost memory of switching on the light to put away Sophie's clean vests and tights). I stand by the cot for a few moments, watching her chest rise and fall while I listen to her breathing. It's a small but forceful and ancient sound, and it reminds me of what you hear when you press a conch to your ear, a noise that is partly your own heart beating, and partly the sound of the ocean, the pull of the moon. The rhythms beneath the surface, the mysterious rhythms that thread us all together. *Love set you going like a fat gold watch.* Hate can do that, too.

She's so very little. Her tiny fists like seashells.

Next door, Christopher's flat on his back, one white foot poking out beyond the duvet. I retrieve the beaker – it's empty, he must have finished it after I said goodnight – and take it downstairs and wash it up, and then I go back into the sitting room and set a few more marbles rolling, *click, click, click,* while I wait for Emma and Ben to come home.

I wasn't going to mention it, but in the end she's a little tipsy from the wine and the excitement of being back in the world – drunk with success and relief – so I think: *why not.* I suppose I'm testing her, sure she'll fail, banking on it; and yet perhaps part of me (a small foolish part) hopes to be surprised.

Ben is helping me into my coat, and I flip my hair over the collar and pretend to be snagged by an afterthought, pointing at the framed photograph on the bookshelf: 'Let me guess: your parents, Emma?'

How strongly Christopher resembles his grandfather, I say,

as she picks up the frame and examines it, as if she hasn't noticed it for a while.

'Really?' she says. So I appeal to Ben, who tells me he never knew them; they both died before he and Emma got together.

'Ah, that's a shame,' I say, and I find the news takes me aback: those two pleasant-looking people, Andrew and Ginnie, glimpsed briefly through hedges and kitchen windows, or in the distance on the marsh, wearing hats against the sun and whistling for the grandmother's terrier.

It wasn't that Emma told me much about them; she didn't. But they were there, behind the things she said. Mild, involved, interested. She took them for granted, and that fascinated me as much as anything else. I'm surprised by how the news affects me.

While we're saying goodbye, she invites us for supper.

'That would be fun,' I say, and then I step out into the night. For some reason, as I walk, I find myself thinking about the marble run. *Click, click, click.*

Emma

Now our evenings are a little more structured, now Cecily's going down pretty heavily at seven, there's absolutely no reason why we shouldn't have some people over for dinner. Who would go with Nina and Charles? I spend a few days agonising over this, and then Ben gets tired of my indecision and says, 'They're not upholstery. They're not *curtains,* for God's sake,' and I'm glad he's making jokes, I'm glad he's forgiven me for the shoes, so I invite Fran and Luke, and Patience (an ex-colleague, I haven't seen her for ages) and her partner Rob. Everyone's up for it, though I know they'll all be doing the mental maths: *please let this be worth the expense of the babysitter.* No pressure, then.

'Do you want to do your beef thing?' I ask Ben one evening during the commercial break.

'What beef thing?'

'You know, the beef thing. Everyone likes that. I'm pretty sure Fran and Luke haven't had it.'

He says OK, he'll do the beef thing.

When Christopher is at playgroup and Cecily is napping or chewing toys, I hurriedly go through cookbooks and google recipes. I compile shopping lists, thinking about salads and soups and puddings. I ring the window cleaner. I iron the wedding-list tablecloth and napkins. I buy some Silvo and tear up an old shirt of Ben's for rags. *Eat your heart out Mrs Dalloway,* I think, as I polish the candlesticks, rubbing and rubbing as the shine is revealed, as the tarnish transfers to the cloth.

Last Christmas, as part of our economy drive (the end of the Royal Academy membership and the organic veg-box scheme; the beginning of my obsession with BOGOFs and discount codes and ebay and 'reduced' stickers) we told our cleaner Magda that we had to let her go. Though Ben never quite articulated it, I know he expected me to take over on that front – after all, I'm at home all day, aren't I? With nothing much to do? – but what with one thing and another, things have gone to pot. So now I attempt to be systematic about it, moving furniture and rugs around to reveal drifts of dust, running a cloth along the window sills, taking up the sofa cushions and shoving the Hoover nozzle deep into its recesses, listening to the subsequent rattles and clatters with a mixture of satisfaction and dread.

It's a fairly superficial transformation, and it only lasts until Christopher gets home and upends his crate of cars – which also contains lolly sticks, crumbs and hard nuggets of Play-Doh – on the rug. I stand over him, my arms crossed, and I don't say any of the things I want to say. I just say, 'Time to wash your hands for tea.'

On the Saturday morning I leave the house quite early, just before nine, and I drive to the supermarket ahead of the rush, cutting down the bright empty aisles with my trolley and my list, scoring things off, efficiently charting my progress. Afterwards, when I've stashed the groceries in the boot, I dart through to the high street in search of a florist. It's a shining blue morning, full of the racket of awnings being pulled down in readiness for the promised sun, the hiss of espresso machines, the chink and clamour as trays of steaming china are removed from industrial dishwashers. I step around a street-sweeper's broom and the soapy spill left by a window cleaner's bucket.

Outside the cafés, the tables are slowly filling up: people reading papers, admiring strangers' spaniels, commenting on the weather. There's something so optimistic about being out first thing on an early summer's day: the air softening and the definite shadows shrinking as the sun soars up and up. I'm poised to cross the road towards the florist when something catches my eye: it's a shop sign being flipped from 'closed' to 'open'. In the window, a gilded merry-go-round horse is mid-canter, eyes rolling, hooves suspended over an artificial daisy lawn. For a moment, I'm transported: the wheeze and skirl of the calliope; the scent of frying onions and burning sugar; strings of coloured bulbs against a stormy sky. The cheapness of dreams back then.

The bell chimes as I push the door and step inside.

It's one of those lifestyle emporiums, the point where brass neck meets hard currency: old street signs, vintage cash registers lined up on a '60s sideboard, a basket of knitted owls, a pharmacist's cabinet, Parker Knoll chairs upholstered in a natty fabric. Candles poured into china cups picked up from the local hospice shop, now priced at £15. The smell of a reed diffuser ('Nantucket', perhaps, or 'Provence') and lavender soap.

A woman with a mug in her hand says good morning, dipping her head to turn on the iPod. Supper jazz, of course.

Oh, this is ludicrous, I think, wandering around, picking up things – pop-guns, felt-cupcake key rings, funky Italian bottle openers – and pausing in front of the row of polished wooden lasts, the collection of glass jelly moulds. *Ridiculous*, I think, unable to stop myself picturing two or three of the moulds back at Carmody Street: displayed on a kitchen shelf, perhaps, or on the landing windowsill. I bend forward to flip over a price tag and then drop it, fast.

Seeing the movement, the shop assistant leans over the counter and says, 'Can I help you with anything?' For a moment, I hesitate, half-tempted by my shame, and then I remember what Ben said when he found the receipt for those shoes, and I say, 'No thanks, I'm just browsing.'

In the end, because I'm out (and who is he to tell me not to?), I buy a pair of yellow socks with bumblebees on the toes for Cecily, and a pocket-sized kaleidoscope for Christopher.

'That's £22.98,' says the woman behind the counter.

'Thank you,' I say, as she hands me my credit card and the paper bag patterned with Edwardian puddings: blancmanges, trifles, syllabubs in fluted dishes.

When I get home, Christopher is bug-eyed in front of cartoons, Cecily needs a change and Ben is laid out on the sofa reading the *Guardian* magazine. He glances up and says, 'Ah, good, you're back. I'll jump in the bath.'

I go into the kitchen and clear a space on the table, between the cereal bowls and the butter, where I can drop the flowers, and then I start to make as much noise as I can, dragging in the bags from the hall, slamming plates into the dishwasher, banging cupboard doors and turning the taps on so that I'm drenched in spray. When the sink is full, I shut off the water and hear the sound of Ben hopping upstairs, and the bathroom door closing, and with that I feel some relief, even if it also feels like a cauterisation of sorts: give it up, there's no point in hoping he'll understand how you feel.

When he comes down an hour later, fresh-shaven, I'm whipping mascarpone into the eggs while singing to Cecily, who is propped up in the highchair, chewing on a wooden spoon. It's sometimes easier to sing to her than to think of things to say.

'Looks good,' Ben says, coming up behind me and putting his arms around my shoulders. I flinch a little at it – *someone else pawing at me, wanting something* – but I make myself smile, and then I ask him to fetch down the big glass dish for the tiramisu. I won't say anything about the mess he left for me, I won't. I'm better than that. And anyway, I don't have the energy for a row. Sometimes it's less trouble just to let things go.

During that Saturday there are many moments when I wish I'd never done this, never had the idea and set it in motion. But at a quarter to eight – once the children are safely in bed and I've found a clean top – I go around the house putting tea lights into glass holders, and I feel a queer burst of hope: the house doesn't look so bad, the food should be fine, we've got plenty of booze. Perhaps people will enjoy themselves.

I stand in the doorway, and the sitting room looks fairly attractive and orderly: the little lamps casting cosy pools of amber light over the polished table and the smooth pelt of the vacuumed carpet, the vases of ranunculus and white roses set out beside the dishes of nuts and olives. Does it look as if we've made an effort? Does it look as if we're trying too hard? I take a match from the box and strike it, and the little flame bobs and dips as I put it to the wicks, creeping up the match, shrivelling and blackening it. 'Harvest Moon' shuffles into 'The Goodbye Look'.

As I blow out the flame, I sense movement behind me. A small pale face pressed between the banisters. 'Bed,' I say, in a cool and steady voice, turning away, moving the flowers an inch to the left. When I glance back a moment later, he has gone.

In the kitchen, Ben is stationed in front of the fridge, gazing uncertainly into its recesses; I can tell he has forgotten what he was looking for. He shuts the fridge door and together we inspect the table, extended to fill the bay, laid with the jaunty pink-striped tablecloth, and crowded round with an assortment of mismatching chairs and stools culled from bedrooms and bathroom. I adjust the jam jars with posies in them, wondering whether they look stupid. 'What do you think?' I ask, hoping he'll reassure me, but he just says it's fine, leave it. Before I can stop him, he's pouring the dressing on the salad and picking up the servers, starting to toss the leaves around in the bowl. 'Just getting ahead of ourselves,' he says, giving me a wink.

By the time we sit down to eat, the salad will be darkly sodden, limp. Too late now.

'You look nice,' he says, and I remember I've forgotten to put on any makeup. I'm upstairs with my little pots and brushes, trying to find a mascara that hasn't completely dried out, when Fran and Luke arrive, knocking (the parents' courtesy) rather than ringing the bell. Patience and Rob are just behind them on the step.

We stand in the hall, exchanging jackets and bottles and bunches of flowers, and then everyone's pressing through to the sitting room, marvelling at how pretty it's looking, introducing themselves, while Ben picks up one of the bottles.

I'm in the kitchen dealing with Fran's freesias when the Bremners arrive. Of course, I haven't met Charles before. He's much older than I was expecting, late fifties, or even early sixties: tall, patrician-looking, in a dark blue shirt and large black-framed spectacles, receding hair swept back in two wings at his temple. I think of him taking a seat on the ugly sofa, making conversation with Rob, who is in marketing strategy, and my courage fails me a little.

'Go through!' I say, ushering them into the sitting room, conscious that I am glad to have an excuse to abandon them there, and not only because Fran's freesias have left a wet patch on my top. Ben, who doesn't know either of them, is so busy gassing away – something about *Breaking Bad* – that he hasn't got around to opening the bottle yet. 'Ben!' I say, sharply, hating the sound I'm making. 'Do you need some help with that? Nina and Charles, this is Ben . . .'

I hear the cork pop as I stir the cream into the soup.

Over supper, I remember why I haven't seen Patience much recently. She is missing in action, subsumed by the quicksand of motherhood. As the evening goes on, I have an image of her, stuck in it up to her chin, like a character in a Beckett play. Only her mouth is mobile. 'Oh, they're vermin,' she says. 'There's a woman on our street who puts food out for them last thing at night. I'd report her, only I'm not sure who to call.' She keeps seeing the same fox hanging out by the bins. She thinks it must have mange or something, it's covered in bald patches. She turns to me. 'I hope you're not leaving your back door open? You know they've been known to take babies?'

She refers to Audrey and Alfred as if they're famous wits and sages, the key players in her social landscape. Often they are produced as trump cards, hijacking conversations, taking us off in unexpected directions, towards the things she really feels impassioned about: Ofsted reports, a column in the *Guardian*'s family section, the celebrated rudeness of the local butcher. 'Audrey was only just telling me,' she'll say, laughing hilariously at the memory, or, 'Last week I said to Alfred . . .'

'Alfred?' Fran asks, at the second mention.

'Oh, our seven-year-old,' Patience explains, pinking slightly. Does she assume everyone knows? Or perhaps she wishes she hadn't been called on this particular point.

As we clear the soup and bring out the beef, I can hear Charles is making quite an effort with her, asking questions, listening to the answers, and finally being asked one himself. 'No, Nina and I don't have children together, but we both have daughters from our first marriages,' he says. 'My Jessica is in her thirties, but Sophie, Nina's daughter, lives with us. She's seventeen.'

'Ah, the babysitter,' says Fran, half-remembering the story.

Patience helps herself to salad, which is every bit as limp as I'd known it would be. 'Goodness, a teenager,' she says, with an ornithologist's curiosity about a rarely seen species. 'What's that like? Hard work?'

'Oh, I wouldn't say that,' Charles says easily. 'OK, there's the usual stuff. Picking her up from parties at 2 a.m. The lost phones. The falling in and out with friends . . .'

'Teenage girls, they're worse than the Borgias,' says Nina, shrugging.

'And I must confess,' says Charles, 'that I make a very bad driving instructor. I think she must have mounted every kerb in north London.'

'Charles has always been very good with Sophie,' says Nina, lifting her glass, not putting it to her lips. The candlelight winks though the wine. She's wearing the black necklace, a large green cocktail ring, one of her narrow dark dresses, a little cardigan slung over her shoulders. If I wore that, I'd look hopelessly dowdy. Part of it must be expensive tailoring, of course, but that's not the whole story.

'Well, there's one key rule,' Charles says. 'I learned it from Jess. *It'll all be fine, as long as you don't ask too many questions.* Isn't that so, darling?'

Nina smiles. 'She's a good girl,' she says. 'As seventeen-year-old girls go. She could be a lot worse.'

Having ascertained where Sophie is at school, Patience (concerned eyes) says she heard from a neighbour that some sixth-formers were recently expelled for drugs.

'That's true,' says Nina. 'The school came down on it like a tonne of bricks. And somehow, they always find out. Zero tolerance, I'm glad to say.'

A moment of silence. I glance around the table. We are all

thinking about this: thinking, of course, of our own children, tucked up in darkened rooms decorated with spaceships and fairy castles, faithful constellations of glow-stars fading on the ceiling; sleepers watched over by tender vigilant squadrons of bears and monkeys. We are contemplating the effort involved in keeping these children safe and healthy and happy. Sensing how little we understand what's coming next; sensing, if only in the vaguest, most theoretical of ways, our approaching powerlessness.

Patience will not linger here, of course. She embarks on another monologue about Audrey's secondary transfer, the choices they have made for her. Listening to Patience, I remember how her febrile nervous energy – her bloody-mindedness, her tenacity, her twitchy inability to let things go – was once usefully deployed in making hard-hitting current-affairs documentaries. Is this where it has all gone? On securing the services of the famous Mr Cowper, a gnome-like maths tutor who 'only takes the brightest' and charges £55 per hour? On driving Audrey to cello practice, to swim team and street dance? How can Audrey survive a mother like this, a mother with so much to prove?

I met Audrey once, as she and Patience came out of the stationers. A flat-faced child in orange earmuffs, who surreptitiously picked her nose while I joggled the buggy and discussed the weather with her mother. I didn't warm to her then, but now I feel a wave of sympathy. *You'll take it with you forever*, I think. *Your mother needs you to be exceptional. She has staked everything on your exceptionality.* But perhaps I'm being unfair. Perhaps Patience will settle, when it comes down to it, for less than this.

I wonder if Nina is judging me, holding Patience against me, slyly identifying our shared characteristics. I imagine she is. The thought fills me with gloom. I finish my wine and Charles refills my glass. 'The beef's delicious,' he says, so I say it's all Ben's work, I can't take the credit. He asks me how long we've lived here, and we talk a little about the strange way I came to know his wife. How she has saved me on several occasions: returning the wallet; finding Christopher on the street (an episode I'm now able to discuss quite calmly); the babysitting, of course. He hadn't heard about the wallet.

He's genial, attentive, pleasant company, but I'm aware of the chasm between us: I'm probably closer to his daughter's age than to his. As, I imagine, is Nina. Nina and I must be in the same demographic, though in important ways she seems so much older: more sophisticated, more polished. The way she moves through a room in her dark clothes, somehow catching the light without seeming to court attention.

I hear Rob telling her about the marketing strategy he's working on for a digital radio station. Suddenly I feel rash, not really caring very much, and I ask Charles how long he and Nina have been together.

Nearly ten years, he says. 'I did some work for her father, his house in the south of France. She was recently divorced, as I was . . . It wasn't a happy time for either of us. But then things started to look up.' Nina's father isn't French, he explains, but he's married to a Frenchwoman. This is just a holiday place by the sea. Although, he implies, it's hardly basic.

I'm conscious of Nina suddenly turning away from Rob, easing herself into our conversation. 'Oh, the house,' she says. 'It's one of the best things Charles has done.' She describes it: the position on the coast, the light. The scent of pine and lavender.

Fran says, 'Butlin's Minehead again for us this year,' and we all laugh, partly at the Bremners and our own resentment, and then the conversation moves on, to Crossrail and the redevelopment of King's Cross, and on again, to the crazy facial hair – the biblical or Romanov beards – that all the

Soho kids are cultivating, and at some point Nina catches my gaze and mouths, 'Back in a sec,' and slips away from the table. When she comes back a few moments later, she pauses by my chair, drops a hand on my shoulder, and says in a low voice, 'Cecily's crying . . . I didn't know what to do . . .'

But before I rise, I run my spoon over my plate, greedily and hurriedly scraping up the last smears of sweet cream, conscious that the party's over.

I can hear her bellowing when I step out of the kitchen. When I push open her door, she's sitting up in her cot, fists clamped to the bars, her face wet with tears. Somehow she has wriggled out of her sleeping bag. Her feet are icy cold. I zip her in and pick her up and lay her over my shoulder as she quietens, patting her small firm back, murmuring reassurances, and gradually I feel the fury draining away as she softens and relaxes against me, the little hiccups fading, her breathing slowing down. I let her have a sip of water from the beaker on the mantelpiece, and then we stay still for another few moments. But when I try to lower her back in to the cot, she stiffens again, and I feel her inhale, preparing another wail, so I give in and sit down on the chair, letting her curl against me. *Sod's law,* I think, pushing back the curtain, looking out over the back gardens, incidentally lit by kitchens and landings: the spectral washing hung on the Callaghans' line, the movement of a cat on a wall. The sky is the colour of a bruise.

There's a burst of conversation from downstairs as someone comes out of the kitchen, and then the noise shuts off again.

Footsteps on the stairs; Fran pops her head around the door. 'Oh, Cecily,' she whispers. 'Give your mother a break.'

'That'll teach me,' I say. 'I thought we had the nights sorted. She hasn't done this for weeks. I'll have to sit with her until she goes back to sleep.'

'We were too noisy,' Fran says. 'Maybe she could hear how much fun we were having.'

Fran's awfully sorry, but she and Luke won't stay for coffee, they promised the sitter they wouldn't be back too late. 'It's been a lovely evening,' she says. 'Such a treat!' But I have a feeling that she and Luke will have a few laughs on the way home: about Patience, of course, but also probably Charles, so much older than the rest of us, and a little ponderous; and his wife, the noncommittal Nina, intimidating in the way that only chic slight women can be, perched on the pine stool in her neat dark dress and her thick teal-coloured tights, her crazy shoes, the shoes of an architect's wife. *Where did Emma find that couple?* they might say to each other. *And why are they bothering with her?*

I find I'm unable to answer that question. I have no idea. The party, now that I've stepped away from it, seems ludicrous, a doomed exercise: a ragbag of ill-assorted strangers with ironed linen on their knees, cranking through the usual topics of conversation. As embarrassing as my ambition.

Cecily's head droops. She's nearly asleep. I won't jinx it by trying to put her back too soon. I'll sit here for another few minutes, listening as Ben ushers Fran and Luke out into the night. A moment later, another burst of repressed noise as Patience and Rob depart, passing on commiserations and best wishes to me. Through the curtain, the crescent moon dances free of clouds, the sky suddenly clear and velvet-dark. More activity downstairs as Ben leads Nina and Charles through to the sitting room, and then I hear someone on the stairs. But the person who comes into Cecily's room isn't Ben. It's Nina, her necklace glittering in the half-light.

'I brought you a camomile, that's what Ben said you'd want,' she says, carrying the cup over to me and placing it on the little table. Cecily glances up at her briefly, without curiosity, and then her head falls back against me, heavy with weariness. In the house opposite, the frosted window goes black as someone leaves the bathroom.

Nina stands behind us for a moment, looking out at the gardens. I can smell her strange spicy scent: I realise that it's so tied up with how I feel about her that I've begun, almost, to love it.

'I'm sorry everyone had to leave,' I say. 'I guess Cecily rather killed the party.'

'We're not in any hurry,' Nina says. 'Charles and Ben are having a whisky and talking about the Bexhill Pavilion. It was a lovely evening. You went to a lot of trouble.'

'Oh, hardly,' I say, but it's true, we did, we tried, and it was fine, pleasant, workmanlike, but no one could really call it a particular success. If anyone thinks about it tomorrow, they'll be drawn back to the sharp moments of comedy and awkwardness: Patience on catchment areas, Luke breaking a wine glass as he reached for the potatoes, a confusion over newspaper columnists.

'I like Fran,' Nina is saying. 'She's funny. That thing about the shoe on the tube . . .' She leans into the window. The curtains move slightly in the mild air. 'In a week or two, it'll be summer,' she says. 'Sophie's breaking up soon for the holidays. Are you planning to go away?'

'Don't think so,' I say. 'Can't really afford it this year. Things aren't great at Ben's work. There's some contract . . . But it'll be fine. He's taking some time off, we'll probably go and visit his family for a few days. A few trips to the seaside, that sort of thing.' I think of an old picture book I've recently read to Christopher: a jaunt on the train, a short walk to a sandy beach, rock-pooling and paddling and kite-flying and a picnic on a rug, and then nodding off contentedly on the return leg, pockets full of shells and sand. No one forgets to bring the sandwiches, no one gets sunburned or stung by wasps, no one slips and falls in fully clothed. Where is this beach? How can I get there?

'Because if you were interested, my dad's house in France is free for most of August,' she's saying. 'You can get quite cheap flights, even at that time of year.'

'Oh,' I say. 'We couldn't possibly—'

'Don't be silly,' she says. 'The house is empty, my dad keeps on at me to use it. Charles and I are going there for the last week of August, right after Sophie comes back from her father's, but you should go anyway, whenever suits you. There's plenty of room, it's not far from the sea, and it's well set up for children, because of my half-sister.'

'I don't think . . .'

'Well, talk about it with Ben. It's a good idea. You'll find I'm fairly tenacious.'

She flashes a smile at me in the darkness, comes closer and extends a hand, placing it over Cecily's skull, long slim fingers carefully resting on the peach-fuzz of hair, the warm curve of bone.

In that instant, as well as being conscious of my own shock at being so very close to her, I'm aware of hers. 'Oh!' Nina murmurs, barely moving. 'That thing, the fontanelle . . . So peculiar. I'd forgotten about it. What a funny feeling.' She waits, then laughingly takes away her hand. 'I mean it,' she says, as she goes towards the door. 'You think about it.'

'I will,' I say, as if I mightn't.

Nina

I'm keen, now, to get back to work. For the weekend following the babysitting, while I dance attendance on Sophie (allowing her to colonise the sitting room with her duvet and iPad and bins spilling Kleenex, bringing her bowls of soup and green glass bottles of mineral water, popping out for oranges and the little saffron-yellow Portuguese cakes she has a weakness for), I'm greedy for Monday, itching to get back into the studio. I want to follow this new idea, this golden thread. I want to see where it will take me. My sense of it is so strong that I can almost smell it and feel its texture. It's like an itch, an ache and a burn, all at the same time.

I recognise this feeling. It fills me with joy.

The pull of this other reality is so strong and so appealing that it makes the real world – the world of eating and tidying and paperwork – feel very flat and dull by comparison.

For a long time I've been preoccupied by coldness, but now, having seen that photograph, I'm thinking about heat: an exposed restless sort of heat blowing over salt flats and close-cropped grass, settling for a moment in a sandy hollow and then moving on again: impulsive, scatterbrained, careless. The dry wind murmuring in miles of barbed wire and humming in the power cables strung between the relentless procession of pylons. Skies so high and pale they seem to have no colour at all.

These ideas come to me in snatches, like visions or ghosts or dreams, only briefly revealed in the quiet moments as I brush my teeth or stand in front of Sophie's wardrobe, putting shirts on hangers. The land laid out in the heat, the silence of the farm tracks, the sprays of cow parsley. The sweet mealy smell of the barn interior, the way your eyes fought the darkness to find the shapes in there: the sacks of feed, the hay bales and pieces of rusting machinery.

These ideas need solitude and time to develop, but Sophie is demanding, carelessly possessive, entirely confident of my attention. She won't wait her turn. For the last year or so she has been pulling away from me, trying to shake me off, and so this dependence – the way she calls for me, in a baby voice, from the sofa: *Ma-ma!* – feels novel yet nostalgic, and also claustrophobic. I love it, I always have; and yet now, for the first time, I find myself resenting it. Perhaps while Sophie has been moving on, I have moved on too.

In any case, I'm unable to think usefully about work when I'm at home. The tyranny of domesticity is just too strong. There's always something else that needs addressing. Something that must be put away or bought or fixed or folded or picked up or wiped down. The little things I won't leave for Lenka, the unimportant details that no one else bothers with. The questions no one else can answer.

Sophie goes back to school on the Tuesday, protesting a little, coughing like an urchin, and as I let myself out of the house and walk down the street in the weak sunshine, I feel that old luxurious exhilaration: the hope of a new idea.

My walk to the studio is always valuable, whatever the weather. I like being out in the world, yet detached from it: meditative yet purposeful.

Today, as I leave the high street and enter the park by the

wrought-iron gates, passing beneath the candles of magnolia buds, the sherbet bubbles of apple and cherry blossom, I feel light, alive, full of possibility. I step onto the bright fresh grass, avoiding the static clusters of mothers whose buggies are snarling up the path. A dog flies after an acid-yellow ball. Above the trees in the clear promising sky a flock of birds: twisting and bobbing, rolling and weaving, cohesive as mercury.

I put my hands in my jacket pocket, and my fingers find the leather tassel keyring Charles brought back from Milan, an expensive pointless trinket, one that pleases me when I remember to think about it. The cold hard shock of the keys.

Out through the lower gate, past the white tiers of Sixties housing, cutting between the Victorian terraces and down a narrow leafy alleyway leading to a footbridge over the railway line. As usual, I walk a little faster at this point, not wanting to meet anyone here, in this enclosed suspended space that seems to belong to no one, to neither side; not looking down, through the bars and the wire, at the black mouth of the tunnel, the graffiti and broken bottles, the insistent push and creep of weeds between the gravel.

Far below me, the tracks are humming: a tiny sound. Something approaching, or travelling further away. I cannot tell which.

I keep walking. On the other side, I pass the school – the playgrounds over the wall empty and silent at this time of day – and the percussion of the main road starts to build: the distant wail of a siren, the sighs and expostulations of buses.

As I unlock the studio door, I can see the fruitlessness of the last few weeks laid out there, on the racks and propped up against the walls, on the large pieces of paper strewn over the floor. It feels good to collect the rough work and to put it away, out of sight; to open the metal-framed windows and let in the air. I fill the kettle and switch it on. While I'm waiting for it to boil I go to the plan chest and pull open the drawer, looking for the old manila envelope hidden under other papers that mean far less. I pull it out. It's soft with age, as soft as chamois. The gum under the flap is just a dull stain now, no adhesion left.

I haven't looked inside for years, though I've thought about the pictures often; what they show or, more accurately, don't show. Remembering what was happening elsewhere: in the distance, or behind the camera, off to one side.

Gently, I coax out the wad of square white-framed photographs, spacing them over the table. No surprises here, nothing I haven't seen before. Some carefully composed shots of the Downs, the white scored lines of the footpaths drifting and spiralling over the gradient. The view from my bedroom window: lawn and trees and red-brick wall, and the flat reach of fields beyond. A still life of seed heads in a milk bottle. A girl in green jeans, seen from behind as she stands at a farm gate, one tennis shoe resting on the lowest bar: a tangled fall of fair hair, a terrier at her heels. Cakes and vegetables and flowers set out on a trestle between some 'Best in Show' cards. The old lighthouse, with the boxy grey sprawl of the power station in the background. My mother in a headscarf, standing in the porch, holding out a bowl of redcurrants. My father's pale face among the shadows as he sits at the piano, the sinuous twist of cigarette smoke as it rises from the ashtray the only other point of illumination. I pick out this picture: the best of the lot, I think. Accidentally, I caught something about him that was true then and remains so now.

We're not quite finished. There's still something in the envelope. I upend it, and the bracelet slips out. A knotted circle of dirty string threaded with a brass button stamped with an anchor, ceramic beads in neon green and orange, an Evil Eye, a few cheap silver-plated charms, the sort we used to pick up in Dorothy Perkins for 50p a pop (a star, a pineapple, a horseshoe for luck). With only a little difficulty, I draw it over my wrist.

The weight and sound of it.

'Keep it. You can give it back when we meet up next time,' she said, pulling it off, and dangling it over my open palm. And then, seeing my expression, 'It's not valuable, it's just bits and bobs, silly old stuff. You don't have to wear it if you don't like it.'

I loved her for that, for the sudden doubt, the rare moment of insecurity. And I hated her, too, for the same reason.

The kettle has boiled. I pour the water over a spoonful of granules, and then I stand by the open window with the cup in my hands, the metal and glass beads cool on my wrist, looking out over the rooftops, the unseen landscape of chimney pots and air-conditioning units and broken TV aerials. I know what I want to paint now, and I'm free to enjoy the pleasurable apprehension, the promise of this moment.

I drink the coffee and allow my pencil to catch and shape a few thoughts, the soft graphite racing over the paper, just to ease myself into it; and then I select the brushes I'll need. Most paintings you're unaware of beginning. They appear out of something else quite gradually, even modestly, suggestions rather than statements. A few paintings present themselves, urgently insist on being addressed; and in my experience those are the ones that work the best. This feels like one of those.

The excitement of making a start, of not being held back anymore. Pulling something out of nothing. Shades and tones move across the canvas. The sky comes first, as it usually does, a large pale wash of gradual colour: heat, emptiness. At the edge, I start to imagine the thing that isn't being directly looked at, the vague presence of something: a house, a wall, a hedgerow. Your eyes will slip beyond this, into the bleached air, but you should know it's there, and eventually your attention will come back to it. That's how I want it to work, anyway.

I'm remembering the walk to the Pugh farm, how it seemed miles away, though it was probably less than a kilometre: the listing stile and the footpath over the field, the cracked earth underfoot, the itch of corn stubble against my ankles, the sound of sheep and seagulls and sometimes the raw caw of rooks. This is how it felt to me, as I stood in the hollowness of the hedge, twigs scratching at my arms and legs. Dry leaves and cobwebs in my hair as I watched the empty yard, the perambulations of chickens, the dog asleep in the shade. There were people inside the house. I heard them as they moved to and fro within the rooms, slamming doors, running up and down stairs, calling to each other; but apart from the occasional shadow passing behind dark glass, a brief movement at an open window, they were invisible. Still, I waited.

That evening, Charles says, 'Let me guess. You've started a new painting, and you're happy with it.'

'So far,' I caution, reluctant to say anything more: wary of assuming anything at this point, and also conscious that I mustn't talk about it yet. As if it might benefit from secrecy, even from deceit. 'I don't know exactly where it's going.'

'I can always tell,' he says, and I love him for that: for noticing, for minding, for being glad, for understanding that I don't want to say more about it – that I mustn't. Sophie is slumped over the kitchen counter, fluorescent marker poised over Alain-Fournier. If I say anything to her, she will slink off to her room, so I don't address her directly.

'We've been asked out to dinner,' I tell Charles, remembering the text. 'I've put the date on the calendar.'

'Oh, the dizzy woman,' he says. The one who lost her child. Yes, I say. The new mother. That's her. I can tell he's not much taken with the idea, but he'll go along with it, as he goes along with most things. 'Charles is *so* good-natured,' my friends say, and I smile, thinking: good-natured, or just lazy?

Over supper, having set her books aside, Sophie says, 'Weird bracelet, Ma. Where'd you find it?'

Oh, this piece of tat? I found it at the bottom of a bag, no idea where I picked it up.

The next day, I leave it in a drawer, but I find my thoughts returning to it as I work: the uneven chink of the beads and buttons and charms, the knots in the string, the cool weight of it against my wrist.

Emma's party, when it comes, is an unremarkable affair, the sort of evening that few of the guests will be able to summon up in any detail the following morning. Charles and I walk from our house to hers at the end of a warm spring day: I haven't dressed up because her girlfriends might interpret that as unsisterly. Demure, that's the intention: elegant, yes, but tactfully so. She opens the door to us, clutching flowers, goggle-eyed with panic. The stems have left a damp patch on her top. Her face is shiny.

As Ben manages the introductions, I allow myself to glance around the room, and I can see the effort she has made, all the thought that has gone into all these little decisions: the tea lights and the dishes of almonds and olives; the scent of polish and roses; the music. I know what's behind it all, of course: I know what's kicked under the sofa, shut away in those cupboards. But somehow I can't help being touched by her ambition.

Ben is standing around, clutching a bottle, too distracted to open it. *This is Fran, this is Luke. This is Patience and Rob.* Now we must trace our connections to our hosts in the usual way, trying to find common ground.

'Oh, it's a long story,' I say. 'One of those funny

coincidences.' *Not that funny*, says Ben, and I turn to him and say *no, of course, but it all turned out OK in the end, didn't it*. Fran is familiar with the anecdote, she was there in the park when Christopher went missing. I see Patience processing the facts, horrified by them, unable not to judge. Eyes like saucers. 'Oh, you can't be too careful,' she breathes. 'Was Christopher, you know . . . ?'

'Right as rain,' Ben assures her, not as sharply as I imagine Emma would like. 'Hasn't mentioned it since. We think he's forgotten all about it.'

'Oh, that's just as well,' says Patience, doubtfully. 'Let's hope so, anyway.'

'Whereas Emma . . .' Ben says, with a cheery laugh. 'That's another matter entirely. Olive?'

Over the soup I find myself cornered by Patience who talks and talks, as if she's frightened of what might happen in the silences. She and Emma used to work together, 'in a previous life': a life that she implies was unsatisfactory. 'One has to make a choice,' she says, with a modest little laugh. 'And fortunately, with Rob's business doing so well . . .'

The Audrey and Alfred she cites so often – as she tells me stories about her struggles with the council planning department over the kitchen extension, the epic quest for an 'up to scratch' maths tutor – are, I quickly deduce, her children: such giants in her emotional landscape that she does not feel the need to introduce them. 'Goodness,' I say, when it's expected. 'Wow, that must be . . .'

Halfway through an anecdote about Audrey's school choir, as Patience embarks on yet another witless sub-clause, I look away, slowly and deliberately, and allow my eyes to settle on something over her left shoulder: the back door, a tea towel slung over the taps, it doesn't matter what it is.

Will she notice? Will it bother her? There's a brief but glorious confusion as she momentarily loses her thread;

and then, as I press the napkin to my lips, she regains her composure and carries on as if nothing happened. She must have been imagining it, surely.

In between her remarks, rather than relinquishing control of the conversation, she fills the gaps with obstacles: amused repetitions of her last statement, long complacent 'umm's, blithe little giggles.

She wonders if I've seen that new TV drama set in an Edwardian department store, and when I say I haven't, she starts to describe the plot, quite painstakingly.

Now and then I am aware of Emma glancing in our direction, watching me out of the tail of her eye. And Charles, too, giving me a secret smile, and leaning in to attract Patience's attention, showering her with questions, sacrificing himself.

On the fridge, the coloured magnets spell out harmless family jokes: *help, wine, lunatic.*

In answer to a question, Charles is explaining about Jess and Sophie, pushing the heavy-framed spectacles up on his nose with a genial, professorial air.

Fran, remembering, says, 'Ah, the babysitter.'

Patience is taken aback. 'Goodness, a teenager,' she says rather disagreeably, feeling a challenge to her authority. She imagines that must be hard work.

Charles says no, Sophie's fine, bar the usual.

'Teenage girls, they're worse than the Borgias,' I say, helping myself to some of the bedraggled salad. The beef's not bad, but I can tell Charles isn't taken with the wine. Out of solidarity with my husband, an ally in this room, I say Charles has always been very good with Sophie. I lift my glass, and as I do I notice Emma staring at me, drinking me up: absorbed by my hair and dress, my black jet necklace, the one Cecily liked.

Charles says the key is not to ask too many questions,

and they all take this on board, as if he's the oracle. I smile down at my plate, avoiding Emma's hungry eyes. 'She's a good girl,' I murmur. 'As seventeen-year-old girls go. She could be a lot worse.'

Of course, Patience has heard all about the drugs scandal at Sophie's school and is eager to talk about it. And after that, I must listen to complex tales of secondary transfer, and then I must nod and frown as Rob tells me about the marketing strategy he is working on for a digital radio station. 'What do you do?' he asks eventually (as his wife has not), so I say I paint. In the baffled silence that follows, I hear Charles telling Emma the story of our meeting; and that leads him to mention the house near Nice. I lean towards them. 'It's one of the best things Charles has done.' And I describe it for Emma: the view of the sea, the arc of the sun, the way the heat releases the fragrance of pine and lavender.

I can see her imagining it, just for a moment. Caught, irresistibly, in the images and sounds and scent I've conjured up for her. The shade under the vines; the crickets' hush in the heat of the day.

I excuse myself and slip out of the kitchen into the hall, carefully closing the door behind me. The carapace of order imposed on the sitting room has been dislodged by drinks and snacks, the chaos of our presence: the sofa cushions dented, a heap of pistachio shells loose on the coffee table, the carpet stirred and scarred by our shoes. I go up the stairs, sidestepping the yellow plastic dumper truck, the pile of library books. Oh, she has made quite an effort in the bathroom, too: tidied all the bath toys into a net, lit a lily-scented candle, left out a pair of sand-coloured hand towels, a bottle of hand cream, a spare loo roll. Very thoughtful. I check my makeup and walk out onto the landing.

The kitchen hubbub is faint from here, but suddenly Emma's laugh sounds clear and sharp; and that decides me.

I go to Cecily's door, and turn the handle, and step inside, leaving the door a little ajar so that I can see the cot and hear if anyone comes into the hall.

They've trained her to sleep without any light at all, so perhaps this small disturbance, this open door, will be enough. I stand there for a moment or two, waiting to see if anything will happen; but she doesn't move.

As my eyes adjust, details present themselves: the wide-flung arms, the palms open to the ceiling, the soft muslin bunched up against her cheek.

I stand by the cot, my hand on its pale-painted gate. The colourful letters run around the walls: either holding it together, or crushing the life out of it. A is for acrobat, B is for bear, C is for cloud.

When I unzip her sleeping bag and tug her feet free, they are warm and soft and a little damp, utterly limp in my hands, like bread dough. I let them fall, but nothing happens. Dead to the world.

'Cecily,' I whisper, blowing on her face. She flinches a little in her sleep, but resettles almost immediately. I look around. A plastic beaker of water has been left out on the mantelpiece, and I pull out the spout and shake it gently over her face: once, twice. Just a sprinkle. That does the trick. I feel her startle and tense; I hear the squeak of the mattress against the wood, the rasp of cotton on cotton, the gasp as she starts to fill her lungs with air. So I put the cup back on the mantelpiece and quickly move away, out of the room, shutting the door as I go. And then I pause at the top of the stairs, just to make sure.

When she's really howling I go downstairs and drop my hand on Emma's shoulder and bend to let her know. *Your party's over*, I think, as she slides her chair back, a look of exhaustion on her face.

It's as good as last orders. Spooked by real life, Fran and

Luke leave almost immediately, even though it's not quite eleven; and that's the cue for Patience and Rob to collect their things. 'Good to meet you,' I say, stacking the pudding plates, my hands full of spoons. 'Oh, really, let me, it's no problem.'

Ben says it's very kind. He seems relieved when I say I wouldn't mind a herbal tea, as if this suggests the evening still has the potential to be a success. 'I'll take one up for Emma,' I say.

I find her sitting in the chair, in front of the window. She's pulled the curtain back. As I go in, a light clicks off in the house opposite and the clouds shake themselves free, and then the gardens are illuminated by the moon, a whey-coloured crescent hanging over the chimney pots. Cecily's head droops against her mother's chest. I clear a space on the table and put the cup down so that Emma can reach it, and then I stand behind her, one of Christopher's Schleich horses in my hand, looking at us both, the weak warped reflections in the black glass.

She says she's sorry everyone had to leave so I reassure her: we're not in any hurry, the husbands are downstairs talking over a whisky. I compliment her on the party. I say, 'You went to a lot of trouble.'

'Oh, hardly,' she says, thinking now of the foolishness of ironing all those napkins. Buying those flowers.

I murmur something about liking Fran, enjoying the funny story she told about losing her shoe on the tube. As Emma reaches for her cup, Cecily settles herself deeper, her head lolling back against her mother's upper arm. When Emma sips, I sip too. It's nearly summer, I say. Sophie will be breaking up in few weeks. I ask if they have any plans for the holidays.

Not really, she says. Money's tight. Ben's worried about

work, something about a contract. They might visit his family and do a few day trips to the seaside.

I start to make my offer. I talk about the house in the South of France going begging for August. Cheap flights, even at this time of year.

'Oh,' she says, very unsure. 'We couldn't possibly—'

As I tell her more about it – the house is empty, my dad's keen for me to use it, it would be fun if we overlapped, there's plenty of room – I turn the little palomino over in my hand, feeling the sharpness of its hooves, the prick of its ears. *Gift horse, mouth*, I think.

I suggest she talks it over with Ben. She'll find I'm very persistent, I say with a laugh.

In the darkness, I lean down to place Christopher's horse on the table, and now I'm very close to her. Without meaning to I find I've put out my hand to touch Cecily's head. Beneath the cap of flyaway hair, there's a delicate warmth, like an egg. The porcelain fragility of her skull, and the sudden soft shock of the fontanelle, pulsing under my finger.

'Oh!' I say, not quite meaning to, a bit horrified, but fascinated, too. I wait there for a moment, conscious of the strangeness of it, conscious of Emma's unease as well as her proximity; and then I take my hand away without regret. 'I mean it,' I say, moving towards the door. 'You think about it.'

'I will,' she says, although it's more of an exhalation, really; the relieved sigh of someone presented with the solution to a problem.

On the walk home, I tell Charles what I've done, and I can tell he's not delighted.

'Oh, come on,' I say, my hand on his arm. The sound of our footsteps chases up ahead along the quiet streets; we stop to let a pizza-delivery scooter pull left. 'They're rather sweet. I think Emma's a bit lost. You know, adrift in the baby bit. It's nice to be able to help.'

'Well, of course, if you're sure,' Charles says.

'You won't be there all the time, anyway,' I remind him. 'I'll want some company. It'll be fun.'

'Why didn't you ask Bridget and that lot?' he's saying, and so I tell him Bridget books her summer holiday right after Christmas: Croatia or Greece, I can't remember which she has gone for this year. It's true, or true enough. 'Anyway, you can't stand Fred.'

He protests. Fred's not that bad. He means well. 'But the point is, darling, this lot: they're kids.'

'Well, Emma's my age – almost exactly,' I say, but he pats my hand, reprovingly: 'You know what I mean. Where they are. Babies. Naps. Nappies. I don't quite see the fascination.'

'It's not fascination,' I say, taken aback that he has noticed. I can usually depend on Charles not to notice. 'There's something about her. Something I find . . . affecting. She seems so, so . . .' I hunt for the right word, the word that will do, but I can't quite find it. '. . . It's nice to be able to help.'

'Seems to me you've helped her quite enough,' says Charles. 'Returning her wallet. Handing her toddler in to the police. Seems to me you've done quite a lot of good work here already.'

'Oh, don't tease me,' I say, a little crossly. 'There's something about her. It takes me back.'

'I do wonder what you were like then,' Charles says, folding my hand in his; and for a moment I can't think how to respond, and I'm frightened of saying the wrong thing, of giving myself away. And then I see what he means and, while he releases my hand and feels for his keys, I compose myself. 'What, when Sophie was tiny? Oh,' I say, as he goes up the stone steps ahead of me and opens the front door. 'You wouldn't know me. I was someone else then – someone quite different.' And it's true enough, though the real transformation had happened long before, when I first met Arnold, who for all his faults saw in me the things I barely knew I possessed, and drew them out, letting the bad habits fall away behind me, liberating me from the awkwardness and the doubt rather as he liberated me from my father. I remember Arnold in his earliest incarnation as a dealer, walking around my first studio, being surprised by the work: 'Oh yes, I think we can do something with these,' he said, glancing over at me with a speculative expression, just before he invited me for a drink.

Sometimes it felt as if Arnold, with his confidence and generosity and taste, had willed me into existence, suggesting as much as fostering the characteristics that are now so much a part of me. He turned my shyness into reserve, my guardedness into self-possession. He brought me out of the shadows. All this talk about 'finding yourself'; often, other people show you yourself first. Of course, I was grateful to Arnold for what he did for me; but I also resented him for it. In the end, he knew too much. He'd seen both sides. That was why I had to leave.

In the hall, we step over a pile of parkas and hoodies, dirty cream hi-tops the size of boats. I look into the sitting room, and they're lined up on the sofas and sprawled against the kilim cushions: seven or eight of them, eyes and teeth and empty pizza boxes bright in the fish-tank illumination of the TV. On the screen a woman is being chased through a wood. Crying and panting, the tell-tale snap of undergrowth, panicky strings. 'What're you watching?' I ask, and someone shushes me; and then some of the girls giggle. Sophie takes shape, an apparition in the gloom, brushing past me, heading for the kitchen.

They're all invited to someone's eighteenth in Dartmouth

Park, they got sidetracked by this crappy horror thing on Netflix, it's nearly over.

Beneath the smell of soda pop, her breath, when she speaks, is punchy with spirits.

'Whose party?' I ask. 'Won't it be over by the time you get there?' She shrugs, standing in the glow of the fridge, helping herself to two cans of Diet Coke.

'Back by one-thirty at the latest,' I say as she walks away, towards the darkened room. 'I'll wait up for you.'

One-thirty comes and goes while I lie there beside Charles, the door open to the dark and silent house: the coats on the hooks, the flowers in the vases, the snuffed candles and the pots left to dry by the sink.

I won't call until two. I mustn't. I click on my bedside light, angling it low so it won't disturb Charles, and pick up the *Spectator*, and read a column about first memories: how shock acts as a fixative, preserving fleeting and otherwise insignificant moments of childhood distress (falling down the stairs, leaving a favourite teddy in a taxi, losing a parent in a crowd); and then I try to concentrate on the book reviews, but the words swim like cyphers, refusing to make sense. Just after 2 a.m. I try her mobile: the voicemail kicks in straightaway. I send her a text, a tiny electronic pulse of data and anxiety, which goes unacknowledged. Twisting in the loose cool layers of cotton and linen, I wait, I wait, the phone's glow fading in my hand. The cat comes and lies in the crook of my knees for a little while, and then moves off again, compelled by his own mysterious affairs.

She arrives home around four, refraining from switching on any lights. I listen to her picking her way up the soft grey stairs like a burglar.

The following morning, she's full of excuses as she stands in front of the kettle, spooning cereal into her mouth. It was a mad night, she left her phone in her bag, lost track of time and only picked up my messages on her way home.

I explain that I'm docking her allowance and grounding her for a fortnight. If that means she has to miss Rosie's cinema trip, too bad. She shouts a bit, her eyes full of tears, and then storms off with her mug of tea. Charles, who has been keeping out of it (his particular skill), glances up from the week's brown envelopes. 'That's fair enough, isn't it?' I ask, irritated by his remote, amused expression.

He thinks I handled it very well.

I only ever miss Arnold at times like this. Charles is fond of Sophie. He would say he loves her. But the feelings he has for her are mild and dilute, far removed from my raw involuntary connection with her.

I hear her on her phone, the tone of outrage and injury spliced with giggles and 'God, piss off, you *didn't*!' Later, when I'm unloading the dishwasher, she comes to me, saying she's sorry. 'I should have thought,' she says, picking up the cutlery basket and taking it over to the drawer, picking out the knives and teaspoons: very contrite. 'I just got carried away.'

I put my arms around her, feeling the slight bridling resistance before she softens and permits the embrace. I won't back down about the punishments, I tell her (giving her a kiss, pushing her hair back from her forehead, as I used to do when she was a little girl), but I'm grateful for the apology.

She looks at me, fawn-eyed. 'I screwed up,' she says. 'Fair enough.'

I'm tempted to think I've handled it pretty well. But a few days later, while I'm rootling in my purse to find Lenka's money, I find I'm a bit short: maybe twenty pounds down, or thirty. I'm sure I am not mistaken; but then the doubts creep in. Perhaps it's safest to say nothing.

Emma

Full of apprehension, I find it hard to commit to sleep; and then the alarm is going off, and Ben is staggering out of bed, pulling the duvet off me, turning on the overhead light. Behind the curtains the street lamps shine on empty pavements. The windows in the houses opposite are dark, without motion.

We hurry to and from the shower, not speaking, towelling our hair and concentrating on the last critical elements of packing: toothbrushes, phone chargers, spectacles. The luggage is dragged downstairs. The taxi will be here in ten. We stand in the hall jittery with adrenaline, checking over the car seats, the folded buggy, the buttered Ryvita and dried apple rings stashed in Ziploc bags, wondering what we've missed.

It's time. As Ben goes into Christopher's room, I go into Cecily's. I've removed her sleep suit and changed her nappy and have half-dressed her before she's properly awake. She's too stunned to protest, just sits mute on my hip, swaying and squinting, turning her face to shield her eyes as I take her out onto the landing.

The doorbell, the carrying out of luggage, the fitting of the child seats, the strapping in of the children. I step out of the house, into the startling secret chill of the dawn, and turn the key in the door. We are off. As the cab swings out of our road, Ben says, 'You definitely double-locked it, didn't you?'

It's quiet in the cab: just the soft intermittent ticking of indicators and a crackle every so often as control dispatches drivers to addresses in Bow or Barnsbury. Cecily goes back to sleep almost immediately; Christopher sits holding his sippy cup of milk, huge round eyes fixed on the window. Briefly, I see the world as he sees it: a new world of sodium lights and deserted streets and shuttered shops, the familiar landscape stripped of animation and so rendered magical and mysterious. I can't helping thinking of *The Tiger Who Came to Tea* – Sophie being taken out for supper in her nightie – and I'm about to mention this to him, and then I can't be bothered.

As we join the motorway, switching from one zombie lane to another, the sky opens up and begins to lighten, biblical pink and gold building in the east. A memory of leaving London as a child at the start of the holidays, of being packed in the car in our pyjamas, wedged in by pillows and quilts, and falling asleep, and waking up the next morning in my bed at Jassop, the sun creeping over the top of the blue curtains and into the room, the bookshelves crammed tight with worn hardbacks, the paraffin heater shaped like a tower, the rush-bottomed chair in the corner. The smell of it, of things that stayed the same.

I rest my head on the back of the seat. Just for a moment, I shut my eyes. If someone would only give me permission, I think, I could sleep for days. Weeks, even.

'God, I need a holiday,' murmurs Ben. *Not half as much as I do, sunshine,* I think, keeping my eyes closed. We both know that we won't be getting one anytime soon. Last summer was quite unlike any other holiday we'd taken: our days circumscribed by naps and mealtimes, by a need to avoid mosquitoes and the midday heat and the pool on the mornings when they'd added the chemicals. The constant low-level anxiety. Was it really fine to drink the tap water? Would the chemist be open on a Monday afternoon?

A year on, with a baby in the mix, we've learned our lesson. Neither of us expects much. Better that way. I squeeze his hand.

At various points during the morning – queuing at check-in; shoving items into clear plastic bags; sampling Cecily's purěed butternut and formula to prove they're not bomb components; removing and putting on our shoes; being sheep-dipped into the aircraft – I look at my watch and am aghast to find it's still not 9 a.m. Could time go any slower? Before we've even taken off Ben has read Christopher both of the picture books I bought for the journey and one of the new Hotwheels has gone astray under the seats in front. There is the threat of a tantrum, which I see off with the triumphant flourish of a Chupa Chup.

Conversations die away as the plane accelerates, and then revive once we're securely launched, the moment of terror falling away behind us like England. Taking slow breaths of the cold deodorised atmosphere, holding Cecily in my arms, I feel as much as hear the whine as wheels and flaps are adjusted. Up ahead, secured behind locked doors, are the dials and gauges that hold us up; the dizzying electronic skeins of navigation filling the skies. Behind us, the contrail spilling out like a spider's thread.

Brisk smiles are distributed with breakfast. I hold my cup out for the stewardess's metal coffeepot, trying to keep it steady while Cecily bucks and twists on my knee. While Ben holds my cup, I unwrap the croissant and rip it in half. She sinks her gums into it appreciatively.

Christopher is plugged into a movie about a shy dragon on the iPad. Ben gets out *Private Eye*. 'Would you hold her for a moment?' I say, passing her over. I stand up and stretch and join the queue for the loo, but once I'm locked in there I just rinse the stickiness off my hands and splash some water on my face and pat it dry with a fake-linen disposable towel. And then I look at myself in the mirror, in the merciless blue-white light. Crumbs on my jersey. Shadows under my eyes. My hair has dried with a slight frizz to it, giving me a vague unfinished outline, as if my signal is weak.

For a moment, I remember the holidays Ben and I had in the past: simple little whitewashed cottages with terraces covered with vines, fancy suites with thick swagged curtains and pairs of sofas and complimentary fruit bowls swathed ludicrously in cellophane. The clink of rigging, the rattle of trams, room service's quiet knock, the chiming of ten or twenty bells as the goats come down from the hill. Pointing at something on the menu, not knowing or minding what'll come. Food, wine, sex, books, sleep.

Still, it'll be good to get away. Just to see that it's all still out there, still happening: the world of aperitifs ordered at pavement cafés, of pink tablecloths and floodlit squares and crowded markets. Even if we are, for now, not at ease in it.

I go back to my seat and drink my nasty coffee. Cecily has a shouty twisty episode and then quite unexpectedly falls asleep again.

The descent begins. I find the bottle with the slow teat for Cecily, in case she wakes up.

'You've got another lolly for Christopher?' Ben asks.

Yes, of course I have. It's in the inner pocket of my bag. He reaches over and rummages around while Christopher presses his hands to his cheeks, saying his ears hurt. 'I can't find it,' Ben says, and so I shrug Cecily into my shoulder and take the bag from him and have a look, sorting through the baby wipes, the spare sachets of formula, the children's emergency outfits, the novel I have yet to open. It's not there, I can't find the lolly anywhere. The seat belt bites into my hip as I rake through the contents, finding nothing but loose change and keys and the dry rubble of biscuits.

The plane drops again, sinking through the cloud.

'Mama, it hurts,' wails Christopher, and I hear the injury and accusation in his voice, as if it's my fault, as if I've done it to him. And in a way, he's right. I have.

'We're trying to find you a sucky sweet,' I say. I should be sounding calm and sympathetic rather than irritated and dismissive. Sweat prickles out along my hairline.

'Have you looked in the bottom of your bag?' Ben asks, yawning and turning to 'Street of Shame', as if he's off the hook; and I snap, 'It's not there! Did you see it? I didn't.'

I'm about to press the button to call the stewardess – somehow, I'm always the one who has to ask for help – when a man across the aisle leans over with a tube of fruit gums. Thanks so much, I say, wondering what sort of impression we've been creating during the flight, wondering how I must appear, and suddenly cold with humiliation. Now I've started thinking about this, I find I cannot stop.

Fields and woods begin to assemble between silver snakes of rivers, the formal geometry of motorways. The ugly sprawl of small provincial towns. Lakes, industrial estates, farms. Small sky-blue boxes set in the ground, flashing in the sun.

The plane falls and falls, and then catches the edge of the runway with a great metallic shriek, and indeed it has all been all about this moment, the velocity and the terrible noise and the shaking, and then the relief as the pace begins to slacken and the journey is finally over: the brown grass beyond the asphalt, the little orange vehicles buzzing towards us, the men with paddles. But we're not allowed to move yet: we must sit tight while the plane taxis around and then noses into a berth by the low grey terminal. Someone opens the doors, and the heat sweeps through the cabin like wonderful news you can hardly bring yourself to believe. Ben catches my eye, winks. *Not bad, eh?* But half of me is thinking about Christopher's eczema, wondering if he'll have a flare-up, trying to remember if I packed the hydrocortisone. As we step out into the burning light, I am conscious of how I must look to the aircrew lined up to bid us goodbye. A drained-looking middle-aged person, draped in children and exhaustion, close to saying something she'll regret.

It takes forever, dealing with the luggage carousel and the Avis madam with her lipstick and superior manner, but eventually we're in the multi-storey car park, on the scent of the hire car. Ben's excited about this bit: 'Since we've saved so much on the accommodation, I thought we could have some fun.' It's a flash two-door model (what *was* he thinking?) with a sunroof that we'll never open because of the sun.

While he attempts to get the air-con going, I start to load the boot and then break off to spoon the jar of butternut into Cecily. But there is a problem. Ben doesn't know how to switch on the engine. There's an electronic fob, rather than a key, and he can't make it work. 'Shall I go back and ask her?' I say, sighing, remembering the queue of holidaymakers inching all the way back to the little stall selling Tic-Tacs and *Paris-Match*, featuring unknown personalities whose faked-up bodies and houses and families illuminate the short-comings of our own.

'It's OK,' says Ben, rubbing his sleeve over his forehead and paging furiously through the manual, searching for an English translation. 'It'll be here somewhere.' Christopher starts tugging at Cecily's buggy. 'I'm thirsty,' he says, getting the buggy moving, beginning to propel it towards the ramp. 'I need a wee.' I grab the buggy and kick down the brake. Cecily's face puckers. *Oh, fuck's sake*, I say under my breath, as Ben consults the diagram and – with an experimental, fatalistic air – waves the fob again, an inept magician conscious that he's losing his audience.

I take Christopher off, smiling briskly at a neat French family who walk past while he is pissing in the bush next to the trolley depot, and when we return the car is packed and sealed and cooling down nicely.

According to the email Nina sent me, the journey to her father's place should take no longer than an hour. It takes us over two: loo breaks and nappy changes, an argument over motorway exits, a dash around a supermarket for basics as we don't know whether we'll be able to buy anything locally tonight.

We're all knackered, and it's not yet 3 p.m. The road shimmers up ahead, liquid phantoms coming and going in dips in the tarmac. If you stepped on it, it would feel soft and slightly tacky; it would give a little under your weight.

When we drive through towns and hamlets, the windows in the ochre-coloured villas and low apartment blocks are firmly shuttered. All the shops are closed. Where do the people go in the heat of the day? I think of old couples silently sitting in dim poky kitchens that smell distantly of frying; I think of dogs flat-out on those speckly continental floors that always look a little dirty, no matter how often they're mopped.

'So it's next right, and then straight on until you get to the yellow barn, and the drive is off to the left,' I say, my finger on the print-out, the type faded now in the creases left by the constant superstitious folding and unfolding, like a treasure map.

An avenue of poplars, the yellow barn, and then we turn off onto a dirt track, the car bucking and growling, kicking up a tail of orange dust. Some small birds, surprised, take off as we come around a bend. The children fall silent. Ahead of us the steep rocky hillside tumbles away to reveal the sea, just there, just within reach: a curve of turquoise, perfectly glassy and tranquil, unmarked by wind or boats or rocks.

Ben parks as instructed, at the end of the track, beneath the pergola, and once the dust has settled around the car, coating the windscreen with a parchment film, we open the doors. There's a little hot rush of breeze, and the air smells of ozone and thyme and pine. For the first time today, I feel as if my heart is beating, rather than grinding.

'Looks alright, doesn't it,' says Ben, getting out of the car and stretching.

We bring the children up into the garden, a series of paths and terraces: scented shrubs, shallow channels of water trickling into troughs, metal planters spilling over with herbs, and here and there the rustling silver glitter of olive trees. There's a lawn, surprisingly green, a faded hammock strung in the shade of two tall pines, and behind a long stone terrace is the house: low, discreet, an elegant series of pale interlocking boxes, the windows angled towards the ocean. The glass seems to hold it all – the sky, the garden, the terrace, the sea – just so, exactly so, exactly as it might look in a dream. And then, as we approach the house, our dishevelled reflections appear in its windows.

Ben drops his bag on the terrace and goes up close, pressing his face against the glass, hands cupping his face, trying to look in. I consult the instructions. 'They've left the door at the end unlocked,' I tell him, and I walk down the terrace and reach for the handle knowing that the handle will turn, the door will give. Everything will be just as she has said. And everything she has not told me about will be good, too.

Stunned, winded by our luck, we move through the kitchen and the sitting room. Even the children are silent, awestruck. Cecily, on my hip, inspects everything with sober intensity. In here, the sun is held at bay by the shade of the trees, the grey wooden louvres and the bleached canvas awnings that snap and strain fitfully in the breeze, like a ship's sails.

'It's all very white,' mutters Ben, taking in the sofas, the floor cushions, the drifting lengths of linen at the windows. I tell him what Nina told me: it's all slipcovers and spare sets, a woman from the village comes twice a week, like the gardener, and when you've left she changes everything. Because of the half-sister, it's all geared up for kids, though of course we've got to watch the water features. *Nina told me not to worry about sticky fingers.* I say it airily, with a conviction that I think persuades him, though I can't quite believe it myself.

In the industrial fridge, we find milk and juice and white wine and cheese and a dish of stuffed aubergine in a tomato sauce, ready for the oven. Suddenly aware of my thirst, I pour mineral water into tumblers. We all drink, silently.

There's the high chair. That box is full of toys.

Down the corridor, the two bedrooms assigned to us – the double with the linen chaise and the doors that open onto the terrace, the cot in the corner; Christopher is next door, in a small twin – are made up with smooth acres of ironed cotton: white and pearl-grey. The bathrooms, with their deep stone tubs and twin basins, look out onto the pine wood. There's air-con, but what with the ceiling fans and the breeze, we probably won't need to use it, we agree, pushing back the sliding doors, hearing the church bell tolling up from the village, a single austere note.

While Christopher finds the piano and starts to press the noise out of the keys, Ben and I separate and move on through the rooms, finding hidden doors that lead into pantries or laundry rooms or wet rooms or walk-in wardrobes. I can see what Charles has done here, I can see the way he has eliminated the clutter of everyday by editing it, pushing it out of sight; paring back to this simple, seductive tyranny of space, air and light. Much more than the house in London, this house is a manifesto, an idealised statement of how, properly, with discipline and taste, we should live. It's a fair brief for a holiday house, I suppose, feeling the needle of jealousy beneath the delight that all this – for a week or so – is going to be ours.

In the master bedroom, Cecily on my hip, I pop open the cupboards and a few drawers – it would be strange not to be curious – and find pretty much what I expected to find: the stepmother's capsule summer wardrobe (cotton dresses, some slim-cut, some full-skirted for evening, one in last summer's particular shade of cobalt; a slippery tangle of bikinis in bold prints); the father's Lacoste polo shirts in all colours, swimming trunks printed with seahorses from that ludicrous specialist store in the Burlington Arcade.

'What did Nina say her dad did?' Ben asks, appearing at the door, and I say he's a composer of some sort. We find his name on a few envelopes collected on the kitchen counter: M. Paul Storey. Ben reaches into his pocket for his phone, but has no reception. He'll have to google him later. 'We must be talking big time,' he says, wandering off outside. Then, a moment later, I hear him call for me.

He's found the swimming pool. It stands in its own gated courtyard between banks of dwarf lavender, the purple heads bowing and beginning to turn dusty. Pale grey cushions on the loungers, pale grey sun parasols. The pool – that long unruffled expanse of water – is tiled in grey: but a darker grey, closer to charcoal, nearly black. A dark mirror surrounded by aching light. It's the most glorious thing I've ever seen.

Christopher's blond head appears at the gate, his small hand reaching up for the latch. He tries to lift it, but is thwarted by its height and weight. 'You mustn't come in here without Mummy or Daddy,' I tell him as I let him in. 'That's very important.'

He says OK, and then he stares at the pool, the delicious spectacle.

In the house, we shove Cecily in the high chair with a breadstick and tell Christopher to keep an eye on her, just for a minute. And then we're rushing back through the hot scented garden to the car, dragging the suitcases and shopping bags out of the boot and lugging them up the hill. The impatience of unpacking, of trying to locate the trunks and swim nappies and rash tops, of inflating Christopher's armbands. When I've got everyone changed and ready, I still have to find my own swimsuit, a tired old khaki thing that gapes a bit at the bust; I meant to buy a new one before we left, but I never got around to it. Our bathroom towels are white; pool towels, left folded at the end of the beds, are slate. I wonder if Charles thought all this out, or if it was the French stepmother, Delphine.

Ben carries Cecily into the shallow end. She's rigid with apprehension at first, her limbs stiff and doll-like, and then she's squealing with pleasure and dancing in his arms, blinking in the spray. Christopher bobs between his orange wings, his hair slicked to his head, ghostly legs spinning beneath him. I hear the water gushing over the lip of the pool: an infinity edge, of course. Beyond it, the hazy indistinct line of the sea against the sky.

I walk down the stone steps into the blood-warm water and push off, feeling, as it rises over my shoulders, the tension falling away behind me, along with the heat and the anxiety and the irritation of the day. I dip my head under and kick down, swimming five or ten strokes, stretching, eyes blurred, ears full of a silent roar, my mind suddenly empty. When I come up and tread water in the deep end, droplets falling from my hair, it sounds like glockenspiels.

I flip over and float on my back for a while, considering the sky: the sort of sky where a cloud would be startling, an unexpected novelty. High up, a few birds are patiently riding the thermals in slow lazy spirals, making small adjustments to the angle of their wings while they wait for those tiny giveaways on the hillside: a pebble sent rolling, the twitch of grass, a sudden shadow.

I'm not sure what they are. Buzzards? Eagles? Ben will know. But I don't want to ask him, not at this particular moment. There's lots of time.

Dimly, through the water, I hear Christopher say, 'You look like a marmalade, Mama. When your hair does that.'

Later, when the children are asleep, we sit at the table on the terrace and eat the aubergine dish left for us, watching the light going out of the sky and listening to the dogs barking along the headland. 'We've really fallen on our feet here,' Ben says. 'I think the technical term is "jammy buggers".'

I murmur agreement as he uncorks the second bottle. The air is full of white flowers and herbs, sweet and savoury; and through all this threads the agreeable scent of the mosquito coil burning at our feet. The wine is very cold in the big glass. When he kisses me, I kiss him back, my hands in his hair.

I feel, tonight, like someone else, the sort of person who goes on holiday to a house overlooking the sea, a house with curtains the colour of milk and a swimming pool tiled in slate. I used to know this person, I used to understand her; maybe I'll get to know her again. Now that I'm here, the warmth on my skin and beginning to soften my bones, it seems almost possible.

As the days pass, the house tolerates our frailties without indulging them. Our damp towels slung over the balustrades. Boxes of cereal and crackers left out on the dining table.

Toy trucks in the gravel. Before long, these little things look conspicuously wrong, and we find ourselves tidying up as we go along, as we never quite manage to do at home. And yet it's an easy house to live in, everything so well-planned, so thought-through: so obvious, in many ways. It's the sort of house that reminds you, inevitably, of the shortcomings of other houses, of Carmody Street in particular. We find ourselves marvelling at the water pressure and the kitchen drawers that close with soft, muted adhesion, like the doors of expensive cars.

Even as we fill the house with our noise and clutter, we are steadily succumbing, giving in to it and the way it suggests we live. Without quite realising it, we are being overpowered.

For the first few days, Ben is all go, reading guide books, consulting maps, working out when things will be open. We should go shopping in the village in the cool of the morning; in the late afternoon, we should visit an art gallery or the fishing port where Picasso had his studio (its harbour now filled with shiny black super-yachts that look like arrowheads of jet). Christopher complains as we buckle him into his car seat, and threatens to be sick as the car twists along the hairpin bends. He doesn't care much for Picasso.

But on the third morning Cecily sleeps in until after nine, and so Ben and I wake of our own accord, a novelty that gives him time to reconsider. Perhaps we'll just hang out for now. See how it goes. It's in the quiet uneventfulness of the next few days that I begin to sense her – the other me, the person I thought I'd lost – and the flashes of the ease and happiness she took for granted. When Ben has taken the children for the first swim of the day, I make a second pot of coffee and carry a cup around the garden, discovering that one thought can still lead, quite naturally, to another. In the shade, the grass is damp from the sprinkler. As I step into the sun, I can feel the air rising around me, laden with moisture.

Later, I'm lying on the cushions beneath the arbour as Christopher, not quite believing it's permitted, picks the purple grapes and drops them into my mouth. The skins, warm and grainy against my teeth, give with a pop. To scandalise him, to make him giggle, I spit the bitter gritty pips into the bushes. 'Mama,' he says. 'That's not allowed.'

From time to time – in the hammock or on a lounger, as the sun plays on my eyelids: red and black paisley, a languorous psychedelic swirl – I find myself thinking about home, and it's always a shock. I think of our house, silent and empty beneath fitful skies, its spaces still imprinted with signs of our hasty departure. The half-drawn curtains, the rumpled beds, the children's nightclothes lying on the carpet where we dropped them. As if we had warning of some advancing catastrophe.

Dust falling through the rooms and hallways, falling on the stairs.

But of course life goes on without us. The daily snap of the letterbox, plastic-wrapped catalogues and library reminders and special offers on barbecue coals sliding over the hall floorboards. I open my eyes, and it's a relief. The precise line of the poplars over the hill, the sea's glitter, the boundless clarity of the sky.

In the heat, I feel myself growing, like a plant. I'm conscious that I'm reclaiming some of my old height. It strikes me that I spend so much of my life stooping. Bent double to pick things up, crouching to listen or inspect or rub or commiserate. I imagine my spine unfurling like a time-lapse fern, the spaces between the vertebrae widening and expanding.

The shortcomings that we identify in the house and garden say more about us than it. The pool may be safely gated, but the small shallow channels of water circulating so musically through the garden demand a certain vigilance. Christopher falls over and cuts his knee on the gravel. Later, we discover that he has been busy transporting great quantities of it from the path to the lawn beneath the hammock. The sets of children's crockery are Finnish design classics, so we push them to the back of the kitchen cupboard and buy plastic plates and bowls from the hypermarket, along with ugly pool inflatables and a softball set with a sponge ball.

Ben says he thinks it's odd how little personal stuff there is in the house.

'Well, it's a holiday home,' I say.

'Yeah, but it's a *home*. It's not as if they rent it out or anything. The only people who use it are Nina's family, and their friends, right?'

'I don't really know,' I say, not liking the way he's making me feel: aware that I'm bristling slightly.

'It's strange, isn't it? Not to have any photographs? No books or *objets*?' He says the word with a laugh, gesturing around the living room.

He's right. There's the piano, and the abstract landscape with an arid feel (although the yellows and ochres and hard blues are not the colours I associate with Nina, I assume it's one of hers) over the dining table, and four bone-coloured slipware vases set out with thoughtful irregularity on a shelf, and that's pretty much it, apart from a carefully curated collection of guide books and maps; and the toy box, of course, with its rake and sieve, its bean-filled puppy and baby doll, lips puckered for the dummy, and, right at the bottom, neatly packed away in a wicker hamper, the immaculate china tea set.

Overall, all the spaces are painstakingly neutral: bare, pared-down. Hollow, almost.

I say that it's the *lack* of stuff that makes the house feel so restful.

'Yeah, it's nice for a change,' he says, a little doubtfully. 'I can't imagine living like this for any length of time, though.'

'Oh, I can,' I say, a little too forcefully. 'I love it. It's giving me all sorts of ideas. When I get home, I'm going to build a gigantic bonfire in the back garden, and chuck everything on it. All the crap, all the clutter. Douse it in petrol, light a match. *Ka-boom.*'

He laughs. 'Yeah, right,' he says. 'Because I remember how good you are at donating things to Oxfam. Those little piles of junk which you leave out on the stairs, which we all fall over for a few days, and then the junk just goes back into general circulation. Osmosis.'

'That's not fair,' I protest, but he's right, I find it hard to let things go.

Still, I imagine building a pyre, piling up all the broken toys and picture books with torn or missing pages, the guitar Ben'll never get around to re-stringing, the wonky-legged stool. Flipping the red beak on the tin and squirting lighter fluid over the blanket the moths got at. The rattle as I open the box of matches. I feel the sudden rush of bright heat on my face and neck, smell the bitter smoke.

As we help Christopher over the shingle or buy pistachio ice-creams in the little square, Ben and I have the nostalgic conversations about the summers of our childhood – Ben's in the New Forest; mine at the farm in Kent owned by my grandparents – that we've had on other holidays. It's a relief to be freed from the usual topics: money worries, the creeping stain on the ceiling of Christopher's bedroom, who's spiking a temperature.

Strange, how our children's present summons up our pasts. The things I remember most clearly aren't necessarily the things I put into words: afternoons up a tree with a book, sleeping out in a tent, cycling to the beach with Lucy and building a fire and boiling eggs over it in an enamel saucepan filched from Gamma's cupboard.

Eventually we grew out of that sort of thing; we no longer yearned for the country, we started to make excuses not to go, and when we did visit we were restless, dissatisfied, conscious that we were missing out on what was happening elsewhere.

It's late afternoon and we are in the little playground – shaded by pines, long needles underfoot – not far from the harbour. Cecily is in the swing while Christopher rides a squeaky spring-mounted cartoon motorbike. I look up, through the trees. Sunshine dances and flickers on my face, bursts of light and warmth. I'm telling Ben a story about my grandmother's half-facetious pursuit of the top prizes in the annual Jassop produce show – how she wouldn't let us in the kitchen when the cakes were in the oven, how we had to tiptoe around upstairs, remembering not to slam doors – when I'm struck by a stray memory. I'm remembering watching Gamma, in a dun kilt and forest-green jersey, loading her car with precious commodities (the jars of preserves with their neat muslin mobcaps, the tins containing fruit cake and Victoria sponge, the trays of butterfly cakes bound for the WI's tea stall) while I hold still, barely breathing and yet bursting with suppressed laughter, my hand over my mouth, feeling Lucy shake beside me.

I haven't thought of this for years: the hollow heart we discovered in the hedgerow behind the farmhouse, an ancient secret space enclosed by a living wall of leaves and briars, perfect for spying and secrets. When it rained, you stayed dry in there, the rain pattering around you, darkening the driveway and the slates on the roof, but the earth beneath your sandals remained sandy and friable. Did the grown-ups know about it? We assumed not, but perhaps they were only pretending.

It's a sensation, not an anecdote. I can't find a way of expressing it, I can't see how I could make it into a story, so I fall silent, remembering the rustle and dimness of shouldering my way inside, the scratch of twigs on my arms, the twisted branch that served as a seat. The pleasure of staying hidden as the world carried on with its business, unaware that it was being observed: my grandmother pegging out the washing, the postman's van and once a week the mobile library, my grandfather dragging bags of sheep nuts into the barn. My parents setting off for a walk, my father idly swinging a borrowed walking stick into the nettles and the foaming banks of cowparsley.

It was everything to us: cave, priesthole, crow's nest. We believed it was probably as old as the farmhouse itself, or older. We saved sweets to eat in there, and every year we'd find a few of last summer's wrappers caught under roots, the glitter eroded by the weather, little fluttering scraps of another August's happiness.

Then one visit Lucy lost interest in it; and it wasn't so much fun on my own. The years between the deaths of my grandparents we forgot about it altogether. Strange, how these things come at you out of the blue, a lifetime of summers later. I wonder if the hedgerow is still there; if shreds of purple and gold foil are still caught in the roots. I wonder what, if anything, Christopher will remember of this holiday.

The metal creaks and squeals as Christopher throws his weight around, lurching backward and forward on the motorbike, lost in the ferocity of his enjoyment. 'You're going awfully fast,' Ben says, approvingly. The look on Christopher's face says, *not fast enough*.

It's not that I've forgotten that Nina and Sophie will be arriving on the Thursday; more that I've willingly lost track of time. But if I'm honest, I will accept that at some point I stopped looking forward to their arrival. We've been happy here on our own, our schedule going to pot, the usual rules warping a little in the sun and saltwater. Against all expectations, we've been freed from something.

'A proper lie-in tomorrow,' I say as we sit at what's now our regular table at our favourite restaurant, watching old men in shirtsleeves gathering to smoke and chat in the little dusty square. Between the trees the air is strung with coloured bulbs, red, yellow, green, blue: a carnival illumination against the oncoming dusk.

Christopher glances up quickly from his *frites* and says, 'Are there *lions* here?'

We explain, and then Ben says, 'We have to tidy the place up before they arrive. What time does their flight get in?'

You're kidding, it can't be Wednesday already. There's some truth to my pantomime shock; and beneath that is a sneaking resentment. I'm not looking forward to handing the house over to Nina and Sophie, witness to my bleakest English moments. But it's unfair of me, I know that.

'Not until the afternoon. There's not much to do, anyway,' I say, and it's true. We've given in to the rigorous expectations of the house. Cereal boxes look silly left out. I find myself in the novel position of being unable to tolerate crumbs on the counters. In any case Thérèse (an industrious narrow-faced woman who leaves the house wrinkle-free and smelling of artificial lemon) appears every few days to mop and polish. 'I hope it'll be OK, I hope they won't find us too annoying,' I say.

'We can keep out of their way,' Ben says, spooning some avocado into Cecily's mouth. 'It'll be fine, Em, don't worry.'

But I do. In the run-up to Nina's arrival, I'm aware of an air of finality and mourning, as if I'm preparing to say goodbye. The last easy breakfast beneath the grape arbour, the last noisy family swim, the last mindless wander around the garden with a coffee cup, pinching and sniffing thyme and rosemary while Christopher rakes the gravel into little piles and drives his cars around them. On the shady grass, Cecily is threatening to crawl: lunging off her bottom and dragging herself up on all fours, trembling a little with the effort. Ben's foot dangles from the hammock, just keeping the thing in motion. He's halfway through his second thriller, greedily losing himself in it whenever he can. In a minute, he'll have to put it down and drive Christopher into town to buy baguettes and salad.

I go back into the house to make another pot of coffee and while I'm waiting for the water to boil I walk down the corridor and find myself again in the master bedroom, the room that belongs to Nina's father and his wife, the room that Nina will sleep in tonight. Like the rest of the house, it's a vaguely monastic space, and pleasantly dim in the mornings, the sun held in check by the wooden ribs of the louvres. The high ceiling, the low broad bed, a cane chair at a writing desk, a long marble-topped table against the far wall. A pair of plain wooden candlesticks and a shallow alabaster bowl containing a few pine cones and stones glinting unevenly with quartz. The pale flags are cold beneath my feet. I switch on the ceiling fan, clicking it to the lowest setting. Overhead, the blades in the air. *Wuh-wuh-wuh.*

Thérèse has put out a pair of swimming towels and left a sprig of lavender on both pillows. New soaps by the basins and the big stone bath. I pick up one bar and press it to my nose, inhaling the scent through the thick waxy wrapper. It smells like the rosemary taint on my fingers: stingingly clean, needle-sharp.

The bedroom windows hold the slope of the pine wood, and beyond that the bright V of the sea. Perhaps I'm wondering if Nina's view will be the same as mine, and that is why – without quite formulating the desire – I find myself sitting down on the bed, carefully lying back, placing my head on the pillow and lifting my bare feet to rest on the cotton. The pulse in my ears drowns out the quiet rotation of the fan overhead, while I'm straining to listen, straining to hear the sound of Ben's footsteps in the corridor, appalled at the prospect of being caught here, doing this. *What exactly am I doing?*

When I stand up, the bed is wrecked, in disarray, scored and marked by the messy imprint of my body, a body which is so much larger and more awkward than Nina's. In a panic I tug the linen straight, running my palms over the sheet, trying to smooth and flatten it, and plump up the pillow, replacing the sprig of lavender which has fallen to the floor; but I lack Thérèse's skill and naturally it all looks wrong, hopeless, a giveaway. I go to the door and hesitate, inspecting the bed from a new angle, then I have one last try, tweaking the pillow and the swimming towels. *Fuck's sake, it's fine, get a grip. It'll do.*

On the stove, the coffee pot is burning dry, and I scorch my fingers taking it off the hob.

Nina

After the ceremony in a drab little hall off the Euston Road, we congregate for Ursula and Hugh's wedding reception in a Marylebone garden square. I always appreciate access to these hidden spaces: the black railings and thick banks of shrubs enclosing quiet gravel paths and striped green ovals. It's a muggy afternoon, warm and overcast, the air hardly moving in the yellow and blue bunting that droops between the plane trees. Ursula's daughters press through the crowd, offering scones and butterfly cakes. For those who want it, tea comes in mismatching junk-shop china. There's a Punch and Judy tent near the climbing frame.

Bridget hurries over the lawn. Thank God it hasn't rained, she says, the ground's hard enough for her heels. As I am meant to, I admire her new shoes. 'Fred bought them for me when he was in Paris – anniversary present,' she says. 'I'd sent him the link and the address, not to mention a reminder of my size – but all the same, it was sweet of him.'

'You're very lucky,' I say, but she turns to me, laughing. 'Oh, Nina. Look at him.'

We look. Fred is making conversation with another pink-faced man in a dull tie. Through the clusters of guests, I hear the phrases 'goat rodeo', 'batting average' and 'moving forward'; it's unclear whether they're talking shop or sport.

As we watch, Fred swivels around, reaching out to grab a canapé, a dolly's cucumber sandwich, popping it into his mouth with uncomplicated greed.

The glass of champagne the girl gave me as she let me in the gate is already losing its electrifying chill. 'As you know, I'm very fond of Fred,' I say, smiling down at my silver sandals.

Bridget's just back from the Greek holiday (the villa was a bit of a disappointment: suspect plumbing, and the wi-fi wasn't working, much to Paddy's disgust). 'So, what about your summer?' Bridget is saying. 'Of course you're missing Sophie, but there must be compensations, weekends away when you fancy it, just throwing a bikini and a toothbrush into a bag. Christ, how we travel. Surfboards, golf clubs ... We look like the Mandarina Duck catalogue.'

Why shouldn't Bridget envy me my life, the way it appears to her? My work, my success, my pretty and compliant daughter, the way I look (my flat silver sandals, toenails painted this summer's blackcurrant)? And Charles. I glance over at him. He's talking to Hugh's mother, but raises a glass when he catches my eye.

'And how *is* Sophie?' Bridget is asking. 'Not AS Levels already.'

So I say *I know, isn't it ridiculous.*

Later, we go home and move in and out of the rooms, never quite catching up with each other, like little peg people rotating stiffly around a cuckoo clock. Perhaps we have less in common with Sophie away. I hear the toilet flush, and then he wanders into the sitting room, sighing as he settles down with the newspaper, and the noises irritate me. Perhaps it's the heat, and the champagne. I drink a tall glass of cold water and open the laptop.

The gallery has emailed to say a client who bought one of

my paintings a few years ago would like to visit the studio late on Tuesday morning.

I write back saying I'd be delighted to meet Mr Fisk again, and then I compose a message to Sophie, describing the afternoon and Ursula's dress – though she won't be interested – and saying one of us will be there to pick her up at Heathrow when she gets in.

Some time around eleven, I step outside to collect the chair cushions from the terrace. The sky is muddied with light pollution, orange clouds hanging overhead, the air as warm and still as stewed tea. Henry has made a kill: a small squalid detonation of matter and bloody feathers on the floodlit lawn. Charles pokes the worst of the mess into a bin liner, and then it rains in the night: one of those sudden violent deluges that the city needs every so often. The following morning, there's nothing much left on the grass, and when I run through the park the air feels rinsed, astringent.

On the way back I take a detour down Carmody Street and halt outside Emma's house, bending and stretching as if catching my breath at the end of a sprint. The Nashes haven't been away for long, but the place already has an air of abandonment: the half-closed curtains in the upstairs rooms, the lid off the dustbin, pizza fliers jammed in the maw of the letterbox. It must be just over a year, I think, since I first saw her in the square: the shock of it, the things I remembered, and the things that were new and striking. Her tiredness. Her distress, low-level but constant, impossible to ignore – like a hum, or a whine.

Later I think of this as I wait for the arrival of Mr Fisk, as I line them up along the wall of the studio: the white skies and long spits of land, the sense of heat building and building, caught in the smudges of trees. I'm almost too near to the work now, I realise. A break from it will do me good. Mr Fisk, a quiet Canadian, moves around the studio without saying much; but in the afternoon the gallery calls to say he's interested in two of the most recent pieces, and is thinking about two more.

Over the following days, as I prepare my packing, as I wait for Sophie to come through customs – an inch taller, new hair, neon vests and violet nail varnish – I'm thinking about getting close to Emma's distress signal, perhaps getting so close to it that it stops being noticeable.

To celebrate Sophie's return, we go out to the retro diner: buttermilk chicken, curly fries, slaw in pleated paper tubs. But she only picks at it. She prefers Japanese now. Or Korean. She's crazy for kimchee. She wasn't paying attention earlier in the summer when I told her about inviting the Nashes to France, so she looks pissed off when I remind her, staring at me, twiddling a chip. 'Why'd you do that?' she asks. 'What *is* it with you and that lot?'

'It's your mother's good turn,' Charles says.

'Celestial brownie points,' I say lightly. 'Anyway, they're leaving on Saturday, when Charles flies out to join us. We'll only overlap for a day or two.'

'Of all the people you could have asked, and you asked them!' Sophie says, disgusted. 'Even the Binghams would've been better than that lot.'

'I suppose I felt that Emma would appreciate the invitation more than anyone else,' I say. 'It's nice, to be able to help. The children are cute.'

'I don't *get* it,' she says, toying with an onion ring. After a few weeks with the half-siblings, Astrid and Otto, she has had it up to here with kids. 'Oh, my, God. You know one day while I was at the gallery Astrid went into my room and got hold of my makeup? She denied it of course, Trudy took her side and Dad was so unbelievably wet . . . I never found out what she did with my Mac lipstick. It was that special-edition one, too.' So I don't mention the potential babysitting. In any case, after a month at Arnold's – all that guilt money, the sponsored splurges at Hollister – she'll be feeling flush.

Two days later, we make the journey that we've made so many times before, and yet this time, thinking about Emma going through the same process a week or so earlier, there's a certain sharpened definition to everything: the strung-out families at check-in, the ennui of the cabin staff as they rehearse various catastrophes, the girl on the Avis counter inspecting her nails while I sign the paperwork. As we pull onto the motorway in the late-afternoon sun, Sophie fiddles with the car radio, tutting at the aerated Europop. But this is part of the ritual, the way it has always been: the best you can hope for is the inevitability of Sade or late Springsteen. It's the sound of summer, to me, along with the rasp of crickets in the pine wood, the midnight hiss of the sprinklers.

Dusk is falling by the time we leave the motorway: too dark to see the sunflowers in the surrounding fields, though as the season is ending, their round faces will be blackening and shrivelling, tilting towards the earth. Here it comes. The familiar hairpin bend, the petrol station, a new 'à vendre' sign up next to the boulangerie. The village falls away behind us, and as we come to the yellow barn I switch off the radio and the air-con, and wind down the windows, a thing I like to do here when arriving at night. The car fills with the warmth of dust as the headlights catch on the rocks and grasses along the track, the sudden ghostly lurch of trees pale as bone. Above and beyond, everything is black, blacker than black, and yet restlessly alive with tiny reflective flickers of eyes and wings.

The Nashes' car, dull with dirt, is parked under the vines; and Ben is there, appearing at the gate, smiling, his teeth very white in his face, offering to help us with our bags.

'How good to see you,' I say, and I put my hand on his arm, his crisp blue sleeve, and lean in for the double kiss, getting a hit of aftershave – the soapy citrus of Acqua di Parma, I'm fairly sure – and mosquito repellent. Ben hasn't met Sophie before, and he doesn't quite know how to greet her – should he shake hands? Kiss her, too? – and he makes a hash of it, ducking in and out, trying to relieve her of her suitcase. 'I'm fine, it has wheels,' she says, sidestepping him.

'You must be dying for a drink,' he says as we go up through the garden. Supper'll be ready in a bit, if we're hungry; they weren't sure if we'd have stopped to eat on the way. The baby's already in bed, she's knackered from all the swimming. And the crawling.

'And Christopher?' I ask. 'I hope he's enjoying the pool. How's his swimming coming on?'

Now we're climbing through the fragrant layers of the garden, crossing the lawn and approaching the house, its interlocking illuminated cubes glowing against the dark hill. Sophie's bag drags gravel. Below that, the sound of water as it spills into channels and trickles into troughs.

I think of Charles, the first time I met him: the sketches that he put in front of us, the pen chasing over the yellow tracing paper as he made suggestions and amendments. The confidence of his imagination. *That might work*, he'd said. *Or, how about this? We could try this.* How he made it all seem possible.

We cross the terrace and go inside, and there she is, standing by the long marble counter, holding a bottle of champagne, her face shining with sun and the sudden embarrassment of welcoming us into our own house. She's wearing a red-striped T-shirt that makes her look like Where's Wally. *Oh,* I say, kissing her and feeling the forceful heat of her cheek against mine, *it's so lovely to be back.*

'This place is amazing,' she says, embracing Sophie, who

submits with good grace. 'We can't believe our luck...' And then the cork is released, and she laughs as she fumbles for the glasses. The foam boils up and over. I see Ben noticing this, and finding it annoying. Christopher steps forward, holding up a bowl of nuts like a chalice.

'Oh, Christopher: pistachios! My favourite. And I'd love a drink,' I say, though really I'd prefer Evian at this precise moment. 'I'll just dump my bags.' I catch Emma's anxious look and remind Sophie that we need to keep the noise down because of the baby.

Down the corridor in my father's room – which I prefer to think of as the master bedroom – the ceiling fan is rotating, drowsily stirring the air, as thick and sweet as syrup. When I turn on the bedside lamp, something immediately bangs into the screen at the window and whirrs off again into the night. I unzip my bag and stand looking down at the thin layers of cotton and linen, the black and pale grey and off-white, the paperbacks and shoes tucked in around the edges, and then I take my wash bag out and carry it into the bathroom. I let the water run very cold and cup my palms under the tap and splash my face. Straightening up, I examine myself in the mirror: dark strands of hair stuck to my wet cheeks, the beads of water clinging to my eyelashes. I dry my face on one of the thick towels and while I'm digging around in the wash bag for mosquito repellent my fingers find the bracelet, its greying fibres starting to loosen into individual strands: the pineapple, the star and the Evil Eye. I slide it into the side pocket, and go back to join the rest of them.

'Are you close to your dad?' Emma asks me, once Christopher is in bed. We're sitting outside, encircled by the tiny red embers of mosquito coils. The sweet smell of burning threads through the vines, drifts over the lawn and towards the sea. Over on the other side of the hill, there's a sudden silver flash as a car takes the turning onto the coast road. It's a very sharp bend.

I say, *not particularly*. I say, *He's a bit of a handful, my dad*. As we eat salad and langoustines, I give them the fun, potted version, the award-winning Hollywood version, the one they'd like best. The one that will ring some bells, but not others. When I mention the Oscar nominations for *Crazy Paving* and *Ampersand*, Ben's fork goes down. 'Seriously? I knew the name was familiar, but I couldn't quite place it.' Emma sits tight, drinking her wine. This means nothing to her.

'He's semi-retired now, though he still does the occasional thing, if he likes the set-up. Lives in Paris, mostly, with his third wife. They have a little girl, Clara. Bit older than Christopher.'

'My aunt Clara', says Sophie, as she pulls the head and carapace off, 'is a brat.'

'Oh, Sophie, steady on,' I say, with a laugh, passing the mayonnaise. 'But it's fair to say my father's more indulgent this time around. Clara gets lots of attention.'

While Sophie tells them about the Ladurée birthday cake ('All the macaroons were bubble-gum flavoured. It was as tall as she was!') I see Emma glancing at me surreptitiously, and I know she's feeling sorry for me. *Poor Nina*. Whatever, I think, raking my fork through the salad.

Oh, we moved around a lot, I say, when she asks me where I grew up. 'He and my mother were always buying up rundown places and doing them up, then moving on. Oxfordshire, the south coast. After they split up, my mother settled in Sussex and he got a place in London, and that was the point at which his career really took off. I don't think he was really cut out for country life. Can you imagine him in wellies, Soph?'

She agrees that it's a bit of a stretch. She can't imagine

him with my mother, either, come to that. Sophie's always fairly rude about Paul, though when BBC4 screened that profile of him she made sure everyone at school knew about it.

'He's weird,' she says. And then she tells a story about the last time she saw him, when he came for supper at the house in London a year or so ago. 'And Mum was in the kitchen, and Charles had wandered off somewhere, and I was stuck in the sitting room alone with him, and he just had no idea what to say to me, no idea at all, and he just looked at my shoes, perfectly ordinary Converse, and said: *Great shoes! Where'd you get them?* It was the only thing he could think of to say to me. Like, duh.'

We all laugh at this, quite merrily, as if it's the funniest thing; but I sense Ben and Emma's unease, their realisation that they might easily make the same mistake. It's very hard, finding the right thing to say to teenagers. I see Emma starting to identify with my father, and I don't like that much.

I know she'll come back to the subject of Paul. She'll want to draw me out, bond with me, show me how empathetic she is. There was a chance – a slim chance – that she'd remember his name. But she has seen it written down on envelopes; she has heard me say it aloud. Nothing. It means nothing to her. I'm quite safe.

That night I dream. It's not the dream of walking into a crowded room and being unable to speak; it's the other one, the one I hate even more. Am I chasing someone, or being chased? It's hard to tell, and never really matters anyway. Here I am, climbing a staircase, the shallow steps falling away into shadow behind me, and twisting endlessly into inky darkness up ahead. I can hear someone in front, just out of sight around the bend, and I'm desperately trying to catch up with them; or perhaps they're a flight behind, and just starting to gain on me, despite my best efforts. The sound of their feet, and their breath, quite steady and even; and mine, coming in rough gasps and snatches, reverberating and echoing, bouncing crazily off the walls.

I wake suddenly in the low bed, my feet twisted in the linen, a film of sweat on my neck. It's early, not quite seven.

The house is dim and quiet. When I open the doors and step outside, the shadows lie precisely on the grass and the paths. This is the best time of day: new-minted, before the heat makes everything slovenly. Bees bob and weave between the lavender and the white trumpets of flowers.

The pool, when I unlatch the gate, is an expanse of black glass. As I stand there, holding my towel, the surface briefly ruffles and wrinkles in the breeze, and then grows taut again.

After finishing my lengths, I'm standing in the shallow end, enjoying the sensation of sun on my shoulders, when I become aware that I'm being watched. It's Christopher, standing by the gate in his pyjamas, one hand longingly on the latch.

'Good morning!' I say, coming up the steps towards him, the water noisily falling away. 'You're up early.'

He regards me, silently, not smiling.

I wrap the towel around me and run my fingers through my hair, pressing the water out of it. His clear eyes. I wonder what they see. I wonder what he remembers, or will remember. Distantly, I remember reading something in a magazine – the *Spectator*, I think – about childhood recollection: how distress preserves memory more efficiently than contentment. *I could give you something to remember,* I think.

'Do you want a swim?' I ask, coming up to the gate. 'Only, I don't think you should come in without Mummy or Daddy. It wouldn't be safe.'

He steps back, the gate between us. In his other hand,

Blue Bunny dangles by those long soft ears. 'Are they up yet?' I ask. 'Are they still in bed?' As I come through the gate, I close it behind me, hearing the snap as the arm falls down into the slot. I take his free hand, quite firmly, and he lets me, though I can feel his initial resistance, and together we walk down the long gravel paths while I chant,

> *James James*
> *Morrison Morrison*
> *Weatherby George Dupree*
> *Took great*
> *Care of his mother*
> *Though he was only three,*
> *James James said to his mother,*
> *'Mother,' he said, said he;*
> *'You must never go down to the end of the town*
> *If you don't go down with me.'*

I point out the bees and we stop and listen to the sound they're making, the drowsy industrious hum.

In the kitchen I pour him a glass of milk and spread some butter on a piece of yesterday's baguette and he eats it solemnly, barely speaking, his eyes round and watchful, while I unload the dishwasher.

When Ben appears with the baby, he's full of reprimands and apologies: 'Oh, noodle, you mustn't wander off like that on your own, you mustn't bother Nina . . .' but I tell him not to worry, it was entirely my fault for leaving the door open into the garden, and the pool gate was safely latched, of course. There's an unspoken understanding that we won't mention this to Emma, who would fret unnecessarily about the water features, and when she comes through – wearing the pink linen shift I saw her wearing on the high street all those months ago – Ben and I conspire to talk about other things: how we all slept, the glorious weather, plans for the day.

I suggest an outing. Nothing too taxing: a drive into the hills to visit a monastery, about twenty minutes' away. It's one of my favourite places. It'll be a little cooler up there. The monks keep hives and you can buy the honey. Christopher might find that interesting.

When I bring Sophie a glass of juice in bed and tell her the plan, she says she'd rather stay here; she fancies having the pool to herself.

Once the decision is made, the heavy machinery goes into action: Emma's candy-striped bag is packed with equipment for all eventualities including famine, sunstroke and plagues of insects; nappy changes and trips to the loo are counterbalanced by last-minute drinks of water. 'Not Blue Bunny,' says Ben, trying to remove the toy from his son's grip as we take stock. 'Blue Bunny would much rather stay here and have a rest.'

'Daddy's right,' Emma says, 'We'll leave him here to look after the house,' but as Christopher's face crumples she's giving in, saying, 'Well, if you promise to hold on to him . . .' and Ben is breaking away, walking off towards the car, snorting and muttering to himself.

Once we're all assembled, there's the wait while Emma tries to help Christopher into his seat. 'I can do it! I can do it!' he growls, pushing her hands away, fumbling stubbornly with the safety straps. His arms and legs and neck are chalky, death-white with suncream. To kill time, Emma hops about, picking brown apple cores and half-drained bottles of water out of the footwells, offering the baby – who has started to protest – a rice cake, apologising and insisting that I take the front seat. Ben sits waiting, tapping his fingers on the wheel, miming a whistle. His elaborate unconcerned patience is all tension.

The monastery is apocalypse-quiet, as always: the car park's empty, and as we walk up through the wood – the buggy wheels snagging and bumping on the stony track – there are no signs of any other visitors. As we come to the gatehouse I point out the terracotta Madonna and child set in the recess of the wall, and Emma says she approves of the baby Jesus. She likes his fat cheeks, the fact that he doesn't look like a bank-manager in a loincloth.

Stop, start, stop. Christopher moves in bursts and without method, rushing off at a tangent or doubling back on himself, crouching down without warning to examine things at ground level – ants, his shoe buckle – so that there's always the danger of tripping over him, or kicking him. Fitfully, we follow a smell of soup through a series of halls and cloisters and courtyards, Christopher finding the echo in every space. Now and then we catch snatched glimpses of men in white robes crossing a terrace or vanishing into a stairwell. There's a sense of invisible industry, people one step ahead of us, forever keeping out of sight: the recently watered lemon trees in their terracotta pots, the just-mopped corridors that dry as quickly as we can walk down them.

The refectory is ready for the monks' lunch, the long tables set with heavy worn cutlery and jugs of water, wooden bowls covered with cloths. Quiet hangs beneath the wooden rafters: hundreds of years of silence, of contemplation, of plotting and prayer. In the great scheme of things, Christopher's noises – the sounds of protest and delight and injury – will barely register.

The child is tightrope-walking along a pattern in the tiled floor. He won't be hurried. When the toe of his sandal touches the black, he insists on going back to the beginning and starting all over.

We stand around, smiling and waiting for him to finish. In my pocket, my fingers find a coin. I turn it over and over:

heads, tails, heads. 'Oh, very good, darling,' says Emma. 'What a clever boy.' It's the sort of thing you might say to a dog fetching a stick. She glances at me, self-conscious and yet wanting me to share in the pleasure of his achievement. I pull my hand out of my pocket to applaud. 'Well done!' I say, thinking: *smiley eyes.* Stifling a yawn.

There's no chance of having a conversation with her. Emma is occupied, as if by an army. She's always *touching* them: adjusting hats, wiping noses, patting cream into their soft little limbs, their rounded shoulders. I walk on ahead, suddenly bored and brisk: back through the cloisters, pausing to pick up Blue Bunny (dropped and forgotten, exactly as forecast) and, in the main courtyard, turning left into the chapel.

The thick warm blackness swallows me whole and for a moment I'm blind, halting, my fingers outstretched; and then I see the glow around a pillar, and the tray of candles comes into view. The flames bob and sway, a dozen or so hopes and wishes glittering and winking, using themselves up. I find a chair, the feet scraping as I put my weight on it. The air smells of incense and citrus-scented detergent and, more distantly, of mould or damp. I feel tired, here in the clammy dark, safely away from the rest of them.

When I hear sing-song voices bouncing around the courtyard outside, I push Blue Bunny deep into my bag, beneath my cardigan, and then I sit still, invisible for the time being, waiting for them to find me.

We go to look at the beehives, a series of pastel-coloured boxes a little way into the wood, and the Nashes pick up a jar of honey from the gatehouse, Christopher posting the euros into the wooden box, and then we walk back down the path and get back into the car.

We stop at the market in the next town for crêpes. Between the lace and the bric-a-brac, there's a second-hand stall selling old toys, incomplete sets of Playmobil and Lego and baby dolls with startled eyes and fat waxy cheeks. Christopher persuades his father to buy him a bag of Dinky cars and, once we're back at the house, spends the afternoon lining them up and racing them over the lawn. His parents take it in turn to supervise him and the baby, doing shift work by the pool where Sophie and I nap and read, pulling our loungers in and out of the shade as the sun rolls through the sky.

When Emma lets herself through the gate, I pretend to be dozing, my sunglasses allowing me to monitor her as she drops her towel and rushes down the steps into the water. Even though she believes no one is watching her, she is embarrassed by herself, her paleness, her figure, her lack of definition. The fibres of her khaki swimming costume are weakening, giving way: you can see the white of her buttocks through a thinning patch on the seat. She swims well – a neat confident swim-team crawl – but tires easily. She pulls herself up to the infinity edge, crossing her arms over it and resting her chin on her hands, the water pushing past her as she stares down at the valley.

I should offer to help, I think, shutting my eyes so the blood dances red-black, feeling my skin tighten in the heat.

The gate clangs as she leaves and then ten minutes later it's Ben's turn. I lift my head and adjust my sunglasses, smiling at him. Sophie says, too loudly, 'What time is it?'

I mime at her: *turn it down, too loud*, and when she tugs the earphones out, I say, 'Nearly six.'

She nods and rolls over onto her back, lifting her head to pull her hair away from her neck, trying to catch the breeze. As Ben drops his book and towel on the lounger, I see him looking at her, perhaps without meaning to: the sheen of cream and sweat on her stomach and arms, the bones of her ankles. The white Vs stencilled by her flip-flops.

There's a buzz in the sky, and we both glance towards the noise. Something appears against the guileless blue, a shining capsule, a helicopter heading for a weekend at one of those cliff-top villas built by reclusive golden-era film moguls, properly updated with spas and panic rooms.

'Oligarch,' I say, and then I tell him about the things you can only see from out in the bay: the wedding-cake terraces. The maids, like ants, hurrying to and fro under the yellow-and-white striped awnings. The cars lined up beneath the palm trees.

'It's another world,' he says. 'Crazy stuff.' He walks to the pool, standing on the edge for a moment, self-consciously contemplating the twisting patterns caught on its dark surface, and his own reflection: the orange trunks jauntily printed with octopi, the beginning of a paunch. Then he inhales and swings his arms and dives in: a bellyflop, his legs bending at the knee, like a puppet's. The water surges noisily from side to side. Turning a page of my book, I pretend not to have noticed.

He swims fifteen or twenty lengths of a slow and shambolic front crawl, ploughing up and down, gasping when his arm goes over. Then he comes up the ladder and throws himself down on the lounger, scattering droplets. Sophie flinches, brushing at her arm, then resettles herself.

He picks up his book, reads a page or two, then lets it drop onto his chest; picks it up again, turns back to check something in an earlier chapter.

I say, 'How are you getting on with that?'

He feels it's not quite as good as the first one, and I say, *Oh, that's a pity.*

I don't say that I've read it and enjoyed it, though I found the final plot twist unsatisfying, as plot twists often are: nothing like life, which – it seems to me – turns less on shocks or theatrics than on the small quiet moments, misunderstandings or disappointments, the things that it's easy to overlook.

'I don't think I *like* these characters,' he's saying: an annoying remark, one with which I can't be bothered to engage. The blue-black shade is starting to advance over the shallow end so I say, *time for a last dip*.

When I walk back to the house I find Emma tidying away the children's tea, rinsing the plastic beakers, chasing crumbs off the table into her palm. Christopher is nagging for another chocolate biscuit, and Cecily's tetchy with teething and tiredness, the front of her dress wet with dribble. I say to Christopher, *if you come into the garden with me, I know a game we can play.*

He stares at me for a moment – evaluating me and finding I come up short – and then switches his attention to his mother. 'Another biscuit,' he wheedles: 'I'm *starving*,' and I see Emma twitch, torn between indignation and a desire never, ever to hear her child utter a phrase like that.

I say, 'Oh, but I don't suppose you know how to play Grandmother's Footsteps, do you?' and he's unable to resist it, he needs to correct me and put the record straight. He does know that game, he plays it with Billy and George and George's nanny, only George calls it Dinnertime for Mr Wolf.

'Are the rules the same? Will you show me?' I say. 'Before your bath?'

'OK,' he says, sliding off the chair.

Together, we walk to the end of the lawn, by the hammock. The golden light is cut through with long sharp shadows. Out in the bay, there's the flash of a white sail. 'You stand there,' he says, pointing. 'Shut your eyes. And you have to say: one, two, three, four, five jam tarts.'

'I'm it?'

'Yes, and I'm creeping up on you.'

We give it a try.

'One jam tart, two jam tarts, three jam tarts,' I chant, but he shouts: 'No, you count *in your head*, silly!'

'Oh, right. Sorry,' I say. 'I'd forgotten. It's a while since I played this. When Sophie was little, maybe. Can you imagine Sophie as a little girl?'

He giggles at the idea, taken with its preposterousness. 'She's bigger than me,' he says.

'She is now. OK, let's try again. I'll count to myself, up to five jam tarts, and then I'll turn around, and you freeze, and if I see you moving . . .'

I turn my back and look out to sea, the sun so low and molten that my eyes fill with tears, and yet I can feel it: a cooler wind is coming in, the edge of evening approaching. Dusk is gathering along the coast, in the coves and quay-sides and marinas, where in an hour or so the long strings of coloured bulbs will twinkle and sway; and then it will pass over us – like a visitation: a plague or a blessing – on its way inland, sweeping inkily over the grand tiered villas and fortified ruins and blue-shuttered cottages with Arum lilies growing in olive-oil tins, the hot little bars where old men gather to watch football.

The hammock yawns to my left, moved by the breeze, spilling cushions into the grass.

Silently, I count: *one, two, three, four, five jam tarts.*

I spin round, teeth bared. He has hardly moved. He's standing very still, trying not to laugh, his fists clenched.

'Oh, you're too good at this,' I say. And then I turn my back again.

One, two—

This time, I catch him mid-step, his face puckering into outrage. 'That wasn't *time*!' he shouts, and I say, 'Oh dear, talking *and* moving, I'll have to catch you now—' and I begin to move towards him, my arms outstretched, like wings, and he holds still for a moment, as if we haven't quite resolved the issue, and then his eyes widen at my expression and he turns and starts to run, stumbling a little, heading for the terrace, the house, his mother. As I gain on him, as he starts to scream, I find myself wondering if this, after all, will be his first memory: a sunny lawn, a blue sky, and the horror of being chased by an unsmiling stranger, a woman you barely know, although already you know her to be a cheat.

'Oh no, we're fine, it's just a game,' I say to Emma when she comes out with the baby on her hip.

'For heaven's sake, don't make that noise again, Christopher,' she says. 'Cuts through me like a knife.'

He doesn't want to play anymore and when Ben comes back from the pool and says it's bathtime, Christopher goes off without protest, not looking back.

I kick off my sandals, climb into the hammock and lie there as the sky darkens and the pinpricks of stars come out, listening to the sounds of the house (water running in the sink, someone whistling 'Hickory Dickory Dock', the clatter of saucepan lids and oven doors). She is quite preoccupied in there, doing the usual things in the usual order, as if that is enough to keep her safe. I watch her move through the illuminated cubes, and I think of the first time, all those years ago.

I knew she was coming. We hadn't been in Jassop long (and would be moving away just as soon, though of course I did not know that then) but my mother was on cordial terms with Mrs Pugh, and indeed had gone to Donald Pugh's funeral, feeling she should, though my father thought it ludicrous, to attend the funeral of a stranger. Over the months that followed, I'd overheard my parents talking about the farm sliding out of service: the livestock sold, the machinery auctioned off or allowed to rust in the outbuildings. The fields tenanted to local farmers.

'Marian's granddaughters are coming to stay,' my mother said one day at the start of the summer holidays. 'One of them is your age. I should invite them round for tea.' My mother was still trying to engineer friendships for me, leaving me in rooms with the teenaged children of her new acquaintances, not understanding that this approach now guaranteed failure. I didn't need any more friends. I had Della and Louise, serious girls I'd recently fallen in step with at school, girls who drank black coffee and read poetry during study breaks, and who took the train up to London with me on occasional Saturdays, to visit the National Gallery; but they were both going away over the summer, Della doing a French exchange near Orange, Louise visiting cousins in Dorset.

'Oh, please don't,' I said, and for once she listened to me.

My mother came back from the village one hot quiet afternoon and said the Pugh granddaughters had arrived, she'd seen them buying ice-creams and magazines in the shop. Really, I said, turning the page of my book. Later, when she was safely indoors, when I could hear my father working on the piano – playing the same passage over and over, refining it in some imperceptible way, or maybe just enjoying the accumulating sound of it – I put down my novel and stood up, stretching and yawning a little in the shade of the apple tree, as if someone might be looking.

Into the green 'o' of the overgrown lane, dodging the stinging nettles and the long arms of brambles, and across the stile with its loose treacherous plank. The footpath was snarled and rutted with old dried mud; I watched where I placed my feet. My shadow a small dogged presence, dancing and bobbing as I lifted up the barbed wire and squeezed underneath and climbed into the field. Closer, but keeping out of sight of the low house and its dark little windows.

The hedgerow, healthily dense on the outside, but within

– yes, just here – dry and hollow. I pressed my way in, twigs scraping my arms and neck and dragging at my hair, unsure of what I'd be able to see. Not much, it turned out: a partial view of the farmyard, Mrs Pugh's boxy burgundy car (the doors left open for coolness), the water tank, some rubber doughnuts pitted with teethmarks scattered close to me on the grass verge. The burble of chickens, some pop on a distant radio, but otherwise nothing. I rubbed my arm, the burn of the graze, and then a girl stepped into the sun, very tall and straight. Gold all over.

Now I lie in the hammock, watching, and waiting quite patiently for the moment when Christopher realises it's missing.

She comes out with two glasses of wine, worrying her way down the steps, raising an arm to shield her eyes from the spotlights hidden in the urns and behind the trees. Looking along the floodlit paths, checking by the deck chairs.

'Christopher's lost his bloody rabbit,' she says, passing me a glass. 'Don't suppose you remember when you saw it last? He can't sleep without it.'

'He took it out in the car this morning, didn't he?' I say, efficiently reviving the disagreement and the surrender, the look on Ben's face. 'Did he have it when we stopped for lunch? At the market?'

She can't remember. Perhaps he dropped it when he was looking at those toy cars. 'Oh, bloody hell. Anyway – not your problem,' although, as Christopher's howls start to spill out of the house, I'm not so sure about that. 'Poor little chap,' I say. The sound builds and then fades, and then there's a silence.

'He'll be OK, it'll turn up,' I say. Then I twist sideways and shimmy along, making space for her. 'Hop in,' I say.

She should be indoors, helping put everyone to bed; but she would so much rather be out here, with me. 'Do you think it'll take us both? I'm such a heffalump . . . Oh, what the hell,' she says, and then the hammock lifts and strains and we're locked together in its embarrassing, compelling intimacy, thigh against thigh, bare arm against bare arm. She giggles and pushes at the ground with a toe, setting up a gentle pendulum swing. She smells of sun lotion and, when she lifts the glass to her mouth, there's raw garlic on her fingers. I've never been this close to her before. She coughs and says, 'You'll be glad to see the back of us.'

'Not at all,' I say. 'It's fun having you here. I do think Christopher's a sweetie. He spooked himself during that game we were playing earlier, I should have realised that was going to happen.'

'Everything spooks him,' she says. 'He's at that age. It's all extremes. The highs, the lows.'

'And for you, too,' I say. 'I remember what it's like. That stage . . . fantastic, of course, but it's such hard work. God, I remember Sophie . . .'

'Do you mind me asking,' she says, very hesitantly, very delicately, so I know she has been longing to ask this, 'what happened with you and Sophie's dad?' So – mindful that we may at any time be interrupted – I tell her a little about Arnold, the neat tailored narrative I trot out for acquaintances and the odd analyst, wondering if anyone will ever challenge me on it, make me dig a little deeper. How young I was, what he seemed to represent. How he and Sophie gave me an identity, I suppose, just when I needed a new one, and how I'll always be grateful to them both for that. 'My dad . . .' I say. 'He's a charming man, too charming, probably. My mother was a casualty of all that. She never really got over it. Arnold showed me a way out.'

She listens very carefully, conscious that she's going up a level. Every so often there's a lurch as she stretches a toe to the grass, trying to keep the momentum going. I can feel her willing me on, willing Ben to contain whatever's happening in the house.

'By the end, my parents were pretty ill-suited,' I say. 'They did that thing, they grew apart. Although there was a bit more to it than that.'

She swings and sips. She's feasting on this moment. Loving it.

'He had a bit of an eye,' I say, all understatement, all bravery. 'For most of the time, he was fairly discreet. But right at the end, he made a bit of a fool of himself. There was this girl . . . someone I knew. That was enough.'

Her face. She's appalled. 'No. Seriously? He went off with a friend of yours?'

'Oh, no. It wasn't like that. Nothing *happened*. No one did anything, exactly. No one said anything. It was just the last straw.'

A light comes on in Sophie's bedroom, and I watch the fluid shape on the fly screen as she moves towards the window and pulls the curtain across.

'And she wasn't a friend. I hardly knew her,' I say with a little laugh. Emma doesn't know whether to look at me or not; for now, she keeps her eyes fixed on the house, eager not to spoil the moment of delicious frankness, of confession. 'My father . . . well, he was very taken with her. He made a bit of a fool of himself. I don't think she was even aware of the effect she'd had on him. She was that sort of girl.'

'What do you mean?'

'You know. Beautiful . . . a bit careless.'

We think about these girls, how dangerous they can be.

She asks, 'And you were how old?'

'Oh, sixteen or seventeen. Around Sophie's age. My mother – well, she'd had enough.'

'Oh,' she says. 'Christ.'

'Well, it was a long time ago,' I tell Emma, as if I've been wise enough to let it all go; or most of it, at any rate. As if I've made my peace with it. As if I have no memory of hearing her in the field late one afternoon, shouting for the little dog – whose name I cannot remember – and how I called to her and introduced myself and said I'd look out for him; of returning to the empty house and reading another chapter and then going round the back to the woodstore and unlatching the door, whispering for him to hush, and tying a piece of twine to his collar and walking him through the lanes to the Pugh farm. Staying for a glass of bitter lemon, not saying much, just watching and listening, absorbing it all, the offhand way she spoke, the *ums* and *yeah*s and *kind of*s that showed she was sure her opinions were worth waiting for.

As if I have no memory of saying, 'Well, if you haven't got anything better to do . . .'

Of my mother a day or so later, her hands glossy with oil as she tumbled the watercress in the shallow wooden bowl with the butter lettuce, the red-deckled alabaster slivers of radish, while Emma moved a pile of mail from the kitchen chair. Of my father lowering the piano lid and coming through from the sitting room in a bit of a mood, expecting just another lunch. Of Emma – the colour of her hair, her eyes, her skin – allowing herself to be drawn out, submitting to his attentions as if this sharp approving interest was nothing unusual for her; answering questions about A levels and Greece (where her family had recently holidayed) as if she was the one making a concession.

Noticing the blue glass eye on her bracelet, he told us that the Greeks believed you could bring a curse by praising with envy.

After lunch, she wandered around my yellow bedroom, looking at my pinboard and sketchbooks and the family of owls in a desultory fashion: a little bored, not quite knowing why she was here. I wasn't sure what to do with her, or with myself, so I stood at the dresser and ran a comb through my hair, aware that it needed a wash. Furtively comparing myself with her in the mirror: the toothmarks left in my slightly greasy hair, the streaky fragrant tangle of hers.

And later, when she said *thank you* and *see you soon* and walked off into the hazy afternoon, into the clouds of golden pollen hanging in the lane, my father stood behind me at the door and watched her go, as if something was being taken from him. He said nothing, not then. But later he couldn't help himself, the old fool. 'I'll drive you,' he said the following afternoon, when I mentioned that I was planning to cycle into town to collect my photographs from Boot's. 'And then I'll take you for tea somewhere.'

My father rarely had time for this sort of thing. I sat in the passenger seat holding my canvas bag in my lap, aware of the lit cigarette moving from steering wheel to his mouth and back again. The novelty of this quiet intimacy as the car bowled through the marshland (with its crooked trees and singing lengths of wire; the wind feathering the grasses and dimpling the dark water in the ditches) felt good, promising, as if he might be taking an interest; as if I might finally be learning to feel at ease in his company.

There was a sort of disappointment as the wharves and spires of the town loomed up ahead. The narrow streets were crammed with day-trippers so he dropped me near the station and accelerated away in a burst, furious at the lack of parking spaces. I collected the packet of photographs from the chemist's, and made my way up Mermaid Street to the teashop, as arranged. I'd just claimed a table in the window (the waitress hastily clearing away the sundae glass and teacups, swiping the table with a cloth) and was opening the packet, anticipating the usual disappointments of red-eye and over-exposure and movement blur, when I saw my father coming out of the tobacconist with a newspaper under his arm. Under the canopy – striped like an Everton mint – he paused to pull the foil from a fresh packet of cigarettes; and then he looked up and something caught his eye, and he stepped forward and said something, and he smiled.

It shot through me like horror: a cold dull shock, almost deadening. Entirely new, yet somehow not a surprise. *He never looks at me like that*, I thought. Perhaps at this point I was also thinking, *And he never looks at her like that, either.*

Emma stood there in front of him, her back to me, shifting her weight from one foot to the other, pulling at her hair. *Preening*, I thought, but perhaps that was unfair. Perhaps it was only unease. They stood there beneath the striped canopy, talking for a moment or two; he offered her a cigarette; she refused, seemed to laugh, glanced at her wrist and then all of a sudden she was moving off, nodding, raising her hand, her palm flashing in farewell.

I saw him watching her.

When he found me at the table, he didn't mention Emma at first, and then he couldn't resist, he had to say her name; and it reminded me of my schoolfriend Della and her terrible, humiliating need to talk about Sam, Louise's older brother (who thought we were all pretty awful and didn't bother to hide the fact).

As the tea and cakes were set down in front of us, my father mentioned he'd just bumped into that friend of mine, the Pugh granddaughter, the girl who came for lunch – perhaps I'd seen her? Emma, that's right. He'd asked her to join us, but she was late for her lift, her grandmother was waiting for her at the bottom of the hill. She and her sister were leaving tomorrow. He supposed I'd be staying in touch with her.

Perhaps, I said.

You should make sure of it, he said. Pretty girl. Clever too, he imagined. 'Her whole life ahead of her,' he said, dreamily; and I could tell then that her prospects were far better than my own. He seemed to expect something from me at this point; an anecdote, perhaps, or information, but I didn't know anything about her, really. So we sat in silence as he drank his tea and looked out at the people passing in the street, and at his own dissatisfied expression in the glass. 'You could take a leaf out of her book,' he said eventually, almost absently.

While she was podding peas and waiting for *The Archers*, my mother remembered something. 'Oh, Paul, I meant to say, someone from the studio rang for you.' She couldn't lay hands on the piece of paper, and she couldn't remember the name, and suddenly I saw her through his eyes: the dress with the dirty hem, her face with its lines and pores, the mild chaos that always accompanied her, as clinging as yesterday's woodsmoke. The room upstairs, all the ungainly equipment. I thought of the spinning wheel's pedal noisily rising and falling, the stiff waxy handfuls of wool turning into stringy beaded yarn; the sound of the shuttle as another length of rough fabric emerged from the loom. The pointless stubborn activity of it all.

My father slipped away noncommittally. I wanted to hurt someone, and he was out of my reach. But I could hurt her. So I did. 'We saw Mrs Pugh's granddaughter again today,' I said, as I laid the table for supper, catching my face in the flat blades of the knives. 'In town. Doing some shopping.'

Emma. Such a nice girl.

I said yes, she seemed OK. I left a pause. I said, 'I didn't talk to her, actually. Dad did.' I laughed. I said I'd happened to see them together, talking on the street, they hadn't known I was watching. As I said it, I was thinking, *don't over-egg it, don't embroider, keep it simple. It'll be more powerful if it's simple.*

I put down the salt cellar and the pepper grinder. I said, reluctantly, 'I think he's a bit knocked out by her, if you know what I mean.'

She kept moving between the Raeburn and the sink, the refrigerator and the kitchen table, her face always turned away from me. 'Really?' she said, quite coolly. 'Do you think so? How funny.'

'I don't know, he seems kind of moony about her. He looked . . . idiotic, if you want the truth,' I said with a sigh. And then, 'Oh watch out, the peas are boiling over.'

It was a little thing, but it was enough to make her think. Enough to make her check his pocket diary, his wallet, the phone bill. Enough to ensure she found some evidence of something.

I was unjust to my mother, of course. I see that now. It wasn't her fault, not really. But my father, in his own absurd way, has acknowledged his culpability (and paid for it, and continues to pay, even in ways that infuriate me, like sending his rich ignorant friends, with all their many bare walls, in my direction). Emma, on the other hand, has never shouldered any responsibility for what happened. None at all.

A moment of quiet. The hammock ropes creak against the trunk. A dog howls mournfully on the other side of the valley. 'It's strange,' I say, over the rim of my glass, as if I'm talking to myself. 'I don't often think about it. Perhaps it's because of Sophie being the age she is . . . perhaps that's why.'

It all sounds so tidy, so fake. The edited highlights. I almost want to laugh.

'And you?' I say. 'Tell me your story. Everyone has a story.'

'Nothing to report,' she says, a little shamed.

'Nothing?' I say. 'I don't believe you.'

'It's true,' she says.

'But your parents. I mean . . .'

'Oh, don't get me wrong, it was hard losing them in the way I did, but I can't *reproach* them for anything. I've been so lucky, sometimes I think I must have it coming to me, somewhere down the line.'

We sit together, thinking of her parents. Andrew, Ginnie. My memories are now caught up in the photograph I saw in the Carmody Street sitting room: Andrew's fox-coloured summer beard, Ginnie's smocked top and the big round sunglasses pushed up to hold back her hair. The shadow of the photographer falling towards them, Lucy or Emma herself, a child then, in a nightgown and wellingtons perhaps, or a sundress patterned with poppies, straps knotted into bows over bony fledgling shoulders. I think of the child lifting the black plastic camera, squinting through the viewfinder, fixing them and telling them to say cheese. 'Stilton,' they say. 'Double Gloucester.' And then they smile, and time stops and holds them like that forever.

I say, 'What do you mean?'

She says she always felt lucky, a bit too lucky somehow. She goes on to count her blessings, almost feverishly. She was so fortunate with her parents, her education. Meeting Ben after a string of no-hopers; managing to get pregnant, quite far into her thirties and then again close to her fortieth birthday. Everyone's healthy, touch wood. Money's pretty tight, but then that's hardly unusual. Of course, she misses her career, but perhaps once the kids are both at school she'll be able to resurrect it or retrain – maybe as a primary-school teacher – or set up her own business. 'I've always felt it, I've always felt I'm due for a bit of a kicking,' she's saying, as if it sounds like nonsense.

And then Ben's on the terrace, calling to her, saying he's sorry to break up the party, but Christopher's in a right old state, could she lend a hand? And she sighs and leans forward, sliding out of the hammock.

When I go inside fifteen minutes later, the door to the room Cecily shares with her parents is shut, and I assume she's safely down, but Christopher is glimpsed from the corridor: kneeling up in bed, his face blotchy and desperate, as if no one is listening to him. 'He's all alone!' he's whimpering as his parents move around the bed, picking up towels and pairing sandals. 'He's all alone, no one to take care of him.'

'Darling, he'll be fine,' says Emma. 'I'm sure some lovely family has found him by now. They'll look after him.'

To judge from the wails, this is more painful than the thought of Blue Bunny lost in the wood.

I shower and wash my hair, using Delphine's almond shampoo. I'm wrapped in my towel, applying aftersun, when Sophie comes in without knocking, throwing herself down on the bed. 'He's never going to shut up,' she says, pressing her palms into her eye sockets. 'Oh my God, what a noise.'

'I know, poor creature. You were like that, with Boy. Do you remember Boy? He was a girl, but you cut off his pigtails.'

She lies back on my pillows, yawning, flicking through the books on my bedside table while I get dressed. She's not really watching me as I brush my hair and put on a little mascara, as I pick up the canvas shopper containing Blue Bunny and put it on the top shelf at the back of my cupboard.

Overhead, the fan blades go *wuh wuh wuh*.

'Have you got any nail-varnish remover?' she asks.

'I think so. Check the wash bag by the sink.'

She gets up and I can hear her unzipping it, rummaging around. Got it, she says. When she comes out with the bottle and cotton wool pads, she's wearing Emma's bracelet on her wrist. 'This old thing again,' she says. 'I like the pineapple. So retro.' She angles her wrist, inspecting the beads and trinkets. 'What's this one?' she asks, fingering the blue glass.

I tell her it's to ward off bad luck. And that's all I say, at first. But just before we go through to join the rest of them I say, 'Just pop that back where you found it, please,' and she looks at me suddenly, a quick sharp glance, and asks, 'Can't I just wear it for supper? It's a piece of junk, right? What's it doing here, anyway?'

'Someone gave it to me, a long time ago,' I say, and she smiles dismissively, 'Oh. I see. A *boy*friend.'

It's a risk, and I'm afraid. But Emma's too distracted at supper to notice my daughter's tacky little bracelet. Christopher won't settle, and keeps appearing at the table like a wraith, a small and tragic apparition. She and Ben are up and down all evening like jack-in-the-boxes.

All the time, while Sophie reaches for bread and pours herself more water, the trinkets and beads slide and spin and clink on the string looped around her wrist. It's a tiny sound, a tiny spectacle that catches nobody's interest. It's a signal from the past; but no one can decipher it but me. I'm relieved about this, of course. Yet I'm also conscious of a sense of insult. It meant so very little to her. Nothing, perhaps. 'Keep it,' she'd said. 'You can give it back when we meet up next time.' And then, seeing my expression, 'It's not valuable, it's just bits and bobs, silly old stuff. You don't have to wear it if you don't like it.'

I clear the table and boil the kettle for tisanes. 'I could make some calls tomorrow, before you go,' I say, as the kettle starts to keen. 'I could ring the monastery, see if it has turned up.'

'Would you?' Emma says. 'Not much hope, but . . .'

'You never know,' I say.

When I go in to say goodnight to Sophie, she's already asleep: her lamp still on, white wires trailing from her ears. I ease out the earphones and put the iPod on the bedside table. The bracelet is still on her wrist, the blue glass of the evil eye darkening as I lean across and click off her light. She murmurs something and rolls over, the linen sighing.

I do not dream. The sound of the sprinklers wakes me briefly in the early hours: the soft pattering, like the beating of hundreds of wings.

In the morning I find Cecily goggling at cartoons while Emma sleeps on the sofa in an unflattering oversized T-shirt printed with poodles. I stand by the coffee table for a little while, watching her: the palm under her hot cheek, the wedding ring and the white mark left by the strap of her wristwatch, the fine gold bristles on her shins.

While the others eat breakfast I walk around the lawn holding my phone to my ear, doing a bit of gesticulating, in case anyone is watching; and when I come back into the house I report that there's no sign of the rabbit at the monastery, but I've left my number in case it turns up. And I offer to go back to the little town where we bought the crêpes, 'just in case someone's found it and left it on a bench or something', giving Ben and Emma time to pack up.

'Oh no, you mustn't,' they say. 'Are you sure . . . ? God, that would be so incredibly kind.'

I don't bother, of course. I drive a little way along the coast road and stop to buy melon and aftersun. As I come out of the pharmacy I drop the plastic bag containing Blue Bunny in a bin. Then I go to the main square and order a café au lait and watch the yappy little dogs being exercised. It's fairly early, and there's very little traffic, just the occasional scooter whining through the back streets. Women in housecoats are mopping front steps, or throwing open the upper windows and draping bed linen over the sills. I get out my sketchbook and do a quick drawing of two old men smoking and reading newspapers on a bench.

Soon the Nashes will be putting their cases into the car, and then they'll drive away, and Thérèse's husband will drop her off at the end of the drive. She'll change the sheets and sweep the floors and scour the basins, and quiet order will be restored to all the rooms, as we wait for Charles to arrive.

Emma

'I don't get it,' Ben whispers as we lie beneath pearl-coloured sheets, lamps angled low, mindful of Cecily's cot in the corner. 'It's weird, isn't it?'

'You think it's odd that she took a shine to me? What's so strange about that?' I shiver with laughter, but I'm a little hurt, too. Why shouldn't Nina like me? Why shouldn't she recognise in me the things I'd feared might be lost forever? I can't explain to Ben how this feels: to be seen, again, for who I really am. Not to be a person always in the context of other people. However much I love them.

I think of Nina moving between the soft spots of light in her father's bedroom, the room with the writing desk and the view. Unpacking her bag, the white and navy and dove-grey clothes, her sandals and the small bottle of topaz-coloured scent that smells of figs and spice. Placing her hairbrush and the stack of paperbacks on the bedside table. Is it really so very strange that I have a friend like Nina?

'No, I don't mean that, exactly,' he says. 'It's just – what do you really know about her, anyway?'

'I know enough!' I say. 'Not all friendships hinge on a shared interest in Arsenal and pranks you played on the geography teacher twenty-five years ago.'

'She's a bit... *cagey*,' he's saying, and I say that's rubbish, she seems pretty open, what about all that stuff at supper about her dad: 'I guess that explains this house, anyway.'

'And the one in Pakenham Gardens,' he says, thoughtfully. 'Somehow, I doubt Charles's practice does *that* well. Guilt money. Her father sounds like a nightmare.'

'I think she's a bit lonely,' I whisper, and as I say it I realise it's true: Sophie hardly needs her now, and there's Charles, of course; but for all his easy charm there's something a little detached about him, a little distant. It's a novelty, feeling sorry for Nina, but suddenly I'm overcome with pity.

'Oh, don't get me wrong,' he says. 'I like her. She's great. Very generous. God knows how much it would have cost us, to rent a place like this for ten days.' He knows he has been tedious about money recently, a bit of a killjoy, but he has been mulling things over: 'That stain on Christopher's ceiling. That needs looking at. We should probably think about re-roofing. It'll be tight, but we'll manage. We'll have to.'

I put down my book and turn off my light and a few moments later I hear the rattle as he takes off his spectacles. He reaches out for me in the dark, presses his mouth against my ear and murmurs, 'I'm sure the next contract will work out fine. We'll sort out the roof when we get back.' *Go crazy*, I think. *Knock yourself out.*

Our last full day. I'm woken by the sound of Nina talking quietly in the garden, and then the clear pleasant sound of her singing:

> *James James*
> *Morrison Morrison*
> *Weatherby George Dupree*

As I open the wardrobe and pull the pink linen dress off the hanger, I'm thinking about how little time is left. The holiday is coming to an end, of course, and so is my time with her. The thought of London occurs: the downward slide into another autumn, the afternoon light fading earlier and earlier. The cold and the rain. People taking refuge in their own homes, hunkering down, just getting through.

I'll have to be assertive if I'm going to ask those questions: the questions about her first marriage, her childhood and her parents. The conversations we must have, if we're going to be real friends.

I think she wants to tell me the answers. I'm almost sure she does.

But there are so many obstacles. Ben. Cool, listless Sophie who drifts around yawning, avoiding us and yet constantly nearby. The children, of course, forever teetering on the edge of catastrophe. I once heard someone on the radio saying that a bee is never more than forty minutes away from starving to death, and this fact has stayed with me because it seems to have a certain personal resonance. My children are in a perpetual proximity to catastrophe: concussion, dehydration, drowning or sunstroke. Keeping them safe requires constant vigilance.

I've turned into one of those mothers, full of terror.

Every so often, I steal away from them, thinking: *It'll be fine, nothing will happen,* and I lie down alone on the bed or in the hammock, or I walk a little way into the pine wood; and something always goes wrong, something always happens. Someone always cries for me, and I hear the shrill just accusation beneath the pain or the fear; and I feel it, too, like a burn or a blade, an electric shock.

And then I catch them up and hold them close and kiss it better, pressing my face into their soft skin and flyaway hair, feeling the warmth of their cheeks and sticky fingers, the hope and greed and vitality of them. Working my magic; astonished, as the sobs die away, by how powerful my magic is. *No one else can do this for them.* I watch Nina with Sophie, whose demands are so straightforward – there's a problem with the wi-fi, could she borrow some factor 20 – and feel both envy and a tremendous, sweeping pity.

When Nina suggests an excursion, we go along with it, flattered – I suppose – that she wants to take us somewhere that she considers special. As we assemble in the kitchen before departure, the candy-striped bag filling with sun hats and rice cakes and baby wipes, Ben says, 'Not Blue Bunny. Blue Bunny would much rather stay here and have a rest.'

'Daddy's right,' I say, 'We'll leave him here to look after the house,' but then I see the expression on Christopher's face, and I can't bear it, I can't summon the energy required – not in this heat, not in front of Nina – so I say, 'Well, if you promise to hold on to him . . .' and Ben sighs and walks off.

It is a little cooler in the hills. We park the car under the trees and walk up through the wood, the buggy wheels bumping over the cobbles, and every so often a view opens up: a ruined hamlet on the other side of the valley; the ghost of a stream snaking through the trees. Nina walks on ahead, by herself, but waits for us in the shade of the gatehouse. She points out the little statue of the Madonna and child set in the wall and I look up at it, grateful for the hot dusty wind, taking a swig from a bottle of water and then pouring a little over my wrists. 'He's a proper baby,' I say, admiring his balloon cheeks. So many holy infants look like bank managers or middle-grade civil servants, tiny old men in loin cloths, piously administering peace with a raised finger.

I'm conscious of the noise we make as we walk through the cloisters and courtyards, the library and refectory, Cecily starting to struggle in the buggy, Christopher testing out the various echoes. He's either racing on or lagging behind, bending down to examine a trail of ants bearing away the corpse of a woodlouse. *Hurry up. Slow down.*

In the dining hall we wait as he tiptoes along a narrow path of white tiles, his face blank with concentration, teeth pressed into his soft lower lip. He's almost there, and then he hesitates and wobbles and has to start all over again. I'm aware of Ben's irritation as he pushes the buggy on towards the doorway, and Nina catches my eye and smiles at me, full of solicitude: for me and for Christopher. I experience her kindness as if she has held out a hand to me, to us both. 'Oh very good, darling!' I say, when he's finally done. 'What a clever boy!' and she joins in, applauding him, her eyes shining.

The moment of Nina's kindness stays with me, as clear and reviving as a drink of cold water, while we stand on the terrace counting the twelve tolls of the bell in the tower, and help Christopher to light a candle in the chapel. It stays with me as we go to look at the beehives, as we return to the car, as we stop at the market in a nearby town to buy crêpes from a girl in a van. While I'm lifting Christopher so that he can see the thin batter being ladled onto the hot plate (the pleasing deftness of her movements as she levels it off and fills the crêpe and flips it into a wrapper), I'm thinking of that moment. Feeling better for it.

We wander from stall to stall in the dappled shade, between mahogany behemoths and trestles piled with vegetables and old lace and junk, and I have Christopher's hand in my own, just resting there, soft and pliant, but as we pass the second-hand toy stall it leaps and tugs, his attention hooked like a fish. Instead of hurrying him on as I would in England, I let him stop and choose. It's so easy to allow him to be happy, I think. I should allow him to be happy more often.

Our last afternoon. As we return to the car and drive back to the house, I find myself thinking: this time tomorrow we'll be checking in, we'll be waiting in the departure lounge, we'll be stowing our things in the overhead lockers.

Nina and Sophie vanish off to the pool, and because of this Ben and I are just a little more relaxed, perhaps. Little metal cars gouge passes through the gravel as Christopher creates his world in the garden, keeping up a low contented muttering full of instructions and warnings. Sensing this makes us more available, Cecily is suddenly ambitious: she's trying to pull herself up, wishes to experiment with walking. When Ben takes her round the lawn, she reels along, hanging off his hands, her steps as high as a dressage pony's or a chorus girl's, drunk with delight and self-satisfaction.

I leave them and go out to the black pool to do my twenty lengths.

Side by side under the parasols, Nina and Sophie are dozing. The pages of a book flutter in the breeze. The place is lost.

I pick my way around the flip-flops, the bottles of mineral water and Piz Buin, and as I drop my towel on a lounger my attention catches on the sheen at Nina's temples and the little runnels left in her hair as she rakes her oily fingers through it. For some reason, I'm reminded of something – not even a memory, more of a half or quarter of a memory. The neat sharp bite marks made by the teeth of a comb as a girl pulled it through her dark and dirty hair.

It's a precise impression, but it's isolated, untethered. The girl has no features, no expression. No name, no context. Someone I was at school with, probably. I can't remember.

It must have disturbed me at the time, for some reason. Why else would it stick?

Though no one's watching, I hurry towards the steps and into the shallow end, humiliated by my baggy olive costume, my belly, my rough pale skin. I feel better once I'm in the water. Carving through it, I count out the daily lengths.

In the deep end I fill my lungs and put my face under and let go, gently rotating and tilting in the water as the motion leaves it. I was once so at home in my body that I wasted it, rarely noticing it, never bothering to celebrate its strength and efficiency. I'll never be beautiful again, I think. The water licks at my ears. I hear it slopping through the filter and over the infinity edge; repeatedly knocking Christopher's orange armband against the ladder in an uneven tattoo. I hang there as my shadow drifts over the bottom of the pool, becoming increasingly distinct and definite. My pulse starts to clamour.

I wait as long as I can, until I can't wait any longer. Then I surface, gasping, and swim to the edge, resting my arms on the side as the water pulses over it and spills into the channel beneath. The bell sounds in the valley. The children will be getting hungry.

I'm clearing away their tea things when Nina comes back from the pool, and she's just in time to hear Christopher demanding another biscuit. If she wasn't there, I'd probably give in, but today I feel I can do better. There's a bit of a row, which Nina elegantly defuses. 'If you come into the garden with me,' she tells him, 'I know a game we can play.'

I *never play games with him*, I think. Another thing to feel bad about.

I scoop up Cecily and sit her on my hip and try to interest her in a kiss but she squirms and pushes my face away with her fat little hands, wanting to be released. Dribble has soaked her top, and her cheeks are pink pantomime circles. In our bedroom, she crawls around shouting crossly while I dig for the Calpol in the spongebag patterned with sailing boats, and then I run her a shallow bath. I'm peeling off her sundress while singing 'Old Macdonald' (her favourite, she particularly likes making the piggy noises), when I hear the scream.

It's very high and thin and whippy, a streamer in the wind. I've never heard him make a noise like that before.

I run with her through the house, to the terrace, almost

losing my footing on the steps. 'Christopher!' I say as he hurtles towards me, eyes wide. He throws his arms around my thigh and I put my hand out to the table, steadying myself. 'What on earth was all that about? I'm so sorry,' I call to her as she comes over the grass to join us, laughing and reaching out to ruffle his hair.

'Oh no, we're fine, it's just a game,' she says.

'For heaven's sake, Christopher!' I say, almost furious. 'Don't make that noise again. Cuts through me like a knife.'

He has had enough of the game now, and comes for his bath without complaint.

Ben is just settling down with both children, preparing to read *Goodnight Moon*, when Christopher reaches under his pillow and looks under the bed and says Blue Bunny is missing. 'It's fine, he'll be in my big bag,' I say, but as I say the words I'm pitched into sudden dread, a certainty that the rabbit isn't there, and that I haven't seen it since some time this morning.

I check the bag. The jar of honey, oily napkins from the crêperie, some cards I keep forgetting to post. *Fuck fuck fuck.*

We go through the rooms lifting cushions, dragging furniture away from the walls. Christopher stands in the pale corridor, wailing. Fat glassy tears spill over his cheeks. He rubs them away with a fist. 'I want Blue Bunny,' he moans.

'Well, let's just keep looking,' says Ben. 'I'll go and check in the car.' And when he glances up at me I know he's thinking about the scene that morning, before we set off, and how I gave in. *See? What did I say? This is your fault.*

'Can you remember when you last saw him?' I ask Christopher, but this question is beyond him: I might as well ask him to recite some Larkin or read a bus timetable. Sophie goes off to check the pool. Ben returns from the car empty-handed and then we go back over the morning, charting it, using its most striking features – the drive, the walk through the wood, the beehives, the crêpe van and the toy stall – for navigation. 'Did you have him when I bought you the cars?' Ben asks, and Christopher thinks maybe, maybe he did. His breath comes in ragged bursts. Ben and I exchange a look.

Cecily is tired, rubbing her eyes with her fists, so I take her into our room and lower her into her cot, tucking a thin sheet around her and then moving off to the window, to draw the curtains. It's getting dark, the air full of stars and the surging tidal percussion of crickets. Gently I close the door, and then I say I'll go and have another look around the garden, just in case. Ben is trying to interest Christopher in the story, but it's not going very well.

In the kitchen I take the chicken out of the oven, and then I stand by the open fridge, staring at the cartons of milk and the paper parcels of cheese and pâté, waiting for the adrenalin to subside, just a little. *It'll be OK. He'll go to sleep eventually. Just one of those things.* I uncork the bottle of white wine and pour myself a glass. I drink most of it quite quickly. Then I top it up, and fill another one for Nina.

Out into the garden. The vast soft sky is almost entirely dark. The scents of herbs and flowers rise up like steam. I raise my arm to shield my eyes from the spotlights' glare and look down, at my sandalled feet moving over the tiny glinting stones, between the lines of the hedges and the trickling rills of water.

I step onto the grass. In the hammock, Nina straightens up, beckons to me. I pass her a glass. *Hey, thanks.* Her face is in shadow. I tell her about the rabbit, ask if she remembers seeing it.

Nina thinks. 'He took it out in the car this morning, didn't he? Did he have it when we stopped for lunch? In the market?'

I say we fear he may have dropped it when he was looking

at the toy stall. Then we hear Christopher's wail issuing from the house, a sound of the purest, deepest despair.

'Poor little chap,' Nina says. I'm on the point of giving up and going indoors, but the noise stops. She adjusts her position, scooting sideways and twisting, swinging her bare legs free, issuing an invitation. 'He'll be OK,' she says. 'It'll turn up. Hop in.'

There's a moment when I simply have to trust the bloody thing won't come crashing down, when I just have to let go. I lift my feet and my weight pushes me sideways into her. It's embarrassing, somehow, the friendly physical collision. Her neat taut heat. I laugh too loudly and take a mouthful of wine. It almost goes down the wrong way. I cough.

'You'll be glad to see the back of us,' I say, once we're settled into a rhythm. I look up. A sliver of moon, thin and dissolving, like ice in water. I think I can identify the Plough, endlessly toiling through the sky, but I'm not a hundred per cent. Something bright flashes past at the edge of my vision: it's unlikely to be a shooting star, I think. More likely to be a satellite.

Nina says, *not at all*. She feels bad that he spooked himself earlier, during their game. She should have realised that was going to happen.

I say that everything spooks him at the moment. It goes with the territory. The highs, the lows.

Light slides and darts in her glass as Nina says, 'I remember what it's like. That stage . . . fantastic, of course, but it's such hard work. God, I remember Sophie . . .'

And now, because the wine has started to sing, because it's our last night, because I've always wanted to, I ask what happened with Sophie's father.

She sighs, but it's not a reproachful sound, just a sad and contemplative one. She doesn't mind telling me about this, I can tell, and the relief is delicious, intoxicating, as good as the secret itself. So she tells me how she met Arnold during her foundation year at art school, and then she describes the things he seemed to represent: a new way of defining herself, a chance to pull away from her parents and make her own mark. Having Sophie so young: that helped too. She found her purpose – as a painter, as a mother – through Arnold and Sophie. 'My dad . . .' she says. 'Oh, he's a charming man, too charming, probably. My mother was a casualty of all that. She never really got over it. Arnold showed me a way out.'

I let her talk, willing her on. My toe touches the ground from time to time, just keeping the rhythm.

It's a melancholy story, as melancholy as I'd imagined. Her parents, ill-matched, drifted apart. The clincher came when her father, usually discreet, lost his head over a girl. 'Someone I knew. That was enough.'

God. I wince. 'No. Seriously? He went off with a friend of yours?'

'Oh, no. It wasn't like that. Nothing *happened*. No one did anything. No one said anything. It was just the last straw.' A light comes on in the house and she turns her face towards it. In any case, she adds, this girl wasn't exactly a friend. They barely knew each other.

Her voice is low, almost dreamy, as if she has forgotten I am here. I get the feeling she doesn't often discuss this. It must be good for her, I think. To speak about it.

'My father . . . well, he was very taken with her. He made a bit of a fool of himself. I don't think she was even aware of the effect she'd had on him. She was that sort of girl.'

'What do you mean?'

'You know. Beautiful . . . a bit careless.'

We think about these girls, how dangerous they can be.

Nina was Sophie's age when it happened. For Nina's mother, it was the final insult.

I make a stupid little sound of sympathy, and it breaks the

spell. She shrugs and smiles in the dark, the shadows shifting over her face, and says, 'Well, it was a long time ago.'

I feel her sigh come and go. The hammock ropes creak against the trunk. A dog howls on the other side of the valley. 'It's strange,' she murmurs. 'I don't often think about it. Perhaps it's because of Sophie being the age she is . . . perhaps that's why.'

It all sounds so sad, so messy. Everything swims suddenly: the spotlights in the bushes, the stars, the dissolving moon.

'And you?' she says. She asks me to tell my story. Everyone has a story, she says.

I'm not so sure. I blink away the tears, grateful for the dark; conscious that after her story mine looks very dull, as good fortune sometimes appears. I tell her a little about my parents, whom I cannot reproach for anything, not even their dying. I whisper my confession. 'I've been so lucky, sometimes I think I must have it coming to me, somewhere down the line.'

We sit there, our shoulders and elbows and hips pressed close, cradled by the gentle motion of the hammock.

Nina says, 'What do you mean?'

I say I've always felt lucky, a bit too lucky perhaps; and I rush on, listing all the other things in my favour, the stars that happened to be in alignment: my education, my career; finding Ben just when I was on the point of giving up. The babies. (The babies, who drive me mad and run me ragged, who wear me out and show me up. The babies, who make it all wonderful. I can't put that into words, so I don't try.) As I list the advantages I've enjoyed, I'm thinking of the fairies crowding round Aurora's cot, all but one. *I mustn't forget any of the fairies.* Everyone's healthy, touch wood. OK, there's not very much money, but there's enough, we'll squeak by. I miss my career, but I've begun to think about how life will change once Cecily starts school. I have some plans.

'I've always felt it, I've always felt I'm due for a bit of a kicking,' I say, with a little gasp of embarrassment, because it does sound ridiculous, and I've never articulated it before.

But now Ben's on the terrace, calling to me, saying he's sorry to break up the party, but Christopher's in a right old state, and could I lend a hand? I put my foot on the grass, and the rocking stops.

Christopher's hot and panicky, so I take him into the bathroom and sit on the edge of the bath and hold him on my lap, pressing a damp flannel over his cheeks and his eyes, to cool him down, and then I wipe the flannel over his neck and his hands, and I stroke his hair and kiss him and tell him it'll be OK, we're doing what we can, and would he like something of mine to sleep with, just for tonight? His lip trembles, but he's very brave, he chooses the T-shirt with the stars on it, so I tiptoe into our room and find it and bring it back to him. I think I've got him settled, but every time we try to leave, he flings back the covers and clings to us, and the tears start again.

He appears at regular intervals, barefoot and desolate, while we eat. And every time he materialises, I see Ben's expression, and I know what he's thinking.

It's not much of a last supper.

While we're clearing the table, Nina offers to make some calls first thing tomorrow, just in case Blue Bunny has turned up at the monastery.

'Would you?' I say. 'Not much hope, but . . .'

'You never know,' Nina says.

When we say goodnight, we find Christopher has crept in and put himself to sleep in our bed and because we can't face the repercussions of waking him Ben says he'll swap places.

My boy is as restless in sleep as he is awake: twisting,

turning, chattering for a moment or two, breaking into slow delighted giggles, catching his breath in terror. Every so often I'll feel his knees pressing into my back, or he'll fling out an arm so his fingers catch in my hair. Radiating heat and energy even in his dreams.

Cecily's teeth wake us both at six. I'm anxious to let Christopher sleep as late as possible, so instead of waiting to see if she'll resettle herself, I grab her out of the cot and hurry her from the room.

Once I've given her some Calpol and a bit of milk, I shove in a cartoon DVD, one of the half-sister's, and Cecily sits on the rug staring at the screen while I lie down on one of the white sofas. My gaze drifts over Nina's oil painting while I compose my mental lists, fretting about all the packing we have to do this morning, the things I'll need to put aside for the flight.

And then I start thinking about how it'll feel, returning to Carmody Street: the pot of wilted basil on the kitchen table, the laundry airer balanced in the bath, the brown stain spreading over the corner of Christopher's ceiling. The grey skies. The Callaghans' arguments coming through the wall.

Ben wakes me with a cup of coffee. Nina's up, wandering around barefoot on the lawn, making calls as promised. Her gesticulations seem every bit as properly French as her accent. She's wearing a sleeveless black dress, and I can see the small flat muscles moving in her bicep as she raises her left hand and opens it, spreading her fingers, as if she's catching something, or letting it go.

She walks across the grass and up the steps. *Nothing at the monastery*, she reports, keeping her voice low so Christopher doesn't hear. She offers to drive back to the town where we had lunch, just in case someone picked it up and left it on a bench in the square. If she sets off now, she'll be home in plenty of time before we have to leave. 'You've got your packing to worry about,' she says, very firmly. She fetches her bag and collects her car keys from the wooden bowl on the counter.

By the time she returns, we've had our final swim and our luggage is ready. The sun sails high overhead, a pale ball in a white sky, shrinking the shadows and speed-drying the slate-coloured towels draped over the chairs on the terrace. Christopher is sitting on the shaded steps with Sophie, a toy ambulance in one hand, a piece of bread spread with runny brie in the other, leaning against her as she reads him a Richard Scarry book. He hasn't mentioned Blue Bunny for an hour or so, and misses the little gesture (*No, nothing*) that Nina makes as she comes through the garden.

Maybe when we get back to London he'll be so glad to see all his other toys that the rabbit will be forgotten, turning into something he'll only vaguely remember when we scroll through the photographs of this holiday on the MacBook.

Nina passes me: a small shrug of apology and commiseration, that peculiar spicy fragrance. I stand behind Christopher and Sophie thinking, *oh well*, finishing my sandwich and looking out over the garden, trying to fix this moment in my mind: the smell, the temperature, the view of the sea. For a moment I think of the small window on the half-landing at Carmody Street, the not-quite-a-view glimpsed countless times a day as I descend and climb the stairs with my armfuls of clean and dirty laundry. The overgrown hedge, the long snaking shoots of bindweed, the galloping bamboo. The shed door that's still hanging off its hinges. Maybe when the man comes to look at Christopher's ceiling, I could ask him to fix the shed door, too.

'The house was painted inside and outside,' reads Sophie. 'A truck brought furniture, a television set, a radio, rugs, pictures, a stove and lots of other things. The house was ready for the new family.' She turns the page. A blue glass bead twists and spins on the string knotted around her wrist. An evil eye. Someone once told me they're not actually evil at all; they're amulets, worn to ward off bad luck or injury. The name's a bit misleading.

'That's pretty,' I say. She looks up at me. I nod at it.

'Some weird old thing of my mother's,' she says. At the corner of my vision, I see Nina darting through the garden, a small shadow moving between the tidy lines of light and dark green.

Ben is sitting on our bed, sorting through the plane tickets and checking the passports while Cecily pulls herself to her feet, using the bars of the cot for stability. Once she's up, quaking a little, her expression – smug, ecstatic – makes us laugh. 'Yes, you *are* clever,' I say, and Ben reaches over and takes my hand, and says, 'Oh well . . .' and I know when we get into bed tonight he will say *East, west, home's best,* because one of us always says that when we've been away, it's our ritual, and usually we mean it, too. One of the little things that makes us us.

I press my damp swimming costume into my case and zip it up and roll it through the house. Sophie and Christopher are in the hammock now, I can hear her talking to him, laughing. I can't help feeling slightly irritated that she waited until the final minutes of our holiday to take an interest in him; but I know that's unfair. I was much the same at seventeen, I suppose. Easily bored. Always eager for the next thing.

I drag the case down through the garden and leave it in the shade by the car, and then I carry the children's bag down, too. When I come back up through the tiers of herbs, the low walls of lavender, I hear Sophie giggling, the sound of it over the trickling water, and then she says, quite loudly, as if in outrage, 'The fuck she did!' and I can see she's on her phone, and Christopher isn't with her in the hammock after all. Perhaps he never was.

I scan the garden but I can't see him, and when I go back indoors he's not in the living room or in the kitchen area, and he's not in his room, or ours, or any of the bathrooms. I push open the door to Sophie's room – the open suitcase, the clothes trailing over the floor – and then Nina's, which is dim, cool, perfectly ordered, much as it was before she arrived.

Ben has Cecily in his arms. He says, 'Maybe he went into the wood.' I run back out onto the lawn and shout his name. The sound makes Sophie end her call and tip herself out of the hammock. She crosses the grass and she's saying, 'But he was just here a minute ago.'

Nina comes around the corner of her father's house. She moves towards me. The look on her face. She passes me quite fast, already running, and as she passes she says, over her shoulder, 'You and Ben do the woods, I'll check the pool.'

But I'm right behind her, my hands flying up, reaching for her, clutching at her hard bare arms, the grain of her linen dress, and I'm saying something, my voice shrill and wild, a sound that would ordinarily embarrass me, and I'm trying to get hold of her so I can push past her, but she won't stand back, she's in my way, she's blocking me, she's moving so extraordinarily slowly, and she won't get out of the way. So I grab her shoulder, bony under my fingers, and I'm holding her, trying to push her aside, and we're both running, but the path leading to the pool gate seems tremendously long and elastic, as if it is a hallucination, as if the gate is sliding further away from us, retreating with every step we take towards it, and she's still in the way. The little fiddly hedges, the tall trees, the dense smell of hot grass and scorched earth and white flowers. Hands turning salad. Runnels in dirty hair. A blue glass bead, winking in the sun. Time sags and screams. It spills away from me, like the gravel sliding under my bare feet, the hard vicious glitter of it.

I'm right behind her, I'm right behind her, why won't she let me pass? The white stones rattle and skitter.

I see it, the damp towel slung over the gate so the latch hasn't caught. I see it, the toy ambulance on its side by the steel ladder, the tiny wet tracks its tyres have left, parallel lines seeping into the limestone.

The black glass. The water rises up around me. I do not know if I'll be in time.

Acknowledgements

My editors Arzu Tahsin, Judy Clain and Gail Paten; my agents Cat Ledger, Gráinne Fox and Karolina Sutton; Sophie Buchan; Rachel Thomas; Susie Steiner; Amanda Coe and Andrew Clifford; Morag Preston and Damian Whitworth; Lucy Darwin; Anna Mazzega; Daisy Cook and David Masters; Aisling Crowley, Chipo Mumba, Becky Crowley, Holly Kershaw and Zara Janmohamed; Anna Chrempinska; Elizabeth Loding; Deborah Dooley and Bob Cooper at Sheepwash; all the readers who enjoyed *Alys, Always* and took the trouble to tell me so.

David, Sara and Victoria Lane.

Stafford, Poppy and Barnaby Critchlow.

W&N
blog and newsletter